FORTUNE FAVORS THE DEAD

FORTUNE FAVORS THE DEAD

SUSAN JANE WRIGHT

ROAN IMPRINT

ISBN 978-1-7390380-2-1 (Paperback Edition)
ISBN 978-1-7390380-3-8 (eBook Edition)

Editing by Pip Wallace
Front cover image by Leonor Oom
Front cover design by Roan Imprint

Published by Roan Imprint
1500 14 St SW Suite 119
Calgary, AB T3C 1C9
Canada

Printed and bound in Canada

Visit www.SusanJaneWright.ca

For my mother
There was never a problem she
couldn't fix

CHAPTER 1

AN EVENING WITH FINN TANBERG

While Hadiza Paramar raged at the chef and I suggested we substitute fiddlehead ferns for wild asparagus because yelling at the poor man wasn't doing any good, Finn Tanberg lay dying behind a dumpster at the Banff Springs Hotel. This all happened two hours before he was supposed to appear on stage at a gala event celebrating his retirement from the university.

An Evening with Finn Tanberg was in Finn's opinion an overblown, pompous affair. What started as dinner with a few close friends and family blew up like a wedding run amok. Now it was a formal banquet with one hundred and twenty academics, environmental activists, students, and former students coming to Banff to honour my former law prof and mentor.

He hated it.

His son, Peter, was adamant. "Dad, you're in transition. You're not shuffling off to a seniors' home, here's your gold watch, wham, bam, thank you ma'am; you're a hotshot consultant now. This is huge. It needs a big promotional push."

Peter always talked like that. "Promotion" should be his middle name. He was brilliant and highly educated like his father—he'd obtained a Ph. D in material science from Stanford—but that's where the similarity ended. Peter flat out refused to follow Finn into academia. The very idea of burying himself at a dusty, old university horrified him. Ever since he was a kid winkling money off his dad's friends by doing math problems in his head faster than they could, he'd had his heart set on becoming an entrepreneur, preferably a rich one.

Finn hated the idea of a fancy-dress dinner. It was too flashy, too expensive. "What's next, bouncy castles and clowns?" We ignored him. We wanted to make it perfect. That's why I spent the last afternoon of Finn's life persuading a chef to go with fiddlehead ferns—yes, it's a Canadian cliché, but we had no other option—before running back upstairs to change for dinner.

* * *

Pretty black patent heels, a silky black jacket, slim leg pants and a sparkly bangle on my wrist, I twirled around in front of the mirror. *You look like a nun.* My mother's voice. She's been gone for years, but I carry her around in my memory. I smiled. No problem, Mom. Hadiza will be decked out like a peacock, splashy enough for the both of us.

I found Hadiza outside the banquet hall dragging a 'private event' sign closer to the heavy oak doors. Mount Stephen Hall was in a quiet state of anticipation. The bright evening light bled the colours out of the soaring stained-glass windows, the medieval chandeliers glittered and the pale stone floors gleamed. Flowers, silver, and glassware crowded the tables; everything sparkled, waiting for the guests who would soon arrive.

"It's so beautiful, Hadiza. It's a shame to let them come in and mess it up."

She laughed and grabbed my elbow, propelling me inside. Her long red skirt swished across the stone floor.

"What a magnificent view," she said with a sigh. Outside, the green-grey mountains marched westward into the setting sun. "Evie, after all that hassle, it was worth it."

Hadiza made it sound like she'd organized the event single-handedly, taking all the credit was one of her less endearing qualities, but after weeks of frantic calls from her staff I knew she'd dragooned every last one of them into service. This created havoc at the university—she too was a professor in the law department, it was the end of term, and her admins were swamped—but the event had to be perfect. Finn was leaving the university, this was the last thing she could do for him. So that was that.

Today her mood verged on panic. All her staff were back in Calgary, leaving just the two of us to cope with the inevitable last-minute snags like the TV monitor that had inexplicably gone missing. "Just how do you expect me to tell Finn's story without a monitor," she'd barked at a beleaguered hotel staffer who scuttled off to find one. Finn hated being the centre of attention; for all I knew he'd stolen it himself.

Finally, everything was in place.

We helped ourselves to a bottle of wine from the bar and ambled over to our table in front of the podium, our heels echoing softly on the pale stone floor. All we had to do was wait for the guest of honour to arrive.

CHAPTER 2

PETER AND ANYA

The sound of impatient guests filled the dining hall, their laughter amplified by the high ceilings and stone floors. The food was delayed and the liquor flowed freely. This was supposed to distract everyone from the fact that the guest of honour was a no-show. All it did was make them raucous.

Peter fidgeted in his chair. He pulled his cell out of his jacket pocket and placed it face up on the pristine white tablecloth, glancing at it every three seconds or so. Anya, his wife, rested a pale hand on his arm. "Darling, you know Finn, he's always late, give him time."

Peter glanced at his watch, a chunky gold thing, and grumbled, "Seven-twenty, he was supposed to meet us in our room a half an hour ago." Unlike many of the other guests who'd traded their baggy sweaters and tired corduroy slacks for ill-fitting suits, Peter and Anya looked stunning. They always did. They were one of those power couples who bore the burden of celebrity, in this case being a member of the super-rich, with unerring grace. Tall, slim, elegant, Peter was comfortable in his bespoke suit and his perfectly knotted bow tie. Anya was luminous in a strapless black dress, her wide blue eyes sparkled under sharp black bangs, and a single piece of jewelry, a diamond encrusted ammolite pendant, rested in the notch in her collarbone. She slipped her arm across Peter's shoulders, leaning into him.

"Five more minutes, darling, then you can go upstairs and bang his door down." She gave him a gentle smile and he relaxed a little and smiled back.

I nodded in agreement. Finn was the first law prof I'd encountered upon entering law school. A compact man with ginger hair, striding down the centre aisle in the lecture hall; even in his early forties he looked more like a student than a professor. But then again, I expected them all to look like Dumbledore. Finn offered a curt apology for his tardiness and immediately plunged into his lecture. We soon discovered that Finn was chronically late for everything and there wasn't a damn thing we could do about it. Luckily, he was a brilliant teacher, his classes were packed and his 'rate my professor' scores were excellent.

It was almost fitting that Finn would be late for his own retirement party.

Peter drummed his fingertips on his phone and fixed his eyes on the empty podium up on the stage. Anya picked at her purse, it was small, hard, and shaped like a bejeweled butterfly. She fiddled with the clasp, clicking it open and closed, the sound was irritating. As if she'd read my mind, she set it down and cast her eyes around the room.

"It's a shame Patrice didn't make it." Anya's flawless complexion and full red lips made her one of the most beautiful women I'd ever seen.

Patrice was Finn's wife, a military historian who'd

spent the last two weeks touring a group of Canadian veterans around the French countryside, revisiting key battle sites. She should have been on a plane heading home yesterday but a volcano erupted in Iceland, spewing ash across Europe. The risk of clogged engines and planes plummeting to earth was too great and all the major airlines were grounded. It struck me that in all the years I'd known them, Finn and Patrice were rarely in the same place at the same time.

I glanced at my watch. *Seven forty-one.* Finn was seriously late. I was about to suggest that Peter go up and check Finn's room when Peter's phone rang. He read the display, then frowned at Anya. "It's Mom." He lifted his cell to his ear, cupping his hand over the other ear to block out the din. His eyes grew wide. "Christ." He shoved the phone into his pocket and stumbled to his feet. Touching Anya's bare shoulder, he said, "We've got to go! Now!"

"What's happened? Is Patrice here?" Her pale cheeks grew even paler.

He shook his head, "No, she's just boarding at Heathrow."

"Peter, what is it?" I asked, catching his sleeve. The commotion at our table caught Hadiza's eye. She was two tables over, hobnobbing with some guests who were well on their way to getting plastered.

He turned to me. "There's been an accident. Dad's in the hospital."

"I don't understand," Anya said. "We just saw him this morning."

"They called Mom, his primary contact. Anya, move it, we've got to go!" He hurried out of the room with Anya struggling to keep up, running on her tiptoes to avoid tripping on her hem.

Hadiza lifted her hands, palms up. *What?* I gestured for her to join me and before she could say a word, I explained that Finn was in hospital.

"Are you kidding me?" Finn had mentored Hadiza for years, ever since she joined the faculty. She was more than a work colleague; she was a close friend.

"I don't know what happened. All I know is we have to carry on the dinner without him."

"An evening with Finn, *without* Finn?" Her tone went from worried to sarcastic. "That's bloody brilliant. And just what am I supposed to say?"

"I don't know Hadiza, do your speech, wing it, I don't care. I'll tell the waitstaff to start the dinner service. Look at them." I gestured at the crowd. "They're getting hammered." Diplomacy has never been my strong suit. "Just do your speech. I'll accept the award on his behalf and we'll get out of here."

She thought about it for a full three seconds, then straightened her back and marched regally up onto the stage, her iridescent red dress glittering in the spotlights. She touched the microphone, bending it toward her lips like a tulip, then checked over a smooth brown shoulder to confirm Finn's image was displayed on the big screen behind her before calling for everyone's attention.

A loud groan rose from the crowd when Hadiza said that due to unforeseen circumstances Finn would not be joining us on this, his special night, but he wanted us to proceed in his absence. A bustle of waitstaff darted around the tables placing plates of lukewarm chicken in front of the guests. The tightly coiled fiddlehead ferns were limp and spongy and I wondered whether they were still safe to eat.

Hadiza's clear voice reeled off Finn's achievements: a thirty-five-year career in teaching, a world-renowned expert in environmental law and climate change, global finance, and trade. It was this unusual combination of skills that made him a highly sought-after speaker and expert witness, sitting on commissions investigating everything from mining disasters to money laundering.

She nodded in my direction as she set Finn's lifetime achievement award on the plastic podium.

I stepped up onto the stage, lifted the award—a heavy glass plaque shaped like a flattened diamond—and read the inscription aloud. The audience laughed when I said Finn would be terribly disappointed to have missed this opportunity to bask in the limelight. Finn shied away from awards like a horse confronting a rattlesnake. Like the movie mogul Louis B. Mayer, Finn believed that handing out trinkets was a cheap trick to keep people in line.

"It's too bad," I said to Hadiza after we'd sat down, "we didn't think to tape your speech, so Finn could watch it when he gets out of hospital."

A few weeks later his wife recited an abbreviated version of the speech at Finn's funeral.

CHAPTER 3

SECOND THOUGHTS

Hadiza invited the guests to linger as long as they liked, but the night felt out of joint and everyone gobbled down their dinners, belted back their drinks, and dispersed; leaving a few stragglers hunched in twos and threes in the dim corners of the dining hall.

Hadiza went straight to the bar when I returned to my room. Peter, who was picking up the tab for the entire weekend, had booked us into luxurious rooms on the Gold Floor, right across the hall from Finn's palatial suite. As beautiful as my room was, it was just after ten o'clock and I couldn't settle, so I went back downstairs to find Hadiza.

The elevator opened onto the glittering lobby; windows as black as obsidian swallowed the flickering lights from massive chandeliers. A curved marble staircase and the burble of laughter led me to the bar.

Hadiza was at a small table with a man I didn't recognize. He leaned in, his arm encircled her waist as he whispered in her ear. Her evening gown glittered in the dark, heavily paneled room and she looked like an exotic bird that had blown through an open window quite by accident.

Her smile faded a little when she saw me. She said a few words to her companion, then glanced at me, tipping her head toward the far end of the mahogany bar. We settled on the bar stools and she caught the bartender's eye and mouthed *gin and tonic*. I held up two fingers. He nodded and turned back to the mirrored wall, expertly flicking bottles in the air and dropping slices of lime and juniper berries into two tall glasses.

Hadiza shifted on her bar stool. The sequins on her dress made a scratchy sound when she crossed her legs. "Have you heard anything?" she asked.

"Just a quick text from Peter, they're keeping Finn in hospital. You?"

She shook her head, no. "It looks like a decent hospital, though. Their website says they ship tough cases to Calgary if they don't have the equipment or the specialists to handle them here."

The bartender reappeared with our cocktails. He had white-blond hair and bright blue eyes and looked too young to be serving drinks to paying customers.

"The hospital?" he said. "Sorry. Didn't mean to eavesdrop." He had an Australian accent, no doubt he was part of the seasonal crush of young people who'll take any job so long as they can spend their summers hiking and their winters skiing in the Canadian Rockies. "No worries there, it's pretty good." Then he chuckled. "Has to be, with all those tourists falling off their electric scooters."

When he offered us menus, we almost ripped them out of his hands. Neither of us were satisfied with the rubber chicken we'd choked down a couple of hours ago.

Soon he returned with our food. Hadiza's burger was

massive, my chicken wrap slightly less so, and between noisy slurps of her drink and frenetic chewing she confessed she'd been terrified about tonight's event.

"You're kidding! You were as cool as a cucumber on stage, even when the whole thing went pear-shaped. Finn says you're one of the smoothest and smartest people he knows." I touched her arm. "That couldn't have been easy with him MIA and all. Still, you did a terrific job."

She stared at me, her cheeks were flushed and her eyes were glassy, and took a long and satisfying slurp of her G and T. At this rate I'd have to carry her back up to her room.

"Finn." Her voice had an edge. "Who knows what Finn thinks anymore." Just then I felt a warm presence sidle up behind us. It was the man Hadiza had been talking to when I'd arrived. He shot me what he appeared to think was an endearing grin but before he could open his mouth, I shook my head. "We're fine here, thank you." He glanced at Hadiza who was fixated on a juniper berry at the bottom of her glass, shrugged and returned to a small table at the other end of the room.

"Don't be silly," I said. "Finn wouldn't have asked you to emcee tonight, let alone put you forward as his successor on the Environmental Consortium, if he had any qualms about you."

She pursed her lips, her mouth became a thin line. "I'm not so sure about that."

It was a ridiculous idea. Hadiza was a highly respected environmental law expert, her university career tracked behind Finn's for the last two decades. They'd taught at the same universities, served on the same commissions.

"Finn has nothing but respect for you, he's said as much to me many times." She stared sadly into her drink. "Hadiza, that's just the booze talking."

She raised her eyes, watching me in the mirror behind the bar, then signalled the bartender for another drink. I raised a hand, *belay that*, and asked for two large coffees instead. She gave a pitiful moan, pouting like a spoiled child. My sister Louisa does the same thing when she's trying to get out of doing housework. Hadiza moved me as much as Louisa does, which is to say not at all.

The bartender whisked our plates away and reappeared with a small black tray. He set the coffees, a pitcher of cream, and a bowl stuffed with packets of fake sugar in front of us. The aroma of strong coffee was bracing. I swirled the cream into my mug, making pretty patterns with my spoon while I waited for Hadiza's mood to lighten. Like many drinkers, and I know this from personal experience, she doesn't like to be told no.

Finally she lifted her cup to her lips, took a big gulp and smiled. Her resting bitch face was utterly transformed when she smiled. We turned our minds to tomorrow. Should we hang around and wait for further news of Finn's condition, maybe visit him in the hospital, or stick to our original plan and head back home right after breakfast? After testing a few options, we decided we were too tired to make a decision and we'd figure ourselves out in the morning.

When the bartender presented the bill, I gulped. Peter was covering our rooms and our expenses and could well afford it, but it was an eyewatering sum to fork over for drinks and bar food.

Hadiza grudgingly allowed me to steer her into the elevator and wedge her in a corner while I waved my pass key over the sensor that would let us on to the Gold Floor. She trailed me down the hall in that intensely focused way people have when they're trying to hide the fact they're drunk, then stopped in front of her door. "Shit," she said. "Shit, shit, shit." She'd lost her key.

"Look," I said, "come through my room and use the adjoining door, you didn't lock your side, did you? We'll find your key tomorrow." *Hopefully that guy downstairs in the bar doesn't have it.*

Hadiza wobbled into my room and yanked the adjoining door open with exaggerated gusto, then stumbled across the threshold and flopped facedown on the bed. I pulled off her shoes and covered her with a blanket while she mumbled into the bedspread.

Back in my room I found myself talking to my reflection in the bathroom mirror. "What's happening to everyone?" My image looked back at me, dark hair shining but brown eyes bleary. "I don't know," it said, and I frowned. I'd known Hadiza for over a decade, I'd never seen her get this drunk this fast. Perhaps it was the strain of stepping into Finn's shoes. Imposter syndrome, a stupid affliction that plagues successful women regardless of how competent or deserving they are.

"It's not fair," I told my reflection. My reflection agreed.

CHAPTER 4

THE PHONE CALL

Something was happening in my room, dragging me out of a strange dream. The phone buzzed like a hornet on the nightstand. Peter's name flashed pale blue. It was just after 4:00 A.M. No one calls at this ungodly hour unless it's bad news. I took a deep breath and picked it up.

"Peter, how is he?"

There was a long pause. The faint chatter of voices, nurses perhaps, in the background. Peter said, "Evie, it's really, really bad." He sounded like he was choking.

"Are they sending him to Calgary?" I swung my feet to the floor, toes gripping the Berber carpet, my pulse pounding in my ears.

"I don't know. I don't know what to do." He took a ragged breath. "Mom will be here soon. Bloody volcanic ash. Evie, she says if it's really bad, he wouldn't want to go on. Not this way."

What way?

"She can't do it, can she?" He was sobbing now. "You're a lawyer, tell her she can't do it."

"Peter, slow down. I don't know what you're talking about."

"Take him off life support."

My heart lurched as I pictured Peter huddled in the hospital corridor, whispering into his phone. "Peter, is she there? Let me talk to her."

"She landed in Calgary an hour ago. She'll be here soon, an hour, hour and a half at most. Assuming she doesn't kill herself on the highway." He sounded almost bitter. "She's been on the phone non-stop, to me, to Anya, to the doctors. She'll drive into the side of a mountain if she's not careful."

I was on my feet now, feeling around in the dark for a light switch, groping my way to the desk. *Click.* The desk lamp cast a warm pool of light over pens, room service menus, candy wrappers. Cradling my phone between my shoulder and my chin I flipped open my laptop and brought up the hospital's website. *Patient Information, Lost and Found, General Surgery*, nothing for administrative services. Did they have their own in-house lawyers?

"What did the doctors say? Peter? Tell me exactly what they said, word for word."

It spilled out in fitful spurts. Finn had sustained a very serious head injury. He was exhibiting what they called decorticate posturing, the likelihood of him pulling through was low but not completely out of the question. Out of habit I scribbled down everything he said on the hotel memo pad although I didn't really understand anything beyond the fact that Finn might die.

"Peter, listen to me, listen carefully. Did the doctors tell Patrice about the decort — the decorticate thing? That he might pull out of it. Does Finn have a living will?"

"How the hell would I know?" He sounded desperate and angry.

"Look, you need to talk to Patrice, find out whether Finn has a living will. If he has one, review it with his doctors... Peter, are you listening to me?"

He let out a sob and I kept talking. "If Finn doesn't have a living will, and you and Patrice can't agree on... er... next steps, you need to talk to a lawyer. Make sure the hospital's lawyers know there's a problem."

"You think I can stop her?"

"I don't know Peter, I don't practise that kind of law. Just promise me you'll find out if he has a living will and talk it over with the doctors and the lawyers, okay? Promise me, Peter."

The fizz of silence filled my ear, then, in the distance, a monitor beeped. When I called out Peter's name, he responded in a voice thick with tears; he had to go.

I sat at the desk for a long time, debating whether I should get dressed and race down to the hospital to be with my friend and mentor. In the end I crawled back into bed and cried.

CHAPTER 5

CEDAR JAMES MCQUINN

A horn beeped loudly, breaking up the grey dawn on the other side of my window. Down and off to the right a yellow garbage truck was backing up to a dumpster. A man in a fluorescent vest hopped off the back of the truck and banged the dumpster lid shut with a flick of a heavily gloved hand. He waved at the driver, then stood to one side as the truck scooped up the dumpster and tipped the contents into its belly. The procedure was noisy and surprisingly fast.

It was too early to text Hadiza, she'd awaken soon enough with a head-splitting hangover. I was emerging from the shower when she sent a text:

Any news?

Cinching the belt on my bathrobe tighter, I crossed to the adjoining door. One tap and she flung it open. Her face was puffy and creased with sleep. Tears filled her eyes when I said Peter had called; Finn was in desperate shape and might not make it. "Patrice should be at the hospital by now. We'll know more soon."

"Are they pulling the plug?"

"Why would you say such a thing?" I reacted with alarm. Then I pulled her close and stroked her hair, sorry I'd snapped at her. "I don't know, Hadiza. I just don't know." She sighed and the sour smell of stale booze filled the air.

*   *   *

A half an hour later Hadiza had washed the sleep out of her eyes and run a comb through her tangled hair. The ride in the elevator down to the breakfast room was silent and thick with apprehension, in sharp contrast to the Vermillion Room which was abuzz with energetic corporate types eager to start their day. The wooden floor and fat globe chandeliers gave the place a retro look, like a 1950s dance hall.

Hadiza squinted at the menu while I joined the boisterous queue crowding around the breakfast buffet. The table was heavy with meat and fish, cheese and fruit, the chef offered to whip up an omelet or crepes if I'd prefer. I gave him a weak smile, I had no appetite, and returned to our table empty-handed.

Hadiza stared moodily into her coffee cup, then brightened at the sight of her vegan bowl, a concoction heaped with berries and hemp hearts. I stirred my coffee and waited until she was ready to talk. Eventually she lifted her eyes, red rimmed and hollow, and said, "I still can't believe it. They're talking about pulling the plug."

The first thing that popped into my mind was the trite expression 'he's had a full life' but he hadn't. Finn was only in his late fifties; he was changing careers, moving on from teaching and research to consulting. He swore he'd never retire. "They'll have to drag my cold, dead body out from behind my desk. There's just too much to do and not enough time to do it."

"Why hasn't Peter called?" I muttered, glancing at my phone. Maybe Finn rallied in the pre-dawn hours. It happens. He's a strong man, an outdoor junkie, skiing in the winter, mountain climbing in the summer. How in God's name did he sustain a head injury? The man was so careful he never went anywhere even remotely dangerous without fifty pounds of safety equipment.

My mind wandered back to yesterday. I was in the corridor, fiddling with my card key, panting slightly from my morning run when I heard loud voices coming from Finn's room. His door was ajar and he and Peter were arguing about money. It wasn't the first time.

"I know you can damn well afford it," Finn's tone was sarcastic. "That's not the point, Peter. It's a colossal waste of money. What are you going to do next? Book a rocket trip to Mars?"

"Christ, Dad," Peter shot back. "This is a gift from me to you. Why can't you accept it for once instead of throwing it back in my face?"

Crockery, a cup perhaps, rattled in its saucer and a door slammed shut. "All the money in the world," Finn shouted, "and you still can't get your mother here on time."

These spats had been happening all weekend. I decided to barge in. Finn was hunched over the desk angrily blotting a coffee-soaked newspaper with a snow-white napkin.

"Good morning," I said with exaggerated cheer. Finn raised his head. At the sound of my voice the bedroom door opened and Peter emerged.

His face was flushed, but he shot me a polite grin and said, "Morning, Evie."

To lighten the mood I launched into a story about my

morning run. I'd gone down the big hill into town and almost collided with a bloody great elk on a street corner. "Scared the living daylights out of me," I said, waving my hands for dramatic effect.

Finn's shaggy head jerked up and he said, "Evie, for God's sake, you have to be careful. It's calving season. Female elk are very defensive of their young, they'll strike if they feel the least bit threatened."

"I know, I know, I always check for stray calves."

Another awkward silence, but the tension in the room was subsiding. With a resigned sigh Peter announced he was going to check on Anya, they were going into town after breakfast to do some shopping. I didn't see Peter again until the banquet, but I'd caught a glimpse of Finn later that afternoon.

He was sprinting down the hall with a wide grin on his face. "Forgot my camera!" he shouted over his shoulder, "Evie, you've got to see this!" Whatever *this* was, I didn't have time, I had to deal with a crisis in the kitchen. Finn shrugged and disappeared into his room.

Hadiza made a hmpff noise, nudging me out of my memories. She tilted her chin at the noisy group of businesspeople clustered at one end of the buffet table. A middle-aged woman in a smartly tailored suit was waving a small pitcher around.

A man in chef's whites approached her. He crossed his arms, listening carefully as she complained she'd had her heart set on banana pancakes, but her greedy guts colleagues finished off all the coconut cream topping. Goodness, how pampered we've become.

The chef raised a hand, *wait right here*, and disappeared into the kitchen. When he returned he was carrying a large white pitcher. The woman clapped her hands as he swirled coconut cream over her pancakes. When she rejoined her friends at their table she had a smug smile on her face.

As the chef passed in front of our table, I gave him a small polite nod. He stopped, his deep-set eyes lit up, and he said, "Evie Valentine, I thought it might be you. I saw your name on the planning schedule." He was talking about the menu for Finn's banquet. "I mean, how many Evie Valentines are there in this world?"

"Not enough," Hadiza said, as she waited for me to introduce her. And, as usual, I'd gone completely blank on his name.

He saved me from embarrassing myself by extending a hand to Hadiza and saying, "Hi, I'm James McQuinn. Evie and I went to law school together."

Ah, yes, of course, first year. I'd met James—back then he was known as Cedar James McQuinn thanks to his hippy dippy mother—in Finn's property law class. We were in the same CANS group. The course load in law school is so heavy that the only way to survive is to join a CANS study group. Every member of the group is assigned one CAN, a set of 'condensed annotated notes,' which will be shared with the rest of the group at the end of the term. A good CAN will lift your test scores but a bad CAN will sink you. James' property law CAN was outstanding, clear and analytical, the sign of a good legal mind.

"How are you, James?" I asked. He looked very much like he did in law school, the same curly blond hair, broad face, and high cheekbones.

James swept a hand across the front of his chef's coat as if he were performing a conjuring trick and beamed, "I'm doing great. Are you here long? We could grab a coffee and catch up on old times."

"That would be terrific, but I'm afraid we're leaving today."

His smile dimmed, then he said. "It's a shame about Finn."

Hearing him say Finn's name sent a shock through me. "Have you heard anything? What have you heard?" It was a silly question. Why would the chef at the Banff Springs Hotel know more about Finn's condition than I would?

"Nothing, really, just that he had an accident and the dinner went on without him."

"We muddled through," Hadiza tipped her head at him. "The food, well—"

I broke in, we weren't going to debate rubber chicken and shrivelled fiddleheads at a time like this, and rummaged in my purse for a business card. "Listen, James, if you're ever in Calgary, give me a call."

He slipped his hand into a pocket and passed me his business card.

"Executive Chef," I read it aloud and smiled up at him. "At the Banff Springs Hotel no less. Very impressive."

His ducked his head, a gesture that conveyed both modesty and pride, and said he hoped we could connect before I left.

Hadiza watched James return to the kitchen then leaned across the table and whispered, "How does a lawyer end up working as a chef?"

"It's a bit of a mystery." James was a bright student who appeared to be doing very well, but he didn't return to class after first year. "Rumours flew that he'd had a nervous breakdown, that his mom was pushing him too hard, stuff like that. Anyway, he was a no-show at the start of second year and no one knew why." I glanced at his business card. "He's a really nice guy. I'm glad he landed on his feet."

"Humph," she said, as the server cleared away her plate and topped up our coffees.

"We should have heard something by now," I said, restlessly glancing around the room. It was half empty, the business people had finished their breakfasts and were now rushing off to find the conferences rooms where they would do whatever it was they were here to do.

"Let's call him," Hadiza said.

"We can't call him! Who knows what's happening right now, we can't interrupt them." *From doing what? Pulling the plug?* The Vermillion Room faded in a blur of tears. Finn had had such a profound impact on my life. I'd always wanted to be a lawyer, but I didn't know what kind of lawyer to be. Finn helped me find my way. "The law is like a compass," he'd said. "Decide what you want to accomplish and the law will guide you there."

I settled on energy law and Finn, first alone, then later with Hadiza's help, became my go-to expert witnesses in regulatory hearings that dragged on for months and months. We became fast friends after endless nights of bad coffee, stale doughnuts, and stacks of charts and graphs that almost made us blind. *God, please don't let him die.*

When we returned to the Gold Floor, the housekeeping staff hadn't come through, but even the rumpled bed and towels strewn haphazardly around the bathroom couldn't distract from the magnificent view. Rain drifted across the valley and misted the window. Finn liked this kind of weather. It was good for birdwatching, he said. Although I'm not exactly an outdoorsy type I did enjoy accompanying him on twitching expeditions. One year on a drizzly grey day much like this, we went to Johnston Canyon where the Black Swifts nest and spotted an American Dipper. I said that was a goofy name and Finn replied it was the only true aquatic songbird in North America. He snapped countless photos and meticulously recorded where and when he saw the bird in Merlin, his eBird app.

I pulled the curtains shut, tossed my suitcase onto the bed and flung my clothes inside.

CHAPTER 6

DREAMSTONE

A head rolled across the table and hit the floor. *This can't be real.* "It's not," said the head as it bounced merrily across the carpet. "For the love of God!" it shouted in Hadiza's voice, "I thought you were dead."

I fought my way out of the nightmare. One summer when I was a teenager I'd worked at a Red Cross blood donor clinic. They always put me on juice and cookies. I was supposed to give donors a sugar boost to keep them from passing out after they'd donated blood. Some people, usually men, the big, stubborn ones, refused a shot of O.J. They insisted they were fine and sailed past me, only to keel over in a dead faint before they reached the door. My job was to cradle their heads before they hit the floor. Louisa, my sister, says the bouncing head dream is my helpless dream; given that it comes when something bad is happening and I'm powerless to stop it, she's probably right.

"What?" I mumbled.

"You were yelping and your phone is ringing off the

hook," Hadiza said. "I thought you'd died in here." Hadiza can be melodramatic at times.

I slid my hand across the duvet looking for my cell.

"No," she hooked her thumb in the direction of the desk, "the hotel phone."

Bridget, our law firm's administrative assistant, blasted me when I picked up the receiver. "Evie, why do you have a cell phone if you never answer it?" She had a point.

She explained that in light of Finn's accident, she'd cancelled the meeting I'd booked with DreamStone later that afternoon. "Good call," I said.

DreamStone was a small privately held mining company. Peter was the CEO, Anya, the chief financial officer, and Peter's university buddy, Jeffrey ("Juve") Wens, the chief geologist. I don't usually do corporate work but agreed to represent DreamStone as a favour to Finn. Peter may be brilliant at marketing, Finn said with a hint of skepticism, but he was in over his head when it came to the corporate side of the business. This struck me as odd. Given Anya's MBA from Wharton and her years of experience in cutting edge financing, including crypto markets, I'd have thought she'd be familiar with every kind of corporate structure there was.

I soon learned that DreamStone was unique. It didn't mine precious metals or gemstones, it dug up ammonite fossils and transformed them into jewelry. "You're a snake oil salesman," I would tease Peter, "passing off the broken shells of extinct cephalopods as fine gems."

He countered that the blue, indigo, and violet stones were extremely rare and would one day be more desirable than the Hope Diamond. "They're highly prized in Asia, you know. Feng Shui experts say they absorb the earth's positive energy, that's what gives them their rainbow colours."

Feng Shui, positive energy, it was all woo-woo talk to me, but it fed Finn's belief that Peter was wasting his considerable intellect selling trinkets to pampered housewives when he could be saving the world from climate change.

"Evie?" Bridget bought me back to reality. "If you need some personal time, Keith and AJ said to tell you they'll cover your files."

"No, that's not necessary, but thank the guys for me." Keith, AJ and I were partners in what we describe as a boutique (read: small) green energy law firm. Together with Bridget and Madeline, our paralegal, we're like a little family, supporting each other when the need arises; although now that I think about it, the need seems to arise more often with me than them.

When I hung up, I was surprised to see Hadiza still hanging about in the doorway. She looked terrible, with an ashy complexion and dark smudges under her eyes. "Hey," I said, "we're not in a rush, let's go for a walk."

"In this deluge?" She turned to face the bleak, wet sky beating against the windowpane.

"This is the Banff Springs Hotel," I said, plucking my card key off the dresser, "there's plenty to see inside. Come on, let's do some exploring, get our minds off Finn." The uncertainty was driving both of us mad.

She rummaged in the mess of clothing piled high at the foot of her bed and dragged out a heavy green cardigan and we went downstairs to poke around in the shops.

* * *

We were in a little alcove admiring a black and white

photograph of Marilyn Monroe on crutches—she'd been here in 1953 and people say she faked an injured ankle to stay longer—when I heard Peter's voice.

They were on the opposite side of the room, Peter, Anya, and Patrice, next to a display case packed with sepia photographs. Peter and Anya were dressed alike in light wool slacks and matching navy puffer vests. Patrice, a small woman with curly greying hair, was well turned out in a navy pantsuit with a wine-red scarf twisted around her throat. For someone who'd just flown in from France and spent the night at her husband's bedside she didn't look any worse for wear.

Their heads popped up as if they'd heard a gunshot when I called Peter's name and I was struck by how much Patrice resembled Finn, she had the same inquisitive eyes and thoughtful expression. Maybe it's true that over time married couples start to look alike, although that wasn't the case with my parents. Dad was a tall, thin Englishman while Mom was small, dark, and curvy. Without giving it another thought I rushed over and threw my arms around Peter, then Patrice and Anya. Stepping back I asked, "How's Finn?"

Peter glanced at Patrice, who was rummaging in her pocket for a Kleenex. Hadiza cast her eyes around the room, unsure of what to say, then launched into a detailed account of all the projects she and Finn had worked on over the years. She was babbling.

I drew Peter to one side. "Is he any better?"

"Dad passed at five-thirty this morning." His gaze was fixed on his mother. "She ordered them to take him off life support. She said it was for the best."

My heart clenched. "On my God, Peter. I'm so sorry."

He gave a helpless shrug, his eyes drifted to Hadiza

who was still chattering at his mother. Patrice's face was blank, she bobbed her head a couple of times, like a reflex. Anya said a few words to Hadiza then pulled Patrice into a protective side hug.

"Look, we have to get going," Peter said to me.

"Let me know if there's anything I can do." As I reached up to give him a goodbye hug, Anya appeared by his side. She smiled politely at me and led Peter and Patrice away.

Hadiza's eyes tracked them all the way down the wide staircase to the concierge's desk where we could hear Anya ask the valet to bring their car around.

"Did Peter tell you?" Hadiza asked.

I felt numb. "Yes, he told me."

"She has everything under control, apparently."

"Patrice?"

"Anya."

"That's probably for the best. They've all had a terrible shock; someone has to take charge of, um, the final arrangements." As we returned to our rooms to finish packing, I started thinking about taking charge. Patrice had made the decision to end Finn's life. Anya was in charge of burying him. That left Peter in charge of nothing.

CHAPTER 7

THE BALCONY

An hour later I was sitting in a high-backed, tapestry-covered chair in the lobby, picking at a red thread poking out from under a shiny upholstery button, waiting for the valet to bring up my car. Someone touched my shoulder and I jumped.

"Sorry. Looks like you were lost in thought." It was James. He was in street clothes and looked younger out of his chef's gear. He sat in the chair across from me and took my hands in his. It was an intimate gesture considering we hadn't seen each other since law school.

"Has there been any further news?" His voice was tentative.

I gulped. "Finn died this morning. Five-thirty."

"Shit," he said. "He hung on for hours." James' lips were white, pressed together. "Always stubborn, right to the end."

"Hung on for hours? What do you mean?" I raised my voice a little to be heard over the clatter of rollie bags being dragged across the stone floor to the reception desk.

He dropped my hands and leaned closer. "Didn't anybody tell you? I was the one who found him."

"Hell, no, why would anyone tell me anything?" I stiffened in my chair, the sudden movement made it wobble slightly. "You found him?"

He rubbed his face with his hands. There was a tiny nick at the base of his little finger. My mom, who practiced palmistry and could deliver a spell-binding reading when she put her mind to it, would have tut-tutted and said the scar crossed the marriage line and James would never marry. He shook his head. "I don't know, Evie. It's not my place to talk about it."

"Oh, for God's sake, James! Don't be ridiculous."

He took a deep breath and in the pale light flooding the busy lobby told me that around five o'clock yesterday afternoon, he had been walking around the hotel. "I'm one of the top chefs in the country and here I am cruising the perimeter to check the dumpsters. These kids are so sloppy"—he was referring to the summer students— "half the time they don't latch the bins and before you know it, the bears start coming around. The last thing we need is a guest mauled to death in the parking lot."

James was studying his hands now, picking at the thin line of the scab on his little finger. "I heard a noise like the clang of a dumpster lid when it slams shut. I went around the corner, the dumpster was open, but when I got closer to latch the lid..."

He paused and gazed out the window. A young family was unloading a packed minivan and backpacks and suitcases were falling all over the place on the sidewalk. Quietly, he said, "I saw something glinting in the sunlight. Evie, there was a camera lying on the ground behind the bin. I... ah... I picked it up... and that's when I found him."

"Finn? Behind the dumpster? I don't understand."

James' eyes never left the chaos of kids and bags pouring out of the minivan. "The EMT guys think he fell from a balcony."

"What balcony? There's no balcony in his room."

His cheek twitched, like a small tremor. "The common rooms and some of the restaurants have balconies."

He explained he'd called 9-1-1, then hotel security, and waited with Finn until EMT and security arrived. "He was barely breathing when the paramedics showed up."

James was so deep into his story that he didn't notice the valet come up behind him. I reached up and the valet dropped my keys into my hand. He greeted James who blinked like a startled owl, then flashed a quick smile but said nothing until the valet returned to his station.

"This hotel has been here since 1888, no one has ever died falling off a balcony." He shook his head, then pointed to my bag. "Can I help you with that?"

"Thanks, but I need to run back upstairs."

As James deposited my bag with the valet and made his way through the lobby, I sprinted up the wide staircase looking for balconies. How could Finn fall off a balcony? The man was a safety fanatic, rules are rules. He couldn't go down a staircase without clinging to the railing. When I got to the second floor I stopped. What was I thinking? I had no idea which balcony Finn had fallen from. Even if I knew, then what? What did I hope to find? A voice in my head told me I was trying to do something useful when the time for action had passed. Slowly I retraced my steps back down to the lobby, retrieved my rollie bag from the valet, and went through the heavy glass doors to claim my car.

James was standing outside, chatting with the doorman. The young family had finally unloaded their gear and the children were shuffling into the lobby, trying not to snag their tiny suitcases and backpacks in the revolving doors.

"Good to go?" he asked.

I nodded and stuffed my bag into the trunk of the Mini. "Let's stay in touch," I said.

When he grinned his eyes crinkled. "I'll look you up the next time I'm in town."

It was such an innocent promise.

CHAPTER 8

THE FALL

Louisa was in the kitchen rummaging through the junk drawer when I finally got home. It was almost dinner time, but nothing savory simmered on the stove or broiled in the oven. This was unusual because my sister, a nurse, likes to cook on her days off. Which is a good thing because if she left meal planning to me, we'd starve.

Louisa and her bull terrier, Quincy, moved in after she divorced her wretched husband. It was supposed to be a temporary arrangement, just long enough for Louisa to get back on her feet, but six years later they were still here.

At first my next-door neighbour, an old guy who spends every waking minute tending to his well-manicured lawn, thought he was losing his mind. He couldn't tell us apart—we're both in our mid thirties with shoulder-length brown hair and dark brown eyes. One day when Louisa was on the back deck and I was out front dragging the garbage cans up the driveway to the street he flew out his front door, demanding an explanation. "You can't be in two places at once!" Fighting the urge to gaslight him—petty, I know—I admitted my lookalike baby sister had moved in with me. Louisa welcomed his nosiness, she said it was good to have an eagle-eyed neighbour to watch over the 'hood when we weren't around. Louisa is way more sympathetic than I am.

Quincy galloped to the front door, thumped broadside against my knees, his usual greeting, then darted back into the kitchen to stare at Louisa with two beady black eyes.

I propped my rollie bag next to the stairs leading up to our bedrooms and said, "You're not cooking. Why aren't you cooking? Are we going out?"

"Where's the dryer operating manual?" she asked. "What's d-80?"

"You're doing laundry?" I was skeptical. "Since when do you do laundry?" One reason we get along so well is Louisa cooks and I do the laundry. It's safest for all concerned. I said d-80 was dryer-speak for 'the lint filter is clogged'. All our appliances talk to us now. Close the door, clear the filter, turn me on, turn me off, it's like Alice in Wonderland. I went downstairs to peel the lint off the filter while she rummaged in the cupboards for a cutting board and the cheese grater.

Soon we were sitting at the kitchen table, swilling crisp white wine and eating omelets, while the sun slipped behind the office towers on the other side of the river. My townhouse is in the inner city on the banks of the Elbow River. The front windows face a wide leafy street and the French doors along the back of the house overlook a riverbank lush with wolf willows, birch, and poplar trees. It's Quincy's favourite place to run.

"Any word on Finn?" Louisa asked. She'd met Finn when I launched my law firm and liked him, saying he wasn't pompous like some academics she knew. This was true, you'd never know Finn was a university prof unless someone told you.

A lump formed in my throat. My omelet was stuck and I had trouble swallowing. "He died this morning."

She set down her fork. "Oh Evie, I'm so sorry."

"Yeah, well, they pulled the plug at five-thirty in the morning." I couldn't shake the memory of James finding Finn behind a dumpster. "Louisa, how far would someone have to fall to sustain a serious head injury? One storey? Two?" Where did he fall from? He was a poster child for safety, how was it even possible?

She frowned slightly and said, "The human body is the most resilient and the most fragile thing you'll ever see. You can fall off a curb, crack your skull, and die; or you can fall ten thousand feet and survive."

"Ten thousand feet?"

"Sure, remember Juliane Koepcke?"

I shook my head. Louisa is a repository of weird snippets of information.

"Juliane was a teenager flying with her mom across the Peruvian rainforest when their plane was struck by lightning. The plane broke up and she fell ten thousand feet still strapped into her seat—that's probably what saved her—and all she had to show for it was a broken collarbone."

"What about her mom?"

Louisa shook her head. "Everyone else died. But Juliane was a resourceful kid. It took her eleven days, but she managed to walk out of the jungle."

"So it doesn't matter how far Finn fell?"

"Of course it matters." She eyed me carefully. "Why? What's bothering you? How exactly did he die?"

My hand twitched, my fork slipped out of my fingers and bounced off my plate onto the floor. I scooped it up before Quincy could lick it. "I'm not sure. He was alive when James found him at five o'clock the evening before. They rushed him to hospital. He was still alive at four A.M. when Peter phoned me—he was desperately afraid his mother would take Finn off life support—and by five-thirty he was dead. Patrice pulled the plug."

"Huh," she said. "Usually it's the other way around. It's the wife who's trying to keep her husband alive and the kids who are telling her it's too late, she has to let him go. That's why a living will is so important. How badly injured was he?"

My mind went back to Peter's phone call. He'd used an obscure medical term. What was it he'd said? I rose from the table and went to the closet to pull a scrap of paper out of my coat pocket. Here it was, the hotel memo pad on which I'd scribbled fragments of sentences, *bad fall, brain injury, very bad, decorticate posturing, living will?*

I read the words out to Louisa when I returned to the table.

"Wait," she stopped me. "You're sure he said 'decorticate' and not 'decerebrate'?" She enunciated the words very carefully.

I spelled out the word.

She lifted her eyebrows.

"Why?" I asked. "What difference does it make?"

She said they both referred to a type of posture exhibited by patients who've suffered serious brain injury. The type of posture is a response to pain stimuli. Decorticate posture pulls away, but decerebrate leans into it.

"Evie, decorticate is bad, but decerebrate is much worse, it's the result of brain stem swelling, there's absolutely nothing that can bring the patient back."

I pushed my plate aside and picked up the crumpled

note. "Decorticate. You're saying there was a chance Finn may have recovered from his injuries?"

Louisa's shoulders lifted in a tiny shrug. "I don't know, Evie. All I'm saying is patients with decorticate posture are more likely to come back. They will never be the same, they may have lifelong paralysis and seizures, but at least they're alive."

My stomach heaved; I couldn't eat. I picked up my plate and tipped the rest of my omelet into Quincy's bowl. Finn was the kind of man who zinged with energy. Wouldn't he want his family to fight for his life if he had even the slightest chance of recovery?

CHAPTER 9

DOCTOR DEATH

Some mornings it's impossible to get to work on time; this morning was particularly bad, every single traffic light turned red, taunting me as I approached the intersection. When I'm late, I'm impatient and forget the little things like saying "Good morning," before I launch into whatever is bugging me at the time. I sailed into the lobby and trapped Bridget at the reception desk, demanding to know whether she had a living will.

Bridget gave me a bewildered stare from her workstation. "I don't have a will, living or unliving. Is that a problem?"

"Damn right, it's a problem," Madeline said as she swept out of her office and into reception. If anyone knows about wills, it's Madeline. Her estate might rival that of Bill Gates. She informed Bridget that everyone should have a will and promised to hook our admin assistant up with her wills and estates guy. "He'll give you a good rate."

"Living wills?" AJ emerged from the coffee room carrying two mugs of coffee. He put the bunny mug on Bridget's desk and raised the sports car mug to his lips. "Why are we talking about living wills?"

Before I could respond Keith strolled out of his office and echoed AJ's question. "What's this about living wills?" Keith sounded weary, more so than usual for a Monday morning. I put it down to fresh air and country living. He lives on a large acreage south of town with his wife, an artist, and their eight-year-old daughter. He moved to the country for the wide open spaces and the slower pace of life but spends every waking minute chopping and hewing and building things. The Marlboro Man may have been an actor but Keith was the real thing, sans the cigarettes of course.

"This is about Finn, isn't it?" As usual Madeline saw right through me. It's uncanny. She'd taken me under her wing on my first day at Gates, Case and White, the biggest law firm in town, and has been by my side ever since.

They all trailed after me as I went down the hall to the coffee room. Madeline and Bridget squeezed in around the tiny table by the window overlooking the parking lot, the guys propped themselves up against the kitchen counters.

I shrugged and said, "I still can't get my head around it. One minute Finn's arguing with Peter about the cost of his hotel room, the next he's in hospital fighting for his life and Patrice, who's racing down the highway, is telling Peter she's going to turn off his life support. Poor Peter. He called me in hysterics, he was dead set against it."

Everyone was silent while I poured myself a coffee and rummaged in the fridge for creamer. "Ninety minutes later Patrice gets her way and poof, just like that, Finn is gone," I said, slowly stirring the creamer into my coffee. The spoon in my hand quivered against the side of the mug.

Bridget broke the silence by asking the question on everyone's mind. "How exactly did he die?"

I took a breath. Where to start? Hadiza and I had been swamped with emails, phone messages, and texts as the news spread through the academic and legal community.

"Apparently, he fell from the third-floor balcony, but no one knows how it happened. Rumours are running rampant. Did Finn commit suicide? Did someone push him, a rival, a lunatic. Finn was as famous as David Suzuki, not everybody liked him. Why do people do that? Spread malicious gossip and wild theories when they don't have a fu—, a *clue* what they're yabbering about?"

My coffee slopped over the rim of my mug. If I didn't stop stirring it would be all over the countertop. "Patrice called me last night," I took a deep breath. "She filled me in."

Bridget said, "I'm amazed she can even talk about it."

So was I. I'd known Patrice almost as long as I'd known Finn. She never struck me as the strong-under-pressure type. She called to thank me for organizing Finn's banquet and to request a copy of Hadiza's speech. Then she told me what had happened. "Finn was on a balcony, taking photos."

I forgot my camera, Finn had said to me as he raced down the corridor to his room. Why didn't I go with him?

"Something must have caught his eye," I said, staring out the window into the parking lot and the woods beyond. "The hotel is pressed up against the mountain, the view is so beautiful. Patrice thinks he must have lost his balance and fell." Here I had to stop and clear my throat. This was the awful part, the part I'd learned from James, the chef. "Finn, um, hit a large metal dumpster on the way down, then rolled behind the bin and got wedged between the dumpster and the exterior wall of the hotel. It's stone." Why did I say that; it didn't matter if the wall was stone or stucco. Finn was dead.

"Why didn't he call for help?" I glanced at Bridget. When she asked the question her eyes became huge, a clear innocent blue.

Madeline interrupted. "So the fall didn't kill him?"

"Um, no. They think the camera strap may have snagged on the lid of the dumpster as he fell. It was around his neck and may have impaired his air supply, but he was alive when he was discovered by a hotel employee. They rushed him to hospital and the doctors tried to stabilize him. They couldn't do much, it's not like the Foothills which is state-of-the-art for strokes and such." Foothills was the hospital where my mom, and later my dad, had died. It was an outstanding facility but more than an hour's drive away from Banff.

Bridget rose from her seat and crossed the room to give me a tight hug. "He was a nice man, Evie. Remember when he was going to smash a champagne bottle over my desk?"

The memory made me smile. Finn and Patrice came to the grand opening of our law firm and Finn said the office needed a proper launch, like the Queen Mary. I thought Bridget was going to tackle him when he brandished a bottle of champagne over her desk.

*　*　*

Later that afternoon Bridget charged into my office. "Why are you still here?" she demanded as she whipped my raincoat off the hook on the back of the door and threw it at me.

Nonplussed, I accepted it. "Am I supposed to be somewhere?"

"The law school reception, happy hour to fete the newest Supreme Court of Canada judge. Jeez, Evie! Keith's already left and AJ is waiting for you in the parking lot."

I cocked an eyebrow at her. "Fete?" I said. "That sounds like a Theo word."

Bridget turned bright pink. Theo was her new significant other. She'd met him last year on a dating app after she decided come hell or high water she'd find a date for the company Christmas party. Five months later they were still together and by all accounts madly in love.

AJ was revving his engine when I got to the parking lot. "Yes, yes, I know I'm late," I said as I scrambled into the front seat, "unleash the beast and drive."

AJ's car is a vintage MGB roadster. British racing green. It got us to the university in record time. When I mentioned that he might be a little heavy on the gas pedal, AJ said it was for the MGB's own good; she needed an Italian tune up now and then. Why he doesn't have a wall plastered with speeding tickets is beyond me.

We parked in a visitor's lot and strolled across the leafy green campus to Murray Fraser Hall. The university is relatively new, lacking the venerable ivy-covered buildings of an eastern university, but the modern architecture, a blend of exposed beams and bright, vibrant colours, gives it a youthful exuberance.

Once inside AJ stopped at the top of a short flight of stairs. "Have you ever noticed that all law schools look the same inside?" He pointed to a wall mural, a large photograph of a smiling professor lecturing a group of students who were hanging on his every word. "Look at the caption. 'Tradition of excellence', or that one." He indicated another photo of a well-known politician who'd attended the school decades ago. "'Auspicious roots'."

"What can I tell you, AJ? They hire the same PR firm."

His reply was cut off by the excited buzz rolling out of the reception hall. The room was packed. I squashed my raincoat into a wheel-in coat rack and joined the mob of students, professors, lawyers, and alumni milling about. AJ, who's a good foot taller than I am spotted Keith talking to an ancient professor who looked vaguely familiar. *Yikes!* Before I could stop him, AJ charged through the crowd, calling out Keith's name.

"You haven't missed a thing yet," Keith said. "She was supposed to be here ten minutes ago." 'She' was my second-year commercial transactions professor who had just been appointed to the Supreme Court of Canada.

The professor standing next to Keith eyed me with suspicion. I nodded hello at him. Fifteen years ago he was ancient. Now he was positively prehistoric. What was his name? His real name, not the name we'd all known him by: Doctor Death. Keith turned to AJ and introduced the geezer, Dr. Gideon Gold. I reached out a hand and introduced myself, surely by now he'd forgotten who I was, but his lips puffed into a smirk and he said, "Ah yes, Evie Valentine, one of the many who cut and run."

I smiled as sweetly as I could under the circumstances, refusing to acknowledge that I'd signed up for his tax course then bailed two weeks later when I realized Doctor Death was a fitting sobriquet. If I didn't withdraw while I had the chance, there was no question in my mind that he'd tank my grade point average.

I said I was going to check out the bar and was dismayed to find Doctor Death trailing after me, chattering like an unhinged parakeet. God, I was going to be stuck with him all night. He was even more loquacious than I remembered. Maybe it was the booze, but he spieled off his life story which actually was quite sad. His wife died ten years ago, they had no children and he'd been retired for eight apparently glorious years. I wondered whether he was lonely. His long yellow teeth sank into a quiche puff and he raised a bushy white eyebrow, pronouncing it far superior to the meal at the Banff Springs Hotel for Finn Tanberg. Pastry crumbs drifted down to settle on his clumsily-knotted tie.

I bristled. "Yes, well, the food had been sitting on the warming table too long. We all thought Finn was just running late, not—"

The assistant dean appeared at the front of the room and announced that the dean and 'our newest Supreme Court Justice' would be arriving soon. A murmur of excitement rippled across the room.

Doctor Death gripped my arm with an age-flecked hand and said, "What do you think of her?"

"She's fantastic."

"No, not her," he sounded impatient. "*Her.*" He pointed to Hadiza who was standing on the other side of the room, deep in conversation with a man with suede patches on the elbows of his tweed jacket. Must be a professor, no downtown lawyer would be caught dead in that jacket.

"Hadiza? I like her a lot. I— "

"She's not a patch on Finn," he said, draining the last of his wine and casting about for another. "Finn, now he was a crackerjack." Doctor Death reached around with surprising agility for someone his age and scooped a glass of wine off the bar counter. "I've known Finn for years. Met him back when I was a sessional at NYU. He was just a young kid then; whip smart. In his second year at McGill. He was in New York for the summer... for the life of me, I can't recall how we met." Doctor Death laughed, inhaled a crumb and began to hack and cough.

He took a deep swig of his wine, settled himself and continued, his face a fiery red. "That was a glorious summer. My apartment building was half finished. It got caught in a strike, the cement and concrete union, I believe. Half the floor plates were still under construction but the building manager rented every unit they could. Nice and cheap." His rheumy eyes began to shine. "I threw one hell of a party on the other side of the floor. It was nothing but raw concrete. Like partying at the top of a twenty-storey parking garage, no walls, just the wind whistling through ripped orange tarps."

I eyed him suspiciously. Was this even true? "That sounds terribly unsafe," I tutted. "Even for New York. Especially if people were drinking."

"Drinking, smoking, doing drugs, anything you needed to get high. Not like today when you need a permit and a bloody babysitter if you want to have some fun." He began to chortle. "Finn, the scoundrel, he scared the bejesus out of the ladies, sitting at the very edge and swinging his legs over the big black void of New York."

A shudder ran down my spine. This young and reckless Finn was nothing like my Finn, the mature, level-headed academic who wouldn't break a rule if his life depended on it.

I was about to challenge him when the room exploded in a wild burst of applause. The dean and Justice Rinfret had arrived and were making their way through the crowd to the front of the room. The Justice smiled kindly as the dean began a lengthy introduction, starting with Rinfret's accomplishments while teaching at the university, then meandering off into an arcane review of the school's history. The room murmured impatiently. The dean took the hint and quickly turned the floor over to Rinfret.

She was a little dumpling of a woman, with fluffy blond hair, a round open face, and a radiant smile. Keith caught my eye from across the room, then winked: don't let that sweet façade fool you. Professor Rinfret did not tolerate underperformers in her classroom and was not above destroying slackers with a few caustic barbs. Anyone appearing in her court had better come fully prepared.

Doctor Death continued droning in my ear until I whispered, "Shhh, don't be rude. Justice Rinfret is speaking." He rolled his eyes theatrically and clamped his mouth shut.

As soon as she finished her speech the Justice was swarmed by well wishers offering their heartfelt congratulations.

"Well, this has been lovely," I said to Doctor Death as I edged away. "I suppose I'll see you again at Hadiza's event." The old man scowled. Had he forgotten? "When she's formally appointed, I mean. I thought the school would host a cocktail party for her as the new Chair of the Environmental Consortium." As soon as I said it, I realized a cocktail party might be unseemly. Finn had not yet been buried, a party honouring his successor would be like dancing on his grave. "Or," I backtracked, "maybe the school will put a quiet announcement in the professional journals or something..." my voice trailed away.

A light crept into Gideon's eyes when he finally figured out what I was talking about. Then came the sly smile. "Hadiza, poor girl, she'll be glad when Finn's finally in the ground." He tapped his finger on the side of his nose and gave me a cunning nod.

I spluttered on my drink.

He laughed and said, "Perhaps 'glad' is putting it too strongly, let's just say 'relieved'."

I knew my mouth had fallen open because I had to think about closing it. Doctor Death raised one woolly eyebrow and took noisy slurp of wine.

"Evie," AJ swept up behind me with my raincoat, "time to go."

Doctor Death gave me a two-fingered salute and faded into the crowd.

As we walked back to AJ's car, I muttered, "I've been stuck with that miserable old coot for an hour and you chose that exact moment to whisk me away?"

He had no idea what I was talking about.

CHAPTER 10

THE STARSHIP ENTERPRISE

I slipped three smooth stones out of a felt bag, purple edged with gold rather like a miniature Crown Royal bag. When I rolled them in my fingers they glistened and flashed in the late afternoon sunshine. Ammolite.

"Ooh, what have you got there?" Louisa asked, unclipping Quincy from his harness. He scrabbled across the kitchen floor and sniffed disdainfully at his empty food dish.

The stones clicked softly like dice when they bumped against each other. It was strangely soothing. Maybe Peter was right, maybe they do have good Feng Shui.

"What would you pay for earrings made of these?" I showed them to Louisa. "Or a pendant?"

"I don't know. What is it?"

"Ammolite jewelry. Peter's company, DreamStone, makes it."

"They're very pretty." She picked a stone out of my hand. "Did you see that story about the robbery at that jewelry store in Vancouver? Thieves smashed a plate glass window and made off with a chunk of ammolite worth more than five hundred thousand dollars. In broad daylight."

She dropped the stone back into my palm and went to the fridge to pull out a tin of dog food. I slipped the stones back in the purple bag and filled Quincy's bowl with kibble from the monster Tupperware container in the pantry. Quincy bunted my legs as Louisa scooped two heaping spoonfuls of something called turkey stew into his food dish and placed it in front of him. Then she picked up her iPad, googled the story, and showed me a photo. "It was as big as a man's shoe. Five hundred thousand dollars. That's a lot of money, and that was a few years ago."

I sat down beside her at the kitchen island and pinched the photo bigger. The fossilized gem was rounded and lumpy, resting on two little wooden supports. "It looks like an armadillo."

"A precious armadillo. How would thieves fence a thing like that? It's so unique." This was true. People buy ammolite at jewelry stores, trade shows, and auction houses like Christies. A distinctive stone like this would be hard to unload.

I shook the stones out of the purple bag again and set them in a line on the counter. They were alluring in a weird way. "It would probably end up in a private collection somewhere on the other side of the world. Still, stealing it in broad daylight like that was a brazen thing to do."

I resolved to ask Peter about it when we met later in the week. About six months ago DreamStone landed two big contracts with Asian distributors, and Peter and Anya were working feverishly to meet a very tight delivery deadline.

The fossil ammonite, with an 'n' when it's pulled out of the ground, is a priceless cultural treasure. Before the delicate stone can be sanded and polished into the gemstone ammolite, with an 'l', scientists at the Tyrrell Museum have to sign off that it has no scientific or display value. Only then will the bureaucrats in the provincial and federal governments issue the permits required to ship the ammolite out of the country.

The application process is tedious and time-consuming, and the deadline for delivery under the Asian distribution contract was fast approaching. Still Peter and Anya didn't buckle under the pressure. Perhaps it distracted them, giving them something to think about other than Finn's tragic death.

I too needed the distraction. Ever since I'd returned from Banff, I'd been haunted by the thought of Finn's crumpled body wedged behind a garbage bin. Such a senseless death. The image of him racing down the hall was still with me, he'd found something and wanted to show it to me, but no, I was too busy putting the final touches on *An Evening with Finn Tanberg*. God, he was right, it did sound pompous.

Distraction came a couple of days later. With a quiet announcement in a legal periodical, Hadiza was officially the Chair of the Environmental Consortium, and she invited me over to her new office in Murray Fraser Hall to celebrate. It was the first week in June, the regular term was over and the campus was semi-deserted. I rounded a corner and came upon a clutch of students sunning themselves on the lawn at the foot of the Prairie Chicken. The sun glinted off the tall stainless steel sculpture and flashed across the grass.

A few floors up I stopped in a large circular landing, trying to get my bearings. These modern buildings with their off-centre windows and strange angles never fail to disorient me. Eventually I found Hadiza at the end of a long corridor in Finn's old office. Anything that smacked of Finn's presence, his very existence, had disappeared: his wobbly stacks of books on the floor; the ancient notices pinned to the wall; and the whale's eardrum jammed into a corner of his bookshelf. All gone. Replaced by Hadiza's sleek computer and minimalist artwork.

"That wall looks like a pin cushion," I said.

She grimaced "You should see the one behind the bookcase. But this will have to do until maintenance comes around to patch and paint. I'm not holding my breath." She stood up and grabbed her purse. Her ID card bounced on the lanyard around her neck and we went back downstairs into the quad.

Her sour mood improved when we got out into the sunlight. She slipped on her sunglasses and said, "Remember that hearing, the one for that massive solar farm south of town?"

My firm represented a solar power company that was investing $700 million to cover five square miles of agricultural land with solar panels. The local farmers opposed the project but Hadiza's research and Finn's testimony that you could use the land to produce both energy and agriculture convinced the regulator the project was in the public interest.

I laughed. "What I remember is Finn taking us out to the site to get a feel for the topography and us getting caught in a horrendous hailstorm on our way back to town."

"Entirely his fault," she said with an indulgent smile. "He had to replace his windshield if I remember correctly. We'd have made it back in plenty of time if he hadn't insisted on stopping in Vulcan to check out the Starship Enterprise."

I'd forgotten that along with being a leading expert

in renewable energy, Finn was a diehard Trekkie. "We've come this far," he'd said, "it's only an hour out of our way." The car forged through the smattering rain and darkening clouds until we reached the town of Vulcan, population 1,900, give or take a few. We stood at the base of an enormous replica of the starship and exchanged greetings in Vulcan, Klingon, and English. When Finn laughed at our attempts I could see the boy behind his eyes. The skies suddenly opened sending us tearing back to his car.

"He had the best alien accent," Hadiza said as we crossed a university courtyard.

"How would you know, you don't speak Klingon."

We joined the queue at Good Earth, picked up our orders and were able to snag a booth next to the window when its occupant, a tall, gangly student, swung his legs up and walked across the long vinyl bench instead of sliding out on his butt.

"These kids," Hadiza tsked. "No manners. None whatsoever." She ran her serviette across the bench before sitting down.

She drew the back of her hand across her cheekbone, pushing her hair back off her face. It was a delicate gesture and reminded me of a cat, which was funny because she hates cats. Her long fingers picked at the plastic wrap on her slice of banana loaf. I had the impression she wanted to say something and was stalling for time. After a gulp of scalding hot coffee, I asked whether she'd picked up all of Finn's responsibilities yet.

"The day-to-day stuff, yes. The committee work is proving to be more of a challenge."

"Challenge? That's corporate-speak for problem. What's going on?"

She ignored my question. "So, you got trapped by

Doctor Death at the Rinfret affair." She was referring to the reception for the Supreme Court Justice.

I laughed. "I thought only students called him that."

"Everyone calls him that." She smiled, then asked in an off-hand tone, "What were you two talking about? It looked serious."

"*We* didn't talk about anything; *he* wouldn't stop babbling in my ear."

She'd picked apart the cello wrap, tore off a piece of banana loaf and popped it in her mouth. I took a bite of my chocolate muffin and said, "He was reminiscing about Finn. I didn't realize he'd known Finn for decades or that he liked him so much."

Someone squealed behind us. Two girls were jumping around and hugging each other, their backpacks bouncing wildly on their shoulders. Their enthusiasm made us both smile. "Oh yes," Hadiza said, "Doctor Death—Gideon—and Finn were thick as thieves."

"An odd combination, I would have thought."

"Not really. They had the same ornery disposition." She freed another hunk of banana loaf and stuffed it in her mouth, followed by a gulp of coffee.

I shook my head. "Ornery? Doctor Death maybe, but not Finn. Doctor Death must hold the all-time record for students signing up for his class and withdrawing after a couple of days."

Hadiza carefully rewrapped what was left of her pastry and slipped it into her purse. "Doctor Death may have the record for the most students quitting his class, but Finn has had his share of student complaints."

"You're joking!" I leaned closer. "What kind of complaints?" Trysts with students and other lurid scenarios flashed through my mind. No, I shook my head, that was out of the question. Would Hadiza tell me?

She leaned back, stretching her arms along the top of the bench. "Nothing really horrible. Just students complaining about his teaching style."

"What's wrong with his teaching style? He used the Socratic method." I'd taken classes with Finn all three years of law school, he was my mooting coach to boot. He believed that law school was more than memorizing precedents, students had to learn reasoning and critical thinking or they were lost.

"You can't teach reasoning," he'd said after a particularly gruelling class, "you can only model it." Sure, the Socratic method was intimidating if you weren't prepared, but Finn never used his sharp analytical skills to badger or humiliate a student. If he didn't get the answers he wanted he'd move on to the next student and the one after that until everyone understood the precedent and the legal reasoning behind it.

"Oh, he was a Socratic teacher right to the very end," Hadiza said, "but some of his students complained his teaching methods made them feel vulnerable."

"*Vulnerable*? How are these thin-skinned kids going to survive in the real world if they can't cope with the Socratic method? This is law school, not kindergarten."

"You sound just like Finn," she said with a slow smile, "but the world has changed. Kids expect profs to accommodate their different learning styles."

"Since when is someone's learning style a protected human right... assuming there isn't something else going on that we need to take into consideration?"

"I know. And to Finn's credit, he did try to accommodate

them. The night before class he'd distribute the questions he planned to ask, to give students time to prepare."

I huffed. "I'm surprised they didn't ask for the answers as well."

Hadiza's face softened and she said, "Actually some did, but he refused, saying that was a bridge too far." She reached across the table and patted my hand. "Evie, unlike you, not everyone enjoys being thrust into the spotlight."

Later that evening when I related this conversation to Louisa I said, "I don't crave the spotlight, do I?"

She laughed and said, "Seems to me, every time you step into the spotlight, someone tries to kill you."

"Not helpful, Louisa. Not helpful at all."

CHAPTER 11

———

LAURA BAZIN

When someone you care about dies, they become a negative space, like a hole with no edges, and make themselves felt at the strangest times. This was one of those times. I was preparing for a meeting with Peter and Anya but all I could think about was Finn. He used to grumble that Peter was wasting his talents in commerce instead of serving humanity and the common good—Finn liked to use phrases like that—but in the weeks before he died his complaints about Peter took on a strange undertone. "Watch them, Evie," he'd said, "don't let them push you around." I wish I'd asked him to elaborate, but I was up to my eyeballs in a messy trial and put it off until later. And now it was too late.

Stop it, I thought as I went out into the lobby to greet Peter and Anya, *no more remorse*. They greeted me with smiles, looking serene and well rested. I led them back to the conference room which was gloomy in the grey morning light. Or maybe it was just me, fed up with the endless days of constant rain.

Bridget brought in the coffee and fixings. She was just about to close the door when Peter told her to wait, Juve would be joining us shortly.

Anya glanced at her watch, a delicate gold band encrusted with tiny diamonds clamped onto her slender wrist. "You gave him this address? He knows to meet us here, not at the house?" She fussed as if she was Juve's mother. Peter nodded.

"I'm looking forward to finally meeting the notorious Jeffrey Wens," I said.

Peter laughed. "Don't let him hear you call him that."

"Notorious?"

"Jeffrey. He only answers to Juve."

Juve had been with DreamStone since the beginning, but I'd never met him, he was always out at the mine or travelling to Asia or something. From what little I'd been able to glean from the internet, the elusive Mr. Wens was a hardscrabble miner who believed in the magic of ammolite with the same feverish intensity as the miners seeking gold in the Klondike. The few photos of Juve on the DreamStone website showed an attractive, flinty-eyed man in his mid forties, tall and lean and bristling with impatience. One could imagine him stalking out of the photo shoot five minutes after it had begun, telling the photographer that like it or not, he was done.

According to Peter, Juve was the best geologist in the business. If there was a speck of ammonite buried somewhere deep in the ground, Juve would find it.

The sound of an expensive car entering the parking lot rumbled on the other side of the windowpane. A minute later we could hear Bridget laughing in reception. She appeared at the conference room door with Juve in tow. I don't know what he said to her but her cheeks were pink and she tossed her curly blond hair around like a teenager as she hustled down the hall to fetch another coffee cup.

"You drove the Lambo?" Peter asked.

Juve nodded. "The bloody Jag's in the shop again."

Bridget reappeared with another mug and I caught a glimpse of Madeline cruising past the conference room door. Obviously Bridget had sounded the alarm, an eligible man was on the premises and Madeline was checking him out, discreetly of course.

When Anya introduced us, Juve smiled and laugh lines appeared around his eyes. There was something about him, a certain raw magnetism that was captivating. I gave my head a tiny shake and focused on what Peter was saying.

DreamStone had hit a brick wall with the government. "If the Department of Culture doesn't issue our disposition certificate immediately, we'll miss the shipment date and be in breach of the Asian distribution contract," Peter said.

"Evie," Anya's intense blue eyes bored into mine. "It'll cost us hundreds of thousands in lost sales and penalties."

I pulled the contract up on my laptop. It was a ridiculously onerous contract and I wished Peter had let me review it before he scrawled his signature and initials all over it.

"I'll make some calls," I said. I don't usually get involved at this stage of the process but sometimes a call from the company's lawyer will cut through the bureaucratic red tape. "You've sent the government the specimen photographs, right?"

"Sure," Juve said, "but I can tell you right now the ammonite has no academic value."

"Or display value," Peter added.

It didn't matter what they thought, this was the

bureaucrats' call. "How long have they been sitting on the application?" I asked.

Peter shot a questioning glance at Anya who frowned and said, "Ten days."

"Ten days?" I raised an eyebrow. "That's nothing. These things take three weeks, minimum."

An angry grumble rose from the other side of the table. "I don't want to hear any fucking excuses for the government." Juve rose and started pacing behind Peter like a caged animal. "You tell them we're running a business here. We've got deadlines to meet and these bloody bureaucrats better get their asses in gear." He stopped pacing and hovered behind Anya's chair. "Speaking of bureaucrats, I know the woman handling our application. Laura Bazin. She's a single mom—"

"And Laura Bazin's marital status is relevant how?"

Resting his hands on the back of Anya's chair, Juve leaned slightly forward. "Hey, look, life's hard nowadays, what with rising costs and inflation. Especially for a single mom with three kids."

There it was again. Another personal detail. My antenna shot up. "Hold on, are suggesting what I think you're suggesting?"

His eyes narrowed and he said, "Oh come on, Evie. Don't be so naïve. How do you think the big mining companies get their leases? That coal company that wants to dig up the Rocky Mountains didn't get its permit by asking nicely. Somebody owed them a favour and the company called in its chit."

Called in its chit? I glanced at Peter and Anya. Did they understand what Juve was saying? Did they agree? Anya looked back at me, her face bland and serene. Peter was staring at something in the woods on the other side of the window.

"Peter," I said his name a little more sharply than I'd intended. "Just to be absolutely clear here, nobody is going to offer Laura Bazin anything to expedite this application. Because that would be a bribe. Got it?"

Without another word, Juve turned on his heel and headed straight to the door. He stopped at the threshold, turned and said, "You tell them we're running a fucking business here. We've got deadlines to meet and they can damn well pull their thumbs out. *Got it?*"

He stalked out, pausing in reception just long enough to bid Bridget good day before getting into his car and roaring out of the parking lot.

The air in the conference room prickled with tension. Juve hadn't shouted or waved his fist at me, but there was no mistaking the aggression in his voice.

Anya broke the silence first. "Don't mind Juve," she said with a chuckle as she turned toward Peter. "He sounds like fury, doesn't he Peter, but deep down, he's just a pussy cat."

Yeah, a cheetah maybe.

Peter smiled at Anya then at me. "Evie, no one is expecting you to perform miracles here, but as Anya says, there's a lot of money riding on this shipment. The damage to DreamStone, financially and reputation-wise if we fail to deliver will be devastating." He caught Anya's eye. A look passed between them.

"Evie," she said in her silky voice, "isn't there something you can do?"

"Beyond making your case to the government in the most persuasive way possible?" I struggled to keep the irritation out of my voice.

Her eyes flicked toward Peter. There was that look

again. For a split second they reminded me of those creepy twins in horror movies who dress the same and have the same haircuts.

I continued. "I'm happy to try to speed things along with a couple of phone calls and a pointed email reminding them that we're on a tight deadline. Who knows, maybe there's something more they need from us, another photo or piece of paper, but I'm afraid that's it. That's all we can do. Are we all clear?" *Don't let them push you around, Finn said.*

Anya nodded and said, "Oh my, yes. Evie, you're the lawyer, we're your clients. We come to you for guidance in navigating the red tape. That's all. Thank you so much for being so patient with us."

Her parting comments was so saccharine, so deferential, it wasn't until they'd left that I realized that Juve may have lost his temper but it was Anya who'd controlled the meeting, subtly nudging it along from the moment she set foot in my office.

I placed the call to Laura Bazin.

CHAPTER 12

THE WHIP

Sometimes conversations have a beginning, a middle, and an end, and other times they're like a bowl of spaghetti, looping around on your fork in a sloppy blob, getting bigger and more unmanageable.

Laura didn't return my call until the end of the day. We talked for twenty minutes and other than my first sentence—*I represent DreamStone and would like to talk with you about clearing up any issues that may be delaying their disposition certificate*—everything else was gibberish. I glanced at the yellow pad next to the phone after I hung up and tried to decipher my notes:

Confirmed, Laura is handling DreamStone Disp. Cert.

Appreciates the call.

DreamStone people always so kind (??)

No outstanding issues. Got everything she needs to complete application.

Why the delay? I'd underlined my question twice.

She'd responded with a question. "Is the company suggesting it would like to expedite the process?"

"I beg your pardon?" There was a long pause on the line, and as she talked my notes degenerated into hastily-scribbled word fragments:

Hard times
Tough making ends meet
Single mom
3 kids

Why does her family status keep coming up? She blamed the high cost of living on inflation then abruptly asked whether a meeting with Juve and her boss would be in order.

"Your boss?" The government website said she was the manager of the dispositions group.

"The minister," she replied.

"The minister?"

"Yes, Cory Russo."

I was beginning to sound like a parrot, repeating everything she said. But my problem was the hierarchy. There were at least three layers of staff, the director, the assistant deputy minister, and the deputy minister, between her and Cory Russo, the cabinet minister. Why would Russo know her name, let alone give her the power to put meetings in his calendar?

"What could he—" I shut my mouth. I didn't want to know how a meeting between Juve and Russo could expedite the disposition certificate, or what Russo and his minion, Laura, would expect in return.

I took a careful breath, thanked her for her assistance and hung up so forcefully that the receiver bounced out of its cradle. Then I started pacing in front of my window.

The river was heaving and tearing at its banks. The 2013 flood started like this. Days of rain and the river rising until it flooded the whole downtown. I wanted to scoop up our building and carry it to safety in the woods behind the parking lot.

Returning to my desk, I collected my thoughts. The words flowed easily out of Laura's mouth, a meeting with Russo, as if this were an everyday occurrence. If Juve was bribing Laura and Russo to expedite the disposition certificate and wanted to 'call in a chit' then Peter and Anya were in big trouble. And so was I if I didn't stop them. I marched down the hall to talk to Keith.

"Let me guess, you're building a fort."

Keith was standing over his desk, picking through the detritus of half-empty water glasses, coffee cups, and dented pop cans searching for his phone and his favourite pen. Despite the disastrous state of his office, he was immaculately dressed. His wife does a great job of keeping him presentable.

He waved me into his office, then sat down in his chair, elbows out, hands gripping the arm rests; he was in 'I'm listening but make it snappy' mode.

"This will only take a minute," I said.

He gave a quick nod but didn't drop his shoulders or look more relaxed. He wanted to get out of here before rush hour became unbearable.

Quickly I described my meeting with the Dream-Stone team and my subsequent conversation with Laura Bazin. "Remind me, again," he said, "who's the Minister of Culture?"

"Cory Russo."

He groaned. Keith and I had met Russo and some other government ministers at a political function a few years ago. While we didn't care for Russo's politics, it's always wise to be friends with the government of the day. Russo had just been demoted in a cabinet shuffle. He went from

Economic Development to Culture, a shocking loss of status, but better than landing in Services and being in charge of paper clips, I suppose.

Rumours flew that the premier had clipped Russo's wings to punish him for abusing his power as party whip. Keith, a hockey fanatic, likened the role of whip to that of an enforcer on a hockey team, but instead of harassing members of the opposing team, the whip puts pressure on his own team mates to ensure they tow the party line. In Keith's vernacular, Russo threw one bodycheck too many and now he was in charge of culture and heritage. Goodbye to swanky trade missions in New York and D.C., hello to ribbon cuttings at rural community halls.

As if Keith had read my mind, he said, "Remember that fundraiser we went to? Four years ago?"

I nodded. "At Gates, Case and White?" Keith and I had left Gates to start our own green energy law firm by then. The rule about being a friend of government applies in equal measure to remaining friends with the law firm you threatened to sue to hell and back for harassment. You just never know where your next file will come from.

Keith and I had been standing in one corner of Gates' impressive conference room, admiring the view of the city from the forty-fifth floor. I'd just made a snarky comment about our colleagues who were tripping all over them-selves trying to make an impression on the woman who'd replaced Russo when he latched onto us.

He's a big, beefy guy, in his early fifties, a loud man who likes to be the centre of attention. He was born in a small bedroom community just north of the city. Before politics he'd worked at his father's real estate firm. His bio on the government website was twice as long as anyone else's, listing every course he'd taken since he was a boy scout. The man was trying too hard to impress.

I'd glanced at Keith, wondering whether we should mention the cabinet shuffle— "I'm sorry you were demoted" sounded a little awkward—but we needn't have worried; Russo crushed our hands in his sweaty palm and launched into a description of his new duties as Culture Minister. Among other things, he was responsible for mining ammolite, Alberta's official gemstone. Did we know that? He made it sound like he was mining titanium on the far side of the moon. We didn't represent DreamStone at the time so I didn't pay much attention but one thing he said stuck in my mind. As minister, Russo had the power to expedite permits or stop them in their tracks. No doubt he was trying to demonstrate he was still a powerful man despite the demotion, but he said it with such relish it sent a shiver down my spine.

"Evie." Keith nudged me back to the present. "What exactly did Laura Bazin say?"

"She suggested a meeting between Juve and Russo."

"A meeting with a cabinet minister? Why? If the company has provided all the information required, what's the point of the meeting?"

I raised my eyebrows. "My guess is bribery."

"*What?*"

"Hey, what's going on?" AJ was rapping on Keith's door frame. "I can hear you two yelling all the way down the hall."

"Come in," I said. "And for the record, we're not yelling. Keith is talking loudly with a lot of enthusiasm."

A tiny smile flickered across Keith's face.

AJ closed the door behind him and dropped into the

chair next to mine. "Go ahead," he said. "Hit me with a shot of enthusiasm."

Alexander James Braxton, as he known to no one but his mother, joined the firm six years ago as an articling student. His quick mind and playful personality made him into what my dad would call a "keeper" and two years ago we asked AJ to join the partnership. He did and other than some nicer clothes, he hadn't changed a bit.

I heaved a theatrical sigh and Keith said, "Evie thinks her clients—"

"*Juve,* not the others."

"Evie thinks Juve may have bribed or wants to bribe a government minister."

"You're joking!" AJ said.

I pulled a face and lifted my hands in a helpless gesture.

Keith explained my concern to AJ just as I had told it to him, but more slowly. Keith and I have radically different thinking styles: he's a slow thinker, an excruciatingly slow thinker, while I leap on problems, wrestle them to the ground, and move on. Workplace psychologists would say our partnership is doomed to fail, but it works.

Ten minutes later AJ knew everything he needed to know about DreamStone's precarious financial position if the disposition certificate was delayed.

"If this is real," Keith said, "if Juve has bribed or intends to bribe Russo through Laura, we have to fire them as clients."

AJ let out a slow whistle. "What's the going rate for a bribe nowadays?"

Keith, who'd been tapping at his keyboard, raised his hand and said, "Hold on, that's a good point. Evie, did Juve or Laura actually say the word 'bribe' or suggest an amount of cash or something else of value that would serve as an inducement?"

I thought back to the meeting. "No, the only one who used the B-word was me. The idea of giving Laura anything of value, monetary or otherwise, wasn't explicitly discussed. But I know in my gut that's where my conversation with Laura was heading."

A few years ago Keith would have been swayed by my gut, but no more. My instincts, for want of a better word, had gotten me into one too many scrapes for Keith's liking so I wasn't surprised when he replied, "Maybe this Laura person is fishing. Testing the waters to see if your client is willing to offer a bribe." He turned to his computer, pecked at a few keys, then looked up at me. "The Code of Conduct says we have obligations to DreamStone. We can't go off half cocked."

I hate it when he brings up the Code.

AJ chimed in, he was scrolling through the Code on his phone. "Exactly. First you have to figure out if you have good cause to fire DreamStone."

"Oh for God's sake," I said. "Juve's intention and Laura's expectation were a plain as the nose on your face."

Keith was staring at his screen, mesmerized by the arcane and wonderfully unhelpful language of the Code. "It says we can't desert them at a critical stage if it will put them in a position of disadvantage or peril," he said.

"*Peril?* I'll put you into peril in a minute. Look, Juve didn't say the word 'bribe' or specify a sum, and Laura was vague when she suggested Juve and Russo should meet, but their intentions were clear." I flashed back to Juve stalking out of our meeting. If he wasn't talking about bribes, then what the hell was he talking about?

Rapidly, I made a decision. "We won't dump them. *Yet.*

I'll talk to Peter and Anya, tell them I suspect Juve might be planning to bribe Laura and her boss to expedite the certificate... and he may have bribed them in the past." I had an unsettling thought: this better come as a shock to them. "And if the disposition certificate comes in too late to make the shipping date, I'll assure them I'll do everything in my power to minimize the penalties under the contract. That's the best I can do."

AJ gave me an appraising look. "And then after their business is a shambles, we'll fire them?"

I lifted my shoulders in a slight shrug, "It depends on how they react to what I have to say."

* * *

I was steaming down the corridor back to my office when Bridget called my name. "I'm transferring a call to your office," she chirped. "It's your law prof friend."

"Hadiza," I said, cradling the receiver between my ear and my shoulder as I rummaged in in my file for Peter's phone number, "how are you?"

A wheezy laugh crackled in my ear. "Hah. Gideon Gold."

Great, Doctor Death. Could this day get any worse?

CHAPTER 13

QUINCY GOES TO SCHOOL

Tell me again why you're having coffee with Doctor Death," Louisa shouted into the wind. "I thought you didn't like the guy."

It was early evening and Louisa and I were at Fish Creek Park running the dog. The wind was high in the treetops, the leaves on the poplar trees fluttered like tiny clapping hands. We don't usually come down here on weeknights but Louisa had enrolled Quincy in an obedience class close by. On the first day of class we discovered that Quincy's classmates were a pack of miniature schnauzers. He kept pestering them, probably thought they were animated stuffies, and we were instructed to give him a good, hard run before class so he'd leave them alone. Which was why he was clipped to a thirty-foot lead and I was standing thirty-one feet away clapping and shouting his name. We didn't dare let him off the lead or he'd never come back. Hence the need for obedience training in the first place.

"'Don't like' is too harsh, let's just say I'm not fond of the guy, but he wants to see me. Apparently, he's got information about Finn that he's dying to share." The circumstances of Finn's death continued to trouble me; he was too careful to fall off a balcony. Something must have distracted him to make him lose his balance.

"He's coming!" Louisa yelled. Quincy was barrelling toward me like a bowling ball heading for the head pin. I flexed my knees. He bounced off my legs, spun around, and charged back to Louisa.

She was squinting into the sun slanting out of the billowing rain clouds. "Louisa, pay attention!" She dropped to one knee, yelling at Quincy to slow down, then whipped a small ball out of her pocket. He skidded to a stop. She let him take the ball while we clipped him into his short lead and strolled back to the car.

She opened the passenger door of the Mini, flipped down her seat and let Quincy scramble into the back. "Yeah," she said, "but why coffee, can't you talk on the phone?"

"Because he insists on meeting in person and originally he suggested we meet for a drink. I talked him down to coffee. It was a compromise." I shuddered at the thought of me and Doctor Death draped across two barstools at the Hyatt Regency.

"Okay, but why you? You didn't even take his class."

"God only knows. Maybe because I was the only one willing to talk to the old codger at the judge's reception." Whatever the reason, I had the feeling that once he'd found me, he'd cling like a limpet mine. Quincy started yipping and prancing in the backseat as we pulled into the parking lot of the obedience school.

Louisa's mouth was set in a determined line. Tonight was the last night of class. Quincy and his miniature schnauzer buddies would either pass or fail. She had high hopes for Quincy. I wasn't so sure. I'd pinch hit as his trainer on the nights she had to work and as far as I could tell Quincy was one of those goofball students who thought school was a lark.

Ninety minutes later we were back in the parking lot. A fat blue ribbon fluttered in Louisa's hand. She was not happy.

"I don't know what you're grumbling about," I said as she watched Quincy clamber across the back seat with a treat bone in his mouth. She made a hmpff noise and strapped on her seat belt, the blue ribbon in her lap. The caption written in gold on the medallion said: *Most Improved Trainer.*

She hmpffed again, saying, "We didn't pay three hundred and fifty bucks for me to improve as a trainer." She glanced over her shoulder at the dog. "I'm not the one who needs improving, he is."

"Aw, give him a break, if a stranger ran his hands down my spine and around to my groin, I'd leap out of my skin too."

"I don't want to talk about it," She said. The silence on the drive home was punctuated by the sound of Quincy slobbering on his treat bone and leaping up to the window to bark at strangers whenever we stopped at an intersection.

* * *

Two days later at precisely ten-thirty in the morning I was sitting at a high-top table in a Kensington coffee shop two blocks from Doctor Death's condo, watching him make slow and steady progress down the sidewalk. It was cooler than usual for June, a rainy gust tugged at his leather coat which flapped around his thighs and he shoved his fists deep into his pockets trying to hold it closed. I hoped he wouldn't trip; he'd never get his hands up in time to stop from cracking his face on the concrete.

He stepped into the coffee shop, peering around until he spotted me and laboriously worked his way over to my table. His coat was barely off before he demanded a large strong drip coffee, black, and a bran muffin. He flicked his fingers at me. "Go on, get going."

"My treat?" I suggested.

"Of course," he replied.

Soon he was mowing through his pastry like a beaver taking down a birch tree. I don't know anyone who enjoys food with such gusto. Now all I had to do was remember to call him by his real name, Doctor Gideon Gold.

The conversation proceeded in fits and starts until he said, "Have you heard that saying by Samuel Johnson?" Samuel Johnson said many things and I shook my head. "'Academic politics are so vicious precisely because the stakes are so small.'" He laughed then coughed into his serviette.

"That's ironic," I said, "Law school is supposed to train lawyers to be fair, I would have expected law profs to be above the political fray."

Still spluttering, he eyed me. "It never ceases to amaze me how naïve students are. Your professors hold your future in their hands and you have no idea how they think." I bit my tongue. We may have 'no idea' but fifteen years ago I knew enough to bail out of his tax law class before he failed me. He continued. "The trajectory of a professor's career is dependent on three things: performance, service, and productivity."

"Performance? The rate-my-professor stuff?"

He gulped down some coffee to clear his throat and

said, "No, those ratings have fallen out of favour, they're far too subjective. Performance refers to whether you're reliable, do you show up for class? Not exactly a high bar, is it. Second is service."

I said I didn't understand the reference.

"Service. Committee work, administrative stuff. Meetings, meetings, meetings. It chews up your day, it's irritating and as boring as hell. But you have to tick the box. And lastly, this is important; Evie, are you paying attention?" *God, this man.* "Research. You must be a productive researcher, publishing peer-reviewed articles in respected national and international journals."

He dabbed his balled-up serviette to his lips. "In my day there weren't as many publishing outlets as there are today. Look at the law school blog. It's been cited by the Supreme Court of Canada, and it's a *blog* for Christ's sake."

I resisted the urge to challenge Doctor Death on the merits of a blog of sufficient quality to influence the highest court in the land, versus a peer-reviewed article published in an obscure magazine that may be seen by three people if you're lucky.

He slurped the remnants of his coffee, set the empty paper cup down on the table and stared mournfully at the dregs. That was my cue. "Another?" I asked, brightly. He beamed, adding that a cranberry scone would go down well.

The sky outside had darkened and the wind was hurling great swaths of rain hard against the windows by the time I returned to our table, and I wondered how Doctor Death would make it home. He'd walked the two blocks over here and barely made it through the door.

Slipping back onto my stool I said, "I don't understand what any of this has to do with Finn. Obviously, he ticked all the right boxes, performance, service, and productivity, and that's why he was so successful."

"Hadiza," he said. With a start I remembered his comment at the judge's reception. *Hadiza will be glad when Finn's finally in the ground.* Doctor Death folded his skinny hands on his belly and watched me. Those milky grey eyes glittering. I leaned forward and lifted my eyebrows. *Well?*

He shifted in his chair, it wobbled a little, alarming us both, and said in a loud whisper, "Finn's recommendation of Hadiza went a long way to convincing the powers that be that she was the right choice to replace him as Chair of the Environmental Consortium. In essence, he made her career. But he could break it just as easily."

"Why would Finn want to break Hadiza's career?" I felt like I was back in Doctor Death's miserable class. He didn't use the Socratic method, instead he talked in riddles, dribbling out information and watching us squirm as we desperately tried to understand the point he was striving to make.

I was ready to dismiss him until he hit me with his reply. "Finn had a change of heart."

"*What?*"

"He decided Hadiza was no longer the best candidate for the job. It demands intelligence and integrity, you know. They were barely on speaking terms at the end."

"That's ridiculous." Of course they were on speaking terms. Although now that I thought about it, they'd barely said two words to each other the entire weekend at Banff. It was as if Peter, Anya, and I had become unwitting go-betweens.

He gave me a long look, then slurped some more coffee, swishing it in his mouth before swallowing. "Say what you will, I know this to be true."

"And…?" I lifted my hand in an impatient gesture, urging him to continue. He'd dragged me all the way down here in the pouring rain, the least he could do was tell me why.

He smiled like a child with a secret he was bursting to tell, then sat back and dabbed the balled-up serviette under his nose again. This deposited cranberry scone crumbs on his upper lip.

"Teaching in a university is a brutally time-consuming endeavour. In the early years you should expect to put in ten hours of prep time for one hour of class time. Later, that drops to two to three hours per one hour of class time. So where do academics find the time to teach, do the admin work, and research on top of that? Performance, service, productivity?"

He stopped and looked at me as if I knew the answer. I shrugged. "I have no idea."

"The smart academics enlist, or dragoon if you will, their students to help them with their research."

"Makes sense to me. It lightens the prof's load and the students get extra credit or some kind of recognition for their contribution, right?"

"Ah," now he looked smug. "Therein lies the rub."

"Oh for God's sake Gideon, spit it out!" I don't know what surprised him more, the fact I'd lost my temper or that I used his first name.

"Right," he huffed. "When Hadiza was a sessional in Joburg many, many years ago, she enlisted a young stu-dent to help her with a research project, something about the law, or lack thereof, relating to internally displaced persons. She presented the student's work as her own. He didn't raise a fuss at the time, but he's since moved to Canada and is practising in Edmonton. When he heard

Hadiza was replacing Finn as Chair of the Consortium, he contacted Finn to lodge a formal complaint."

"I don't believe it," I said, watching the couple beside us slipping on their jackets. Neither of them had an umbrella. They'd be soaked to the bone in this downpour. "When did this happen?"

"The complaint?"

"Yes, this so-called complaint."

"A couple of weeks ago. Finn was going to deal with her after that ridiculous celebration in Banff. But he died—convenient, that—before he had the opportunity to do so."

"Convenient? What are you implying?"

"Nothing," he said, feigning surprise at my question. "It was a simple statement of fact." This was classic Doctor Death, stirring the pot to undermine Hadiza's reputation and my faith in her.

Anger bubbled up inside me. "You have no right—" Outside something metallic smacked into the window then flew out into the street. It looked like a mailbox, tumbling end over end, the metal flap clanking until it came to rest in the middle of the street where it was crushed under the wheels of a semi.

The wind was fierce. There was no time and no point in continuing this conversation. "Let's get you home."

He raised a thin age-specked hand in protest, then looked outside and agreed that would be a good idea.

My car was parked in a small lot four blocks in the wrong direction. It would be quicker for me to walk Gideon to his condo. We pulled up our collars and I looped my arm through his as he weaved and staggered in the wind which caught his hair and whipped the words out of his mouth. But, to my surprise, he managed to utter thank you when we reached his lobby and he ducked inside.

CHAPTER 14

IMPOSTER SYNDROME

By the time I reached the office the sluicing rain had settled into a fine mist, rare in these parts, and a vapid sun glimmered through the clouds. I sloughed off my damp raincoat and hung it on the hook behind the door. Madeline trailed after me. "Where were you this morning? You look like you took a dip in the reservoir." She handed me a fluffy white towel.

"Where did this come from?" We don't have white towels in the bathroom. My words were muffled as I threw the towel over my head and pressed the damp out of my hair.

"My private stash." Of course. One could dip into Madeline's private stash and emerge ready for a night on the town... in St. Moritz. In fact I'm sure that our sophisticated paralegal maintained her stash for precisely that reason.

She reached for the towel and started to fold it, while nodding at my hair. "It's gone all wavy."

I pushed the damp curls off my face and said, "I had coffee with Gideon Gold this morning."

Madeline, who usually glides around the place like a

swan on a placid lake, flung the half-folded towel into one visitor's chair and plopped down into the other. "You're hobnobbing with Doctor Death? Why on earth would you do that?" Then she laughed as the look of surprise crossed my face. "Oh, come on. Every lawyer in town calls him that, I'll bet even his wife calls him that. What could you two possibly have to talk about?"

"His wife is dead, Madeline. And he's pretty lonely as far as I can tell."

"Never mind that, what are you two up to?"

I studied her studying me. Her auburn hair was swept back on one side and cascaded in thick waves over her shoulder. Red hair, pale skin, glittering green eyes, she'd be formidable even if she didn't dress like the Hepburns, Audrey or Katherine, depending on her mood. She'd been my guardian angel since my first day as an articling student at Gates, Case and White. Being mentored by Madeline was not a gentle experience, more like being whacked around by a cricket bat. So naturally I told her.

"Well, to make a long story short, according to Gideon, Finn was going to withdraw his support for Hadiza to succeed him as Chair." Her eyes narrowed as I explained that a former student claimed that Hadiza had passed off his work as her own.

"Years ago?" She wrinkled her nose. "Sounds contrived to me. Just as Hadiza is offered a plum job, some mysterious student pops out of the woodwork claiming plagiarism? I don't believe it. Gideon is just an old white guy miffed that a younger woman, of a different ethnicity to boot, has achieved more than he could dream of."

"Perhaps," I said.

Madeline told me to put the whole thing out of my mind. And I did.

The next day I received an email from a ghost.

CHAPTER 15

MESSAGE FROM A DEAD MAN

Jesus Christ!" I must have shouted because Madeline flew across the hall and into my office. She found me frozen in my chair, eyes locked on my computer screen.

"What?" Madeline was standing over me. Her head bent down to see the screen, so close her hair tickled my cheek.

I pointed, horrified, at the screen. Madeline stood back and yelled for Bridget to get in here. Bridget, who bristles at being bossed around, barreled into my office. "What's wrong?"

"What the hell is this?" I jabbed at the computer screen. Bridget may be an apple-cheeked farm girl but she knows our IT system better than anyone else. "How is this possible?"

I'd been winnowing out the junk mail: Law Society notices, lunch-and-learns, subscription renewals, when I saw something that stopped my heart. A message from Finn Tanberg. "How is this possible? Look at the date. He sent it last night. At midnight. He's been dead for over a week."

"He didn't send it yesterday," Bridget said, turning my laptop to face her.

"Someone hacked his account?" Madeline sounded as mystified as I was.

"No," Bridget said. "This is a scheduled email. He wrote it some time ago and clicked the 'delay delivery' option." A look of incomprehension crossed my face. "It sat in his outbox until the scheduled send date and time, which must have been midnight yesterday given its time stamp."

"Why would he do that?" I wondered. "What's the point?"

Madeline pulled my laptop away from Bridget and read the email aloud:

Evie, need to meet, you and me, re: Dream-
Stone financials. Highest priority. Next week?
Time is of the essence.

"Time is of the essence?" Madeline repeated. "Did he really talk like that?"

"Yes, and he quotes the Bible and John Milton when it suits him. But if it was so bloody urgent, why didn't he pull me aside for a quiet chat in Banff?" An awful thought: Maybe he'd tried and I blew him off because I was sorting out an 'important' detail like the lack of effing asparagus. Damn, the tears were pricking my eyes again.

Madeline closed the laptop gently and said, "Perhaps whatever was bothering him involved one or more of the people at Banff and he didn't want to throw a major monkey wrench into the celebration dinner. Whatever it was, he didn't want it to slide so he fired off this email."

"Bridget," I said, blinking hard a few times, "did Finn send any other delayed emails? Something to explain what specifically he was fussed about?"

"There's no way to tell. All you can do is wait and see if anything else shows up in your inbox."

Wait and see? If there's one thing I hate doing, it's waiting and seeing, especially for a second urgent missive from a dead guy.

So I called Patrice.

She picked up the phone on the second ring and I gulped. I hadn't given any thought to how I was going to broach the idea of Finn sending emails from the grave. After some sympathetic small talk I followed my mom's advice and grabbed the cow by the ears—Mom was Hungarian, she never did get the hang of English idioms—and asked Patrice whether she'd received any notes of any kind from Finn recently.

"Notes? What kind of notes?"

"Emails, postcards, letters, anything like that. Things you may have missed in all the confusion, after Finn died."

"He sent me notes all the time."

"No, Patrice, I'm talking about *after* Finn died."

And she started to cry. She'd just received a call from the Banff RCMP and it rattled her. They had some lingering questions about the circumstances leading up to Finn's death and they wanted a copy of the guest list, everyone who'd been invited to Finn's celebratory dinner and anyone else who was there in support of it.

"Evie, they even asked about you and Hadiza. Finn's celebration of life is coming up soon. Why are the police still calling me and asking about it? I don't understand what's going on."

That made two of us. I had no contacts at the RCMP, but I did know someone with the Calgary police force. I promised Patrice I'd give him a call, anything to put her mind at ease. Then I returned to the reason I'd called in the first place.

"So, just to confirm, you haven't received anything from Finn, nothing that arrived after he died?"

"Nothing. But I'll ask Peter."

My heart skipped a beat. Instinct told me involving Peter was a bad idea although I didn't know why. "No, Patrice, that won't be necessary. Let's not bother Peter and Anya with something as trivial as this right now. They're working on the Asian deliveries, they've got more than enough on their minds." She agreed to let it drop. Or so I thought.

*   *   *

Sergeant Pritchard and I have an odd relationship. Three years ago he was the homicide cop assigned to investigate the murder of a friend and we'd gotten off to a rocky start. My fault, I'll admit it. I wasn't entirely forthright with him—that's lawyer-speak for 'evasive'—and as a result, got myself into a heap of trouble. Nevertheless after the case was solved we continued to meet up for the occasional drink to shoot the breeze or whatever it's called when you no longer have a professional reason to see someone but you see them anyway.

"Valentine," he said when he picked up my call. Caller ID; there's no surprising people anymore.

"Pritchard," I replied. "It's been a while." I could imagine him sitting in his office, squinting out a grimy window at the railway tracks on the other side of the scruffy field behind the station.

"How can I help you?"

He didn't sound like he wanted to help me at all, but

I took him at his word and explained Patrice's situation. "Why are the Banff RCMP asking questions about Finn so many days after he died? Are they investigating it as a suspicious death?"

Pritchard tried to fob me off with a few bland words, but I continued to press until he agreed to call the Banff police on Patrice's behalf. "Don't expect anything," he cautioned. "They have a job to do and they'll do it as they see fit."

That was Pritchard's way of telling me what he'd so often told me in the past: back off.

*   *   *

By the time I pulled up in front of my house I was in a strange mood. It had been a baffling and unproductive day. Peter hadn't returned my umpteen messages—we had to talk about Juve—Finn had sent a cryptic message from the grave and the RCMP were snooping around. The world stopped making sense the day Finn died.

It's the weekend, I reminded myself as I trudged up the front steps, Quincy and I would go for a long run tomorrow, we could have a picnic at Nose Hill Park if it didn't rain.

Louisa greeted me with a big hug. "Pack your bags, Evie, we're going to the Banff Springs Hotel!" Quincy barked in excited puppy yips with no idea of why.

"*We're* going to Banff, you and me? Isn't this your mini getaway with what's his name?"

A tiny line appeared between her eyes and she gave her head a curt shake. "What's his name and I broke up." She glanced at her watch. "About two hours ago."

"Oh no. I'm so sorry, Louisa."

"It's all for the best."

"Yes, it is. To tell you the truth, I didn't like that guy."

She smacked my arm. "You should have said something!"

She was right, I should have said something, but I was trying to spare her feelings, be a supportive sister. What's his name reminded me of Louisa's ex-husband, the odious Doctor Bob, who'd made Louisa's divorce an absolute misery. He got more than he deserved in the settlement because Louisa panicked when he threatened to sue for custody of the dog. He didn't even like the dog.

"Wait, who's going to take care of Quincy?" That was going to be my job while Louisa and what's his name swanned around in the mountains.

"All taken care of. Destiny is coming tomorrow at the crack of dawn." Louisa thinks Destiny is a dog whisperer and Quincy loves that girl.

Louisa caught the flicker of concern in my eye. "Are you okay with going back to Banff? So soon after..." she trailed off.

The idea of staying at the Banff Springs Hotel so soon after Finn's death did unsettle me, but Louisa was coming off fourteen straight days at the hospital and she'd just broken up with what's his name. My little sister desperately needed a change of scenery.

"Sure," I said, "we'll have a great time."

* * *

The next morning Quincy and Destiny waved goodbye from the living room window as Louisa and I roared out of the driveway. Well, Destiny waved, Quincy was riveted on her pocket, waiting for the special treat she'd drop into his mouth the minute we turned the corner and disappeared out of sight.

Traffic was light and we made excellent time. What's

his name had booked them into a tiny room, the website described it as cozy with limited views. Louisa flung open the door and declared it was perfect. We crammed our luggage into the tiny closet and walked down the steep hill into town. I should have brought sunglasses, the sunlight bouncing off the snow-capped mountains was blinding. It was early June, but the air was still crisp and cool. Tourists clogged the shops and restaurants, doing their best to boost the local economy.

"Thank God I brought my jacket." I shivered and zipped my coat right up to my chin when we entered a café.

"You're always cold," she dismissed me with a flip of her hand as we followed the hostess through the restaurant and back out to the packed patio. We'd just placed our lunch order when someone called my name.

"Evie, fancy meeting you here!" Peter and Juve were standing on the other side of the low stone wall that separated us from the throng of tourists crowding the sidewalk. Peter reached over to shake Louisa's hand and Juve gave her a rakish grin. He didn't look the least bit apologetic about stalking out of our meeting the other day. It was as if it had never happened.

"What brings you two to town?" Peter asked. "Here for the gem show?" When we admitted we knew nothing about a gem show he put on an exaggerated shocked face. "It's simply one of the best gem shows in the west." He rummaged in his pockets, pulled out a brochure and pressed it into my hand. The Banff Gem and Mineral Show was running all weekend at the Banff Centre, a glittering glass convention centre nestled on the side of Sleeping Buffalo Mountain. "You've got to drop by. Come see our booth. It's a work of art, isn't it Juve."

When I asked after Anya, Peter smiled indulgently.

Anya hated crowds. They'd left her at the hotel, the Banff Springs naturally, nursing a migraine.

"Oh, and great news, we're exhibiting at the Tucson Gem and Mineral Show next February."

Juve, who'd been standing quietly by Peter's side, suddenly came to life. "It's the biggest and best gem show on the fucking planet. Invitation only." He clapped Peter on the shoulder so hard Peter stumbled. "Peter wrangled us an invite, didn't you, buddy!"

Peter grinned and said, "We'll let you ladies eat in peace." He leaned a little closer. "Look, Evie, I know you've been calling, but we've been crazy busy getting ready for this show, why don't we catch up over a dinner? Anya would love to see you. Juve can man the booth for a couple of hours."

I explained we already had dinner plans. Louisa and I were dining with James McQuinn. "You may remember him, the head chef who took care of the food for Finn's celebration dinner."

"Right—" he sounded uncertain. He probably didn't remember James after all.

Juve gave us a quick salute and said, "Make sure you stop by the gem show tomorrow. You'll be very impressed."

I assured him we'd be there. If nothing else, it would give me a chance to buttonhole Peter and finally get some answers to the questions I had about Juve's relationship with Laura Bazin.

CHAPTER 16

A HARD MAN

What do top chefs do when they're dining out and the food isn't up to their finicky standards? When the mussels are rubbery and the potatoes taste like wallpaper paste do they choke it down or carry their plates back to the kitchen for a 'teaching moment' with the hapless chef? Louisa and I were about to find out.

It was just after seven o'clock. Louisa and I were sitting at a cozy table in the iconic Maple Leaf Grill in the heart of Banff. I scanned the crowd. Nicely dressed but not overly formal. No one dresses for dinner anymore. The aroma of 'Canadian-inspired cuisine', Alberta beef and west coast seafood, wafted out of the kitchen tantalizing the diners with what was to come.

James came through the front door and spent a few moments chatting with the hostess before joining us.

"I've let them know we're here," he said. I assumed he meant he'd let them know *he* was here. "This is a good place. They'll whip up a meal you'll never forget." He glanced around the room which tinkled with the sound of cutlery and laughter and soft jazz.

Louisa met my eye. She'd registered his curly blond hair, high cheekbones, and warm brown eyes. He radiated quiet confidence. I wondered for a fleeting moment whether James had a partner. He'd be more suitable for Louisa than what's his name. Or would he?

I didn't know much about James other than what he'd told me many years ago back in law school. He'd had an unconventional upbringing. His mother, Sky, was the last of the hippies, attending all the big protests, chaining herself to trees and gluing herself to art. He'd said it with a rueful smile. That explained his first name, Cedar, which he stopped using on the first day of law school. He had no idea who his father was and to hear him tell it, he practically raised himself.

As we slowly worked our way through our meal—grilled vegetable gnocchi for Louisa and me, duck for James because he wanted to try the artichoke risotto—the pinot gris flowed and James relaxed. By the time our coffees arrived he was ready to tell me why he'd left law school.

"I really wanted to stay, but Finn forced me out."

No, that can't be true.

James looked deep into his glass, it sparkled in the golden light. "I would have been a damn good lawyer…" His voice trailed off. I glanced at Louisa who shot me a quizzical look that said: *It's been more than fifteen years and he's still hurting?*

"Sky was devastated. For someone who professed to be an anti-establishment troublemaker she'd set her heart on her little boy becoming a whiz-bang lawyer." He glanced up at me for a moment, then returned to staring into his wineglass. "It all came flooding back when you and Hadiza booked that dinner for Finn."

I sat back in my chair; he'd spoken softly but the impact of his words hit me hard. "I don't understand, why would Finn force you out of law school?" Had James been caught cheating? No, that was ridiculous. He wasn't that kind of student.

"Perhaps 'forced out' is too strong a way to put it, but Finn's the reason I quit."

Louisa's wineglass was suspended halfway to her lips. I set mine down, not daring to take a sip for fear I'd choke.

"James, what happened?"

His looked directly into my eyes and said, "That man was obsessed with making a name for himself."

"That's not how I remember him," I said quietly. Finn was driven to excellence, but obsessed? No.

"Yeah well, you were his pet, weren't you."

I could feel the heat rise to my face. "Finn didn't have pets," I said stiffly, "he treated all of his students the same."

"Evie, I shouldn't have said that. Forgive me. All I'm saying is Finn was a hard man, a stickler for 'the rules'"—I could hear the air quotes—"and he made it impossible for me to continue after first year."

"I'm still not following you."

James watched a server light a flame in the massive stone fireplace. It flickered gently in the fading evening light. "I know the rumours, I heard them all. But no, I didn't have a nervous breakdown, I wasn't caught cheating and I wasn't afraid of flunking out. My GPA at the end of the year was more than acceptable."

His face hardened and he was lost in a memory. "Law school's expensive, not as ridiculously expensive as it is today, but still expensive. We didn't have that kind of money. I cobbled together some scholarships and Sky, bless her heart, picked up work as a house cleaner." He rolled his eyes. "What a joke that was, Mom was such a slob. Still, it wasn't enough so I got a part-time job in a restaurant, Santorini's. I think it's still around. Anyway, the scholarship money would keep flowing as long as my grade point didn't drop below a B."

"James, you were brilliant. Maintaining a B average would be no problem for you."

"You're right, I *am* brilliant." He gave a wry smile. "Juggling school and work was no problem until old man Santorini got sick. To help him out I agreed to work extra hours, just until he was well enough to come back. He was supposed to be out for two weeks, but he had complications and was out of commission for six. It almost killed me. I was in school all day, in the restaurant until two or three in the morning, then rushing home and cramming for class. God, what a grind."

He drained his wineglass and lined it up next to his coffee cup. "To make a long story short, I bombed Finn's final exam. That dragged my final grade down to a C. I begged him to give me the benefit of the doubt, to bump it up a letter grade so I wouldn't lose the scholarship, couldn't we plead extenuating circumstances or something. You know what he said?"

I was afraid to ask.

"'James, if I make an exception for you, I'll have to make an exception for everybody. That's how floodgates work. That wouldn't be fair now, would it.'"

"Couldn't you do extra work, write another paper or something?"

"Finn wouldn't hear of it. Rules are rules he said."

"Why didn't you ask the dean for permission to

withdraw from the semester, not write the final exams, and just come back in September?" It had been done before: Two people withdrew in first year, one fell apart when her father was killed in a gruesome boating accident and the other had chronic health problems that flared up during mid-terms. They both returned to class in the fall and graduated a year behind me.

James gazed past me as if I hadn't spoken. Then he shifted in his chair. It was getting late. The moon had risen, coating the streets in a cool white light. "Just think what I could have accomplished," he said it quietly, as if to himself, "if Finn had given me half a chance."

"James," I tried to mollify him. "You've accomplished so much. Your mom must be proud of your culinary success."

"She's dead."

"Oh, I'm—"

"It was a long time ago. But as far as her being 'proud' of my so-called success, back then she thought I was a fucking failure. I was making minimum wage when she died. Working shoulder to shoulder with alcoholics and drug addicts. No better than she was. Stuck in the sewer, nowhere to go but down. She quit working after I dropped out. What was the point?" A puff of cold wind curled around our ankles when a couple pulled open the restaurant door and stepped outside. James shivered. "Before I knew it, she was back on drugs. She died of an overdose in some flophouse in Vancouver."

"Oh James, I am so sorry to hear that," I said, softly.

He took a deep breath. "Like I said, it was a long time ago. I was devastated and went back to Santorini's full time and, surprise, discovered I had a knack for cooking and running a restaurant and," here he made a sweeping gesture that seemed to embrace the restaurant and the entire moonlit town, "as they say, the rest is history.

"It's funny you know, all these years I thought I was fine with it. Reconciled to my fate, the road less travelled and all that. Then Hadiza contacted us to plan Finn's dinner. Did we have wild asparagus, what were the vegetarian options?" He rolled his eyes. "What a fussy little man he was."

That wasn't fair, Hadiza was the fussy one, desperately trying to impress her mentor; Finn just wanted to get the whole thing over and done with.

James caught our waiter's eye and signaled we were ready for the cheque.

I glanced at Louisa, she looked as dismayed as I was. What started as a pleasant evening was ending on a dismal note.

"James," I said, "Focus on where you are now. Look at you. One of the country's top chefs, with an international reputation. I know, I googled you." I chuckled in an effort to lighten the mood.

He smiled and kibbitzed with the waiter, and I wondered whether he believed me.

CHAPTER 17

MURDERERS' GHOSTS

Saturday morning dawned grey and misty. I stepped out of the warmth of the hotel lobby and joined the smattering of guests on the curb waiting for the jitney to take us to the gem show. People complained that it was unusually cold for this time of year. They popped their collars and jammed their hands in their pockets, wondering if they had time to run back inside and grab a coffee to go. Peter and Juve were nowhere to be seen; the show opened at nine o'clock, they would have left for the venue hours ago.

Louisa, that little turncoat, scoffed when I suggested she join me on this junket. She hated tradeshows, had I forgotten? They were too noisy and too crowded. The only things worth seeing were the carnival barkers flogging magic knives that turned the lowly radish into a rose and a zucchini into a pagoda or something. "If there aren't any magic knives, what's the point?"

It turned out she was right about all of it: the noise, the crowds, the absence of magic knives. I flipped the floor map around until the sketch and I were facing the same direction and plowed through the excited babble until I found the DreamStone booth. It was an airy space with two long tables at the front draped with a light blue floor-length tablecloth. The back wall consisted of four towering display cases jammed with stones of varying shapes and sizes, some were cut and polished, others were not. Everything glittered under hundreds of mini spotlights.

Juve was talking to a customer at one end of the table, Peter was standing at the other end, pecking away at an iPad. Next to him was a large glass case containing an intact ammonite fossil four times larger than the one stolen in the smash and grab in Vancouver. It must be worth a fortune.

"Evie, there you are!" Peter came around the table and gave me a long hug.

I smiled and pointed at the massive ammonite fossil. "Is that thing safe here?" He laughed and nodded at a tiny sign at the base of the display case that said the piece was a replica. The original was in the private collection of someone whose name I didn't recognize.

Juve's customer drifted away clutching a small white plastic bag and he was now engrossed in a conversation with two men wearing dealer badges. This was my chance to talk to Peter about Laura Bazin. "Peter," I said in a low voice, "we need to talk."

He glanced at Juve out of the corner of his eye, then put an arm around my shoulders and led me to the opposite corner of the booth. "Okay, what's up?"

"I called Laura about the disposition certificate. She suggested Juve meet with Cory Russo. You know how I feel about this. A meeting with Russo would be completely inappropriate. Why would she even suggest such a thing? Is there—"

He lifted both hands. "Hold on. That's what you're fussed about? Relax, it's all fixed."

"What? When?"

"Last night. Anya got confirmation around eight, Laura approved the application for a certificate. I don't know what you said to her, but it worked." Before I could protest that I'd said nothing he changed the subject, practically crowing with excitement. They'd submitted four pieces of ammolite to Christie's for an auction estimate and learned this morning that two pieces had been accepted. "First the invitation to exhibit in Tucson, and now Christies." He brought his hands together and pivoted as if he were swinging a baseball bat. "We're in the big leagues now!"

Out of the corner of my eye I caught a glimpse of Juve. He was still talking to the two gem dealers, but his back was stiff and his head was cocked in our direction. He gave a loud mirthless laugh, then shook each dealer's hand and ambled over to join us.

"Evie, nice to see you again." He smiled. With his weathered tan his teeth looked very white. "Great job on the certificate. The shipment is on its way to Asia as we speak."

"I didn't do—"

"Excuse me, more customers." He returned to the other end of the table where an elderly woman accompanied by a younger woman, presumably her daughter, pointed at a piece of jewelry in the back display case. The older woman's fluting voice drifted through the excited buzz. Was it true, she asked, that ammolite was the world's most scarce gemstone? Juve leaned close and held out a closed fist. I hadn't seen him pick it up but when he uncurled his fingers a perfect gemstone glistened in his palm. It was the size of an apricot pit. Even from this distance I could see the blue-green colours shimmering at its heart.

"We call it Sunrise." Juve's voice was low, almost seductive. She bent closer and he placed the stone in her hand and turned his attention to the younger woman. "Ammolite has magical Feng Shui properties. Highly prized in the Far East." He must have said it a million times before, but it still sounded fresh. The younger woman watched him with a tentative smile. He reached into the display case and selected some rings and bracelets and arranged them on a dark blue velvet pad. He plucked the gemstone, Sunrise, out of the elderly woman's hand, replacing it with a silver ring studded with ammolites. "Please," he said. "Try it on."

Again he smiled and she smiled back. There was no doubt in my mind he'd nailed the sale.

Someone grazed my shoulder startling me. Anya materialized at my side, her sharp blue eyes searching mine. "Peter mentioned you and your sister were in town." Her tone was low and sweet. "It's a shame you couldn't join us for dinner. I hope James took you somewhere nice." Not waiting for a reply she turned to Peter and said, "Did you tell her about the Christie's contract?" He nodded and she pulled out her phone and emailed it to me.

She opened the glass case housing the large fake ammolite and shifted the display card to make it more visible. As she chatted to Peter my attention drifted back to Juve. The older woman was putting her credit card back in her purse while Juve slipped two rings and a silver bracelet into a small box the same blue as Anya's eyes.

*   *   *

Louisa was sprawled on the bed, her face illuminated by the reflected glow of her iPad, when I returned to our hotel room. The milky skies had darkened with the rapid onset of rain and the room was nothing but shadows. I picked my way over her shoes and the two shopping bags between me and the floor lamp in the corner, clicking on the desk lamp for good measure as I passed. Two more shopping bags slumped in the chair by the desk. I've travelled with Louisa many times and it never ceases to amaze me how tidy she is at home and what a slob she is when we're on vacation.

"What did you do, buy out the shops?" I switched on the floor lamp and the bedside lamp. I hate the dark.

She pointed to a small red plastic bag on the upholstered chair. "Marzipan! I found three pieces at the Rogers' store!" As far as I'm concerned, Rogers' makes the best chocolate-covered marzipan on the planet, but other than Louisa and me, no one seems to like it so it's always in short supply. When we were in Victoria we went back to the store three days running, waiting for the next shipment to come in, but it never did.

I grabbed the bag and flung myself onto the bed beside her. "What on earth are you watching?" I asked, passing her a piece of marzipan. Black and white photos rolled across her screen while eerie music moaned in the background.

"Ghosts!" Louisa devoured her first piece of candy and broke the other in half, passing me the bigger chunk. "This hotel is haunted. Bet you didn't know that."

"I did know that. Some poor young bride fell down a staircase and people swear they've seen her mournfully floating around in her wedding dress ever since."

"Hah! That's nothing. There's the murders in room 873—a man went nuts, killed his wife and little girl, then committed suicide. Evie, we have to go up there. The eighth floor is the only floor in the hotel that doesn't have a room ending in 73. Management says they knocked out the wall to make another room bigger but"—here she wiggled her eyebrows— "the question is why? Could it be because of the piercing screams heard in the middle of the night and the bloody fingerprints that appear on the mirror the next morning? Could it? Hmmm?"

As she snuggled deeper into the pillows her chocolate marzipan slipped out of her fingers and landed on the magazine between us, just missing the pristine white duvet.

"That was lucky," she said. "Look, here's Sam McAuley, the 'friendly old Scottish bellman'. He worked here in the 1960s and swore he'd never retire. Two old ladies say he helped them get back into their room when they lost their keys." She squirmed around to look at me. "*After he was dead!* Evie, isn't this cool?"

I shook my head. "You're a trained medical professional. There are no such things as ghosts."

There may be no such thing as ghosts, but it was all we talked about until room service arrived an hour later. We were already in our hotel bathrobes when a young woman in a brown uniform rolled the room service trolly into our room. After she left, we sat cross-legged at the foot of the bed, feasting on pepperoni pizza and watching M*A*S*H reruns, something we'd never do at home. Later, when I carried our trays to the door and set them on the floor in the hallway, I said to Louisa, "I'll just leave these here for Sam the bellman, shall I?"

She flung a pillow at me.

CHAPTER 18

THE CAVE AND BASIN

It was early Sunday morning and we dragged ourselves out of bed to meet James for a hike before we packed up and returned home. He was waiting for us at the corner of Banff Avenue and Buffalo Street, his windbreaker unzipped and his blond hair poking out from under a brown wide brimmed hat. It looked like a newer version of Finn's beat up Tilley.

James was almost shy when he greeted us and I wondered if he regretted his harsh comments about Finn the night before.

Louisa pulled up her sightseeing app and after a short debate about the relative merits of the various Commonwealth Walkway paths, green, blue, red, or orange, she announced she wanted to see the Cave and Basin, so the Red Walk it was.

James and I fell in side by side while Louisa ambled on ahead. The grey-green mountains towered above us and the clouds were so close we could almost touch them. James took a deep breath; the air was still and cool. "We had a great class, didn't we, Evie? None of that dog-eat-dog competition with pages ripped out of textbooks, all that crap they warn you about."

"That was certainly true in first year," I said, "But it got pretty cutthroat by the end of second year when we were competing for summer jobs that might, fingers crossed, lead to an offer of an articling position after graduation."

His jaw tightened and he glanced at me out of the corner of his eye. "That wouldn't have mattered to me." Then he stopped and stared at the mountain tops rising sharply to our right. "Would it have killed him to cut me a break?"

Not this again. I wanted to grab him by the shoulders and yell in his face, "For the love of God, James, let it go!" Instead I fiddled with my zipper, pulling it up and down, and said, "You've got a stellar career, and look," I opened my arms to embrace the shiny white clouds resting on a thick grove of trees, "you get to live and work here, in this magnificent place."

"Yeah, that's what I kept telling myself. For years. That I was happy with how my life turned out. You know the old saying, 'when life hands you lemons, make lemonade.'" He snorted. "How's that for a cook's cliché?" He stopped and watched Louisa's chestnut brown hair and red jacket move further up the trail. "Did I tell you I became obsessed with his career?"

"Finn's?"

"Yeah. I read everything I could find about the guy, and there was a lot. I've got to hand it to him, he accomplished more than most."

I bit my lip. Finn was dead. He'd accomplish no more.

James sloughed off his jacket and slung it over one shoulder. "I could have achieved a lot, made my mark in the world, if he'd given me a half a chance."

I was about to ask him why so many men were obsessed with making their mark, it's not as if they're dogs peeing up poles, when Louisa shouted for us to get a move on. We hustled up the slope to catch up to her and join a small group of tourists clustered at the museum's entrance.

It wasn't a big museum but Louisa likes to study every single exhibit and read every single label on a display case so our progress was slow. Finally I tugged at her elbow saying I wanted to see the hot springs basin before the next ice age. We went through a rocky tunnel to the cavern. The smell of sulphur was overpowering and Louisa started to cough. She'd be gagging soon if we lingered too long. The pool at the bottom of the cave was a crystalline greeny-blue illuminated by a shaft of golden sunlight spilling down from the vent high above. We dipped our hands in the hot water, no one was allowed to swim here anymore, and went back outside to visit the snails.

James watched as we crouched by the edge of a rough stone pool trying to see these minuscule creatures. "Banff Spring Snails." He said it with pride. "You won't find them anywhere else on the planet, they're on the endangered list."

Louisa squealed; she'd spotted one no bigger than a baby's fingernail. I saw a bunch more about the size of apple seeds clinging to the side of the rocky pool. How could they survive in this hot sulphurous water? The image of the gigantic ammonite shell, the fake one on display at the gem show, came to mind. I realized I knew absolutely nothing about ammonites, other than when they died and were fossilized, they became ammolites with an "l" and their rainbow shells were prized around the world.

"Aren't they lucky?" I said to Louisa. "They're so tiny no one wants to harvest them and turn them into jewelry."

"Well, that was a weird segue," she said, standing up. "James, I think it's time you two went for coffee."

"Aren't you coming?" he asked. She said she wanted to look around in the museum gift shop and maybe pick up something small for her team at work. So I left Louisa and followed James down the path into town.

At the end of every street in Banff is a tall, craggy mountain, blue, green, and white. It looks like the painted backdrop in a Julie Andrews musical, but more vibrant. The streets are jammed with tourists whose eyes aren't fixed on the mountains but the store windows which are packed with souvenirs, art, and expensive clothing.

"We're never going to get a table," James grumbled as I followed him into what he said was *the* primo coffee shop in town. We purchased two coffees and two ham and feta croissants and pushed our way back through the crowd to a bench outside on the sidewalk. His mood had shifted, he was no longer reminiscing about law school. Relieved, I pulled our croissants out of the paper bag and handed him one wrapped in a serviette.

The plastic cap on my coffee cup squeaked but refused to budge. It was dented and I was busy trying to pry it off without spilling hot coffee into my lap when James started talking about the day Finn died. "I told you I found him, right?"

"You did. That must have been very distressing."

"Everything about Finn was distressing." His voice fell and I stopped fiddling with the coffee lid and turned to face him. He stared blankly at the crowd swarming across the intersection two shops down. "Did I tell you about the sparkle?"

"No." I set the unopened coffee cup down on the bench beside me. "What sparkle?"

He lifted his shoulders in a helpless shrug. "When I heard the bang of the bin lid I ran around the corner of the building. At first, I thought someone had stuffed a bundle of old clothes behind the bin. But when I got closer, I could see the camera and a person." A muscle flexed in his jaw.

"Before I could reach him something caught my eye. Up there on the balcony."

"What was it?"

He squinted, as if he were trying to sharpen his memory, then shook his head. "Something strange, flashing in the sunlight. It blinded me for an instant. Then I saw Finn and it went right out of my mind. Until a few days ago."

He was still staring at the tourists jostling across the intersection. I touched his hand; it caught him by surprise and he jerked it away. "What was it, on the balcony? A person?" I asked.

"I wish I knew," he said. "I yelled for help, but got no reply. It flashed, very bright, then vanished."

He rubbed his hands together as if he were cold, then picked up his croissant and finished it.

I walked him back to where he'd chained his bike, we hugged goodbye, and I started the long trek back to the hotel. From the bottom of the hill the Banff Springs Hotel looks quite close, snug up against the mountainside, impregnable as a castle, but once you start the trek it turns out to be much steeper and longer than you'd expect. I was panting by the time I pushed through the heavy glass doors into the lobby. The clerk at the reception desk eyed me curiously as I trudged across the floor and joined a young family in the elevator. The kids chanted the floor numbers, two, three, four as the elevator drifted skyward and it was a relief to step out into the hushed hallway.

The corridor was dimly lit and my mind went to the

man who'd slaughtered his wife and child before killing himself. Where was his room? On eight, four floors up.

My card key beeped in the lock, the little light changed from red to green, I pushed on the door and it jammed. Louisa had set the privacy lock; the metal swing bar was latched shut.

"Louisa," I called out quietly, not wanting to startle her if she was sleeping. "Louisa, it's me, let me in."

Something crashed to the floor. I heard a grunt and a muffled cry.

CHAPTER 19

RANSACKED

Louisa!" In a frenzy I attacked the door, banging it with my fists and slamming into it with my hip. The privacy latch bounced and screeched but refused to give way. "Louisa!" I was screaming at full volume now.

A cart piled high with thick white towels and shampoo bottles trundled into view at the far end of the corridor. A middle-aged woman in a maid's uniform appeared.

A small yelp from our room. "Evie!"

Then a huge crash, the sound of plastic cracking and glass shattering.

"Jesus! Help!" I screamed at the maid, frantically crashing my shoulder into the door again and again. "I have to get there! Let me in!"

The maid froze. Her eyes wide, one hand pressed across her mouth, the other gripping the handle of the linen cart.

The door slammed shut with a mighty bang. Then the click of metal on metal, releasing the privacy lock. The door flew open. A hunched figure barreled out, knocking me to the floor. They raced down the corridor and bolted through the fire door.

I charged into the room shouting Louisa's name.

"Evie?" Her voice sounded small on the other side of the bathroom door. I wrenched the door handle, it was locked. She flung the door open and I almost fell in on top of her.

I grabbed her by the shoulders. "Jesus, Louisa, are you all right?" The tiny bedroom had been ransacked, drawers yanked out of the dresser, clothes flung everywhere. The TV, still plugged into the wall socket, hung off the dresser, halfway to the floor. Louisa's bedside lamp was shattered, lying in pieces in the narrow space between her bed and the window wall. My carryall was unzipped, gaping open on the bed.

Someone brushed past me. I pivoted, fists clenched, then realized it was the maid.

"Oh dear. Oh dear." Her voice shook. "I'll call security." She picked up the desk phone and tapped a couple of buttons. Her eyes darted around the room as she waited for someone to pick up at the other end.

I released Louisa and stepped back to look at her. Her eyes were huge and dark and her hair was wet. "Oh my God, Louisa, what happened? Are you okay?"

She nodded and I noticed she was wearing a white hotel bathrobe. She screwed up her face and declared, "I am never coming back to this stupid hotel again."

* * *

I'll say this for the Banff Springs Hotel: when someone's room is ransacked they go out of their way to make things right. Perhaps it helped that I mentioned ever so casually that I was a lawyer. Not only did they comp our stay but they offered us a free romantic getaway package as well. I think they thought we were a couple and we said nothing to set them right. The hotel manager urged us to please indulge ourselves, everything was on the house, but first we were to meet with hotel security.

Soon a dapper little man in a dark suit appeared. He pulled out the desk chair, sat down and asked Louisa to explain what had happened. Louisa tightened the belt on her terry robe and said she'd wanted a hot bath. "With bubbles and a glass of wine." Did she set the privacy lock? No, because she knew I'd be along soon. She took my laptop into the bathroom and placed it on the vanity. She was going to watch a Dwayne Johnson movie, the one where he saves his family from an earthquake and a tsunami. She's a diehard fan of The Rock.

She'd just settled into a frothy bath when she heard the automatic door click open. Someone had entered the room. Thinking it was me, she called out my name. "When you didn't answer, Evie, I knew I was in trouble. I jumped out of the tub, I almost killed myself, it was so slippery. I cracked open the door to peek out, someone was throwing everything out of the closet." She slammed the door shut and locked it. The intruder banged on the bathroom door and twisted the knob. "By then I was shaking so hard I could hardly stand up. Evie, I was trapped in there, no phone, stark naked. It was horrible!"

I gave her a reassuring smile, but my heart was pounding in my chest.

"I could hear them—"

"Them?" the head of security interrupted.

"—whoever, it was one person, throwing things around and rifling through the closet and the dresser drawers.

They were moving very fast. Then Evie came back. That's when they knocked over the TV."

"Yeah, and the lamp." My heart beat even faster.

"I thought you were going to rip the door off its hinges."

"God knows I tried."

The security guy stopped scribbling in his tiny notepad and asked Louisa, then me, whether we could describe the intruder.

Louisa only saw him from the back, he was wearing a dark hoodie. I shook my head. Everything happened so fast he was just a blurry black shadow to me. The maid was no help, she only saw him from behind as he disappeared through the fire door and down the stairs.

"What do you think he was looking for?" The security guy's eyes flicked from me to Louisa.

"No idea," I said with a shrug.

"I don't know and I don't care," Louisa said before turning to me. "Evie, we're getting out of here. Now."

* * *

Louisa dozed for the first hour of our drive home, then sat up in her seat, refreshed and alert. It's a superpower nurses have, the ability to catnap on their breaks in the middle of a busy twelve-hour shift.

"How was James?" she asked as she poked at the buttons on the radio, reception was spotty and it squawked and hissed until she turned it off.

"I really don't know." When I related James' story about seeing something flash on the balcony, she caught something in my tone.

"You don't believe him?"

"I don't know what to believe anymore. Why didn't he

mention it sooner? To the EMTs or the police? Why wait until now?"

Louisa shifted in her seatbelt to face me. "Because he'd just had a dreadful shock. The traumatized mind does strange things. Adrenaline floods through the body. He was focused on one thing and one thing only, saving Finn. What he may or may not have seen on the balcony was irrelevant at that moment in time."

She sounded awfully calm for someone who'd just been through a traumatic experience herself. Another special skill nurses have. She was staring at my hands on the steering wheel; I realized they were trembling and I tightened my grip, feeling the hum of the highway in my fingertips.

"How are you doing?" she asked.

I glanced at her. My eyes gave me away, they always do, and she said, "Evie, you're overwrought. It was a mistake to come back here so soon after Finn's death... then a creep breaks into our room—"

"Yeah, about that, do you really think it was a random event? Why us, why not the room next door, or the one four floors up? Why didn't he leave when he heard you in the bathroom? He thumped on your door to intimidate you, to ensure you wouldn't come out before he finished tearing our room apart. But he didn't take anything, not your cell, not your wallet. What was he looking for?"

She pressed her lips together and gave me The Look and I knew what she was thinking. When I worked at Gates, Case and White, I'd had a traumatic experience—that's therapist talk for being viciously attacked by a deranged male colleague. I threatened to sue the firm, it wasn't as if I hadn't warned them about this guy, and they paid me a tidy sum to go away quietly. I rarely think about it anymore, but physical contact when I'm not expecting it still makes my blood run cold.

I stared right back at her. "I am not overwrought, Louisa... or being paranoid."

She stared out of her window for a moment, then said, "When we redeem our romantic getaway, we're not staying in any room that ends with a three."

"Why?"

"Ghosts. We were in 473. The haunted room where that guy killed his wife and daughter was 873."

"*Ghosts*? You're talking about ghosts now? Black hoodie guy looked pretty substantial to me."

"And yet you can't identify him, can you?"

"He knocked me down when he barrelled out the door!"

She chuckled and watched the freshly-planted fields flash by her window. I cracked open my window and breathed deeply. Finn loved spring; it was his favourite season. He wasn't a religious man but his respect for nature and the cycle of rebirth and renewal held a significance for him that went beyond any religion I've ever seen.

If he were alive, he'd be preparing for the Great Forage. Finn would search for wild asparagus in secret troves on hillsides and in ditches all over the city. He never revealed their locations and no matter how good an asparagus hunter you were, Finn would always beat you to the prize, leaving nothing but grassy slopes and weedy swales behind.

CHAPTER 20

A SILVER SNAKE

Where is everybody? It was Monday morning and the reception area was deserted. No Bridget to greet me with a cheery "Hello, stranger." No AJ bounding down the hall like a puppy eager to share his hair-raising weekend exploits. No Keith, no Madeline, nobody.

A quiet murmur of voices. I followed the sound to the conference room. There they were, all of them, huddled in front of the windows peering over the cotoneaster hedge that separates our building from the scrubby woods and the river beyond.

"What's going on?" I asked. Four pairs of eyes turned in my direction. Keith and AJ looked stern, jaws clenched and arms crossed. Madeline shook her head. Bridget was gnawing on the side of her thumb. "What is it? You guys are really starting to worry me."

"Come look at the river," Bridget said. "See for yourself."

AJ stepped aside to make room for me at the window. Through the fresh green foliage of the poplar trees the river glistened, fat and swollen like a silver snake. "It's still rising," he said.

For more than a week the local news had been broadcasting reports of excessive rainfall, heavier than usual watershed runoff, and record glacial melts.

"The ranchers are worried," Keith said. He would know. His country acreage was a good forty kilometres south of town in the heart of ranching country. "The ground saturation is worse than they've ever seen it."

AJ lifted his eyebrows. "Saturation? In the sense that the ground's not absorbing the excess rainfall?"

"Yep," Keith said.

Madeline continued to stare out the window. I wondered what was going through her mind. It's not like her to stay silent. She was wearing a stiff herringbone coat dress; a heavy tweed fabric, and yet she was trembling. Without a word she turned and went straight back to her office.

I was about to go after her when Bridget stopped me with a snap of her fingers. "Oh, I almost forgot," she said, "Peter called. He was asking about the status of the Christie's contract."

Of course he was. I went back to my office and was pulling up the file on my lap top when AJ barged in.

"By all means, AJ, make yourself at home." I nodded to one of my visitor's chairs. Madeline was right about AJ. When he'd first joined us, she said he reminded her of Daniel Craig in *Casino Royale*. 'That long straight nose, those intense blue eyes and that strong body.' She sighed when I scolded her, #MeToo goes both ways, and shrugged me off. I still blush when I think about it.

"What's on your mind, AJ?"

He crossed his arms behind his head and interlaced his fingers and asked, "Were you here for the 2013 flood?"

I told him Louisa and I were touring France and Italy when it hit. Day after day we'd return to our hotel room to find distressing stories on CNN and social media. Mom and Dad were still alive back then and we called or texted them every day. The photos of the Saddledome flooded up to the eighth row of seats were the last straw. We were coming home.

Dad wouldn't hear of it. "Don't be silly," he'd said. "Your mother and I are fine up here on the hill." They lived in a lovely old house in Mount Royal and other than the constant racket of sirens and helicopters flying overhead—it drove Molly, their cranky old Bouvier crazy—they were none the worse for wear. Dad said Molly was tranquilized to the eyeballs. Mom laughed in the background, saying the dog was popping more pills than Judy Garland. Louisa and I agreed to finish our vacation on the condition they contact us immediately, day or night, if their situation changed. By the time we returned home the river had receded, leaving behind a mucky slimy mess.

"We missed the whole thing," I said, "what about you?"

AJ said he was lucky. He'd been in Saskatchewan working for the summer at his grandfather's company.

"The world's biggest fertilizer company," I said with a smile.

"A crop inputs and services company," he corrected me. "Some of our rivers ran pretty high and a town was evacuated, but we got through it relatively unscathed."

I studied his face. "But now you're worried?"

He dipped his head, acknowledging my comment. "Yeah, I am, a little. People in my building are saying this constant rain is as bad as it was in 2013." AJ lived in a medium-sized condo building in Sunnyside. He had reason to be worried, Sunnyside was one of the many neighbourhoods that had been evacuated. But it wasn't the prospect of evacuation that bothered him—his unit was up high enough that it was in no danger of flooding—it was the threat of damage to his beloved MGB, which was tucked into a parking space in the underground garage.

"Leave it here in the office lot."

"*This* office lot?" AJ was incredulous. "Are you mad? It'd be stolen before I could get the key out of the ignition. Besides, our lot is barely higher than the river—"

"Sorry to interrupt." Bridget appeared in the doorway and said Peter and Anya were waiting for me in reception.

"What? Do we have a meeting?"

"No, my dear, you do not have a meeting. They were in the neighbourhood and decided to pop in."

Pop in? AJ shot me a skeptical look as he rose to his feet. Clients don't 'pop in' on their lawyers. Not at the rates we charge.

CHAPTER 21

THE DRIVE-IN

Bridget led Peter and Anya into my office. After they settled in their chairs, I told them I'd skimmed the Christie's auction agreement and it appeared to be fine, or as fine as it was going to get given our non-existent bargaining power.

"Christie's?" For a moment Anya looked confused, then she laughed and turned to Peter. "What did I tell you, there was no need to waste our money on a lawyer. Sorry, Evie, no offense." I was tempted to ask her where she'd gone to law school, but that would be petty.

"You're not here about the Christie's contract?" I was perplexed. What did they want?

Anya, who had just sat down, glided up out of her chair and wandered over to the window. She moved gracefully, like someone underwater, and said, "Oh my, Peter, look at this. The river is almost as high here as it is at our place." Last year Peter and Anya bought a very large house on the other side of the river. Peter referred to it as Anya's mansion. In the 2013 flood the entire neighbourhood was submerged under six feet of water, but that didn't dampen property values and they'd paid millions for the place.

Anya picked up the string that controlled the blinds and drew it slowly through her fingers. The plastic bobble on the end clicked as it passed over her massive diamond ring. She turned to me and said, "This may sound like an odd question, Evie, but we were wondering whether you've received any correspondence from Finn?"

"Pardon?"

She returned to sit next to Peter and I noticed that other than her jewelry, an ammolite pendant and her diamond ring, they were dressed alike in expensive black cashmere tops and tan slacks. It was a little unsettling.

"Patrice mentioned something. That you were asking whether Finn had sent her any emails or letters recently. That arrived after his death." She watched me through long dark lashes.

Patrice had told them about Finn's delayed email even through I'd asked her not to. My instinctive reaction was to stonewall. "I'm not sure what you mean. Were you expecting something from Finn?"

"No," she said, "no, it's nothing." Turning to Peter she said, "We have to get going, love, if you want to check on Juve."

"What about Juve?" I glanced at Peter.

"Oh, you know Juve," he replied.

Not really.

"He's killing himself out at the mine. They're working a new parcel; it's a mess out there with all this rain. Sticky and gummy. It's wreaking havoc with the excavation schedule. And," here he heaved a great sigh, "since it's a new parcel we need another disposition certificate."

Instantly my antenna went up. "If it's being shipped

out under the Asian distribution contract you're cutting it awfully close."

"Tell me about it," Peter said. "Laura will have a week at the most to process the application."

It was all I could do not to climb over my desk and throttle him. These deadlines were impossible. "I'm sure I need not remind you that any kind of inducement is out of the question."

Their heads snapped up and I realized my tone was overly sarcastic. Anya waved her hand dismissively. "Oh, stop fussing, Evie, it will be fine."

*   *   *

I was thumping a stack of law books back into my bookshelf, wondering why I hadn't told them about Finn's dead man's email—it's a breach of the Code of Conduct to withhold information from your client—when Keith sailed into my office. He was carrying what looked like an oversized paperback, I recognized its distinctive blue cover: it was a regulator's decision.

"Perfect timing," I said. "I was just thinking about the Code."

He stopped short. Before he could have a heart attack, I assured him it was nothing.

"You're sure?"

I nodded and he flipped the document open to a tagged page. "Look at this."

I sighed and said, "Why do I get the feeling this is something I don't want to read?"

He took a long moment to stare into my face, then pulled the document away. "Okay, you don't need to read it right now, this very instant. Grab your coat," he said with a grin, "we're going for a ride."

Keith and I started 'going for a ride' after that lunatic at Gates, Case and White attacked me. I think Louisa put him up to it. I could imagine her saying *Get her out of the office if she's getting too stressed. The change of scenery will do her good.*

Bridget watched us pass in front of her desk. "Where are you two going? How long will you be gone?"

Keith said, "One hour. Peters' Drive-In."

"Ooh," she squealed, "bring me back a marshmallow shake."

"Pina colada," Madeline's voice rang down the hall.

"Make it two," AJ chimed in.

Keith grinned and shook his head. "They never grow up, do they?" And just like that the world became a nicer place.

* * *

When Gus Pieters, a Dutch pastry chef, set out to make the best hamburgers and milkshakes in town, he developed a secret recipe that's as popular today as it was sixty years ago. And when Mr. Pieters sold the business nothing changed, not even that funny apostrophe in its name.

It was mid afternoon and the place was bustling. Keith placed our orders and I watched the employees buzzing around in their spotless white aprons and blue ball caps. Keith handed me a paper tray which sagged under the weight of four tall milkshakes, mine was 'coca mocha', and we returned to the car.

"Are those fries?" I asked as he peeled back the tin foil and the aroma of freshly fried potatoes filled the car. I haven't eaten fries in a car since I was a teenager and

dumped a tray of ketchup covered French fries all over
the front seat of my boyfriend's Chevy.

"Mm-hum," he said, sprinkling salt all over his lap and
the steering wheel. "Want some?" I set the milkshakes on
the floor and helped him polish them off.

He reached into the backseat and grabbed the regulator's decision with slightly greasy fingertips and handed me
the transcript. "Check out Finn's testimony, it starts at the
top of page 199. He was giving expert evidence at a hearing
investigating the extraction of critical minerals, and he
got into a sparring match with the government lawyer."

"A sparring match. That doesn't sound like Finn." My
former mentor was always calm and exceptionally well
prepared. His fame as an expert witness was legendary.

The first few exchanges with his interlocutor went
like clockwork: question, answer, question, answer. Then
something seemed to rattle him. His answers became
hesitant, the trouble with verbatim transcripts is they
record every 'um', 'er', and stutter. He sounded as if he was
circling around trying to get his bearings. Between sips of
my shake I read the transcript aloud.

> COUNSEL: Doctor Tanberg, what's your view on
> the practice of using critical minerals, indeed any
> minerals, to invest in cryptocurrency?
> TANBERG: I - er, pardon, I - I have no view on
> that. I'm unaware of that practice.
> COUNSEL: You're sure? You're not aware
> of mining companies investing their profits in
> cryptocurrency?
> TANBERG: I'm sure people use income from
> many sources to invest in cryptocurrency.
> COUNSEL: I'm talking about mining companies,

not quote – people – unquote. What's your view
of this practice? Is it wise?
TANBERG: I - I, well, as you know - as you know,
cryptocurrency is a new form of currency, it has
no intrinsic value - um - some consider it to be
a Ponzi scheme, investors unload it for profit on
the next guy before the whole house of cards
falls down.

I glanced at Keith. "He's rambling about the risk of cryptocurrency. Why?" Keith just shrugged and I continued.

COUNSEL: Thank you Doctor Tanberg, I happen
to agree with you, but my question wasn't about
cryptocurrency per se. Let me ask it another way:
are you aware of any instances where profits from
the sale of minerals, critical minerals, gold, silver,
ammolite, have been invested in cryptocurrency?
TANBERG: I... I...
COUNSEL: Or used to back crypto tokens?

Here the chair of the panel interjected.

PANEL: Counsel, this hearing concerns the mining of critical minerals essential for the green
and digital economy. I don't see the relevance
of your question.
COUNSEL: Thank you, Madam Chair, I'll move
on.

I flipped back to the blue cover to find the hearing date.
January, five months before Finn died.
"Keith, what did you make of that exchange?"
Thoughtfully, he rubbed his chin. "It was bizarre. I
know the government lawyer, she's excellent. It's not like

her to go off on a fishing expedition, but that's what she was doing. Did Finn say anything to you about DreamStone investing in cryptocurrency?"

"Nothing. Peter and Anya invested in crypto when it first took off, in their personal capacities. It made them super rich but they're out of it now."

"What about DreamStone?"

"Not as far as I know, why would it?"

"And yet, the Justice lawyer took Finn on a wild goose chase. Why?"

I glanced at the transcript. "It's time to find out. You know the Justice department lawyer? Think she'd be willing to talk to me?"

He hesitated for a moment. "I don't know if she'll tell you what she was looking for, but it's worth a try." He pulled out his phone and made the call.

CHAPTER 22

THE MIST

Louisa was leaning against the railing on the back deck staring at the river when I arrived home that evening. The wind tugged at her scrubs, she'd just returned from the hospital and hadn't changed yet. Quincy paced nervously beside her. His forehead crinkled as he looked up at me, then back at Louisa. I stroked his silky ear and murmured, "Sorry bud, I have no idea why she's still out here in the cold."

The sky was strangely bright, the air filled with mist that softened the contours of the office towers looming in the distance.

Louisa turned to me and said, "This is the weirdest weather I've ever seen." She reached out as if to cup the breeze. "Have you ever seen mist like this?"

"Yes, in Swansea when we walked from the hotel down to the Dylan Thomas Centre. By the time we got there our hair was dripping and we were soaked to the skin."

"Exactly," she said. "That was Wales, this is the prairies. We don't get mist like this on the prairies."

She was right of course. The clinging mist made me feel clammy. "Come back inside." I tugged at her elbow to lead her through the French doors back into the kitchen but she wheeled away from me.

"Have you checked the river?" she asked. I peered through the mist searching for the riverbank. "You can't see it now, but it's really starting to rise. The bank is disappearing awfully fast."

I glanced over to our right, searching for the homeless man's lean-to in the wild zone of poplars and wolf willows that sloped from our house down to the river. There was nothing but a luminous, sparkling drizzle.

"Quincy and I will check the river on our R-U-N after dinner." His ears perked up and he bounced a couple of times. There's no fooling this dog.

She pulled the chicken pasta casserole out of the oven while I set the table. Quincy tilted his head this way and that every time we made eye contact. I flashed my palms at him, "I've got nothing," and he finally gave up and trotted back to his food dish. "Why this sudden concern about the river?" I asked as I poured two glasses of sparking water.

She inhaled deeply and said it wasn't sudden. For weeks the rain was all anyone at work would talk about. "The 2013 flood hit some of our staff really hard." She reeled off some names that sounded vaguely familiar. "Their basements were filled with filthy water and sludge; everything they owned, furniture, exercise equipment, heirlooms, all of it, gone. And no one was properly insured, although insurance can never replace personal mementos, can it."

I remembered the flimsy cardboard boxes filled with ancient Christmas ornaments and odd-sized photo albums we'd retrieved from Mom and Dad's place after they'd died. All of it was stored in our basement.

As we ate our pasta, I tried to reassure her. "We're a good fifteen feet above the river. We'll be fine."

Later that evening, I bundled up in a fleece hoodie and windbreaker and took Quincy for a run. The mist had a raw edge and the wind had picked up, blowing harsh and bitterly cold. We ran along the road then cut down to the narrow path beside the river. The gravel rolled under our feet and we pushed higher up the treacherous slope trying to avoid the mushy pools in the middle of the path.

My chest tightened when I saw it. Murky water drowned the wolf willows lining the river's edge and the poplars leaned against each other at crazy angles, their roots undermined by the water carving away the banks.

Louisa greeted Quincy at the door with an old blue towel, tossing it over his head and vigorously rubbing his paws until he escaped and skidded across the floor to the kitchen.

"Well?" she asked anxiously. "How bad is it?"

I took a deep breath and said it was worse than I'd expected. "But it'll never rise fifteen feet. Not in a million years."

Her eyes searched my face, her expression was determined. "Evie, we can't afford to be complacent. If the river boils over it will happen fast. We have to be ready. We must make a plan."

It sounded so easy, make a plan. And we did. We made an excellent plan. It just wasn't good enough.

CHAPTER 23

———

CRYPTO

Why are government offices so dreary and forbidding? I'd expected the Justice Department to be housed in a building befitting its role as stalwart protector of the rule of law; instead, I was standing in front of a tired old structure that nothing, not even the rebuilt road and fresh new landscaping, could redeem.

Yes, I was overly critical. I'd just spent three hours in the car driving up to Edmonton because the Justice Department lawyer who'd badgered Finn about mining companies investing in crypto, refused to talk to me about it on the phone.

The silence in the reception area was broken only by the solemn ticking of a utilitarian clock hanging on the wall. The receptionist had disappeared and I waited alone until the government lawyer appeared. She ushered me into her nondescript office and we exchanged business cards. She was a tall, no-nonsense woman wearing a blue pantsuit and sensible shoes. She gave me an appraising stare before asking how she could be of help.

I went over it again, explaining my connection to Finn and the company owned by his son and daughter-in-law.

"Ah yes, DreamStone," she said. "I know it."

Why? I wondered, shifting in my chair. "At a recent hearing, you asked Finn some pointed questions. About mining companies and cryptocurrency?" I let the question hang between us, hoping she'd fill the dead air with an explanation.

But she was too smart for that. Instead she responded with a question of her own. "What can you tell me about DreamStone?" Eyes bright, she rolled her chair closer under her desk waiting for my reply. I glanced at her business card. No, she didn't work for a special investigative branch of the Alberta Securities Commission or any branch of enforcement. What was her interest in DreamStone?

And that's when it struck me, she agreed to this meeting because she wanted to pump me as much as I wanted to pump her. Even if I hadn't been bound by client confidentiality and solicitor-client privilege, I couldn't tell her much. What I knew about cryptocurrency could be engraved on the head of a pin. So I tossed her a few crumbs about the company: DreamStone was a small, privately held company that mined and sold ammolite here and abroad. "That's about it," I said when I was finished.

She was silent for a moment, then asked if I'd ever heard of GTX Corporation. I shook my head. "It's an ammolite mining and production company, not much smaller than DreamStone. Recently GTX signed a deal with another company to develop the world's first ammolite-backed cryptocurrency." Soon she was rattling off terms like 'crypto wallets', 'payment gateways', and 'nonfungible token development'.

I held up a hand to stop her. "Sorry, I have no idea what you're talking about."

She closed her eyes for a second, reminding me of a weary elementary school teacher trying to enlighten a recalcitrant student. "Alberta has some of the largest ammonite deposits in the world. Ammolite promoters, dreamers that they are, think they're on the cusp of the next Klondike Gold Rush. And who knows, maybe they're right. But the prospect of fast money makes people greedy... and stupid." She paused and I had the impression she'd wandered off topic. She cleared her throat, then continued. "To make the ammolite market even 'sexier', they're marketing it in digital form." I could hear the air quotes, or maybe it was skepticism, in her voice. "Ammolite tokens allow investors to hold ammolite—remember, it's being pitched as a rare and exotic gemstone more valuable than gold or diamonds—without physically buying it."

She glanced at me. "Are you still with me?"

"Kind of."

"GTX ammolite tokens are pegged to the current wholesale price of a one-thirteenth of a carat of ammolite."

I offered a small smile. "That I understand. But I still don't get the first part."

She gave an impatient huff. "It doesn't matter," she said. "What matters is this: if DreamStone is involved in the crypto market, how shall I put this... it needs to be very, very, very careful. The world of crypto is not what it appears."

"You mean it's plagued with thirty-year-old billionaires who crash the market and get charged with fraud and money laundering?"

Her smile broadened. "That too."

"I still don't understand why you were grilling Finn

Tanberg about this. He had nothing to do with ammolite or crypto."

"He's a DreamStone shareholder. It's a closely held company so its public disclosure is minimal. And his son and daughter-in-law run it. Also, it's the biggest ammolite miner in our jurisdiction, bigger than GTX. The opportunity presented itself, so I took it."

"But why?" She wouldn't give me a straight answer. After ten minutes of sparring with each other she glanced at her watch, then rose to her feet. Our meeting was over. She walked me back into the reception area, still as quiet as a tomb, pointed me in the direction of the elevators, and disappeared.

On the drive back to Calgary I pulled into a coffee shop in Red Deer and called Peter. He surprised me by actually answering his phone; he was on his way out to a meeting but could talk later that evening if I wanted to stop by the house.

* * *

After a three-hour drive, the last hour slogging through rush hour traffic, I finally turned down one of the prettiest streets in the city and pulled up in front of Anya's mansion. Peter called it that so often, that's how I thought of it now. It was a magnificent house. When they bought it, they threw a blow-out housewarming party. Music flowed through the half-empty living room—their furniture had yet to arrive from New York and Milan—and it easily accommodated the two hundred guests who floated through to the kitchen and out through the foldaway glass wall onto the large stone patio.

Peter spent half the night in a panic, chasing after

drunken guests who wandered too close to the edge of the property; the landscaping at the back was not yet finished, the riverbank was unstable, and he was terrified someone would roll down the gentle slope and drown in the river.

Halfway through the evening I ran into Finn in the living room. He was staring into the beautifully lit front garden, his reflection in the window merging with the glimmer of fairy lights outside.

"What do you think, Finn? The landscape architect did a beautiful job, didn't she?" The sound of laughter tinkled on the breeze from the patio. "The backyard will be spectacular once they're finished."

Finn offered a distracted grin, took a thoughtful sip of his whiskey and after some innocuous comments went off in search of Patrice.

The party faded from my memory as I parked my car and passed through the wrought iron gate in the brick wall protecting the house from the street. The front garden in this sheltered space was lush with mountain ash and ornamental shrubs in full leaf. If you didn't know this was a private residence, you'd think it was an embassy.

Peter greeted me at the door with his arms outstretched, he's one of my huggy clients, and led me through to their home office at the back. Anya rose from her desk to greet me. She was wearing a flowing silk outfit, certainly not the jeans and tees I lounge around in at home. The back garden was fully landscaped, finished with full grown Japanese maples, arbours, and a narrow path winding down to the greenhouse in the secret garden next to the river.

"Evie, come look at our new office." Anya pointed to a large plexiglass box sitting on a wooden table next to her desk. They'd moved from a small office building downtown to the mansion during the pandemic and never moved out again. In the box was an elegant white architectural model of a four-storey office building.

"She's finally happy with the design," Peter said with an indulgent smile.

"We have to get it right, Peter, it's the physical manifestation of DreamStone." Her tone implied they'd had this conversation many times before.

"Agreed. Now all we have to do is find somewhere to build it."

"It has to be in the inner city, like Evie's building." Anya glanced at me as she explained that she and Peter would own the building and lease the fourth floor to DreamStone. The second and third floors would be leased to 'quality clients' and the ground floor would contain a full-service café/restaurant and a gym for the workers in the building and the surrounding area.

Peter shrugged helplessly and said Anya was striving for a Google-campus vibe, but on a smaller scale. I stayed quiet about the wisdom of adding luxury office space to a city with a thirty-percent office vacancy rate. Although Anya was right about one thing: the design would fit nicely with the existing architecture in the Mission District.

Peter sat me down at the glass conference table, a modern Italian design with twisted Murano legs, while Anya disappeared into the sprawling kitchen, returning with three tall glasses of white wine. She set the glasses on the table and went back into the kitchen to rummage in a gigantic stainless steel fridge, then reappeared with a wheel of brie and a bowl of dried apricots. She left again to find some large napkins. Would this woman ever sit down, I wondered, then realized that was uncharitable. The line between work and leisure is easily blurred when your office is also your home.

I popped an apricot into my mouth and asked about the Asia shipments. "Any word on the certificate?"

"Yeah," Peter said, "we need to talk to you about that."

Anya finally sat down and said, "DreamStone's penetration of the Asian market is proceeding twice as fast as we expected."

She sounded so formal; if it weren't for the wine sparkling on my tongue, I would have sworn I was on an investors' conference call.

"Good job, Peter." I smiled at him.

He smiled back and said, "Juve's been mining ammonite for decades. He thinks like a miner and used to pitch it as an investment on par with diamonds or gold, but let's face it, ammolite doesn't have the same cache, so—"

"So," Anya interrupted, "we're pushing the Feng Shui angle. They gobble it up in the Far East." As she talked, she touched the ammolite pendant at her throat, stroking it gently as if it were a talisman.

Peter set down his wine glass and said, "We need you to talk to Laura Bazin again, to make her speed up the application process."

I choked on the dried apricot, coughed, and swallowed a big gulp of wine to wash it down.

Then he shot me a wicked grin. "Just kidding, Evie. We heard you loud and clear the last time, no bribes and nothing that looks, sounds, or smells like a bribe. We figure if you talk to Laura, you'll do it the right way."

I nodded, eyes still watering, and took another sip of wine which sparked a fizzy buzz in my head. The room shimmered at the edges; I should have picked up something to eat before I left Edmonton.

"Right, I can do that," I said, setting down my wine glass. "Now, about my meeting with the Department of

Justice lawyer. She's laser-focused on DreamStone and I don't know why. Her interest appears to be related to GTX and its recent move into ammolite-backed cryptocurrency. What can you tell me about that?"

"Not much," Peter admitted, "we're up to our eyeballs in meeting the Asian orders. We don't have time to venture into cryptocurrency."

"Nor the inclination." Anya watched me thoughtfully as she nibbled on a dried apricot.

Peter pulled up the GTX press release on his phone. "Here it is: The AMLT token is fully backed by ammolite resources—" He stopped in mid-sentence.

Squinting at the tiny print on his phone, he said, "Anya, this can't be right. They say their mine is valued at six hundred million dollars. Ours is only slightly larger and we're valued at over a billion." Anya reached out and without a word Peter dropped his phone into her palm.

She barely glanced at the screen before passing it back. "That's much too low. Ammolite has tripled in value over the last twenty years. They're probably talking about proven reserves; that's a much too conservative way to value minerals in today's market. Our valuation is a combination of proven, probable, and possible reserves, with a heavy emphasis on the possibles."

"Calculating value," Peter said to me with a self-deprecating smile, "that's Anya's department." He chuckled and repeated a comment I'd heard him make many times before. "Juve finds it, Anya values it, and I sell it. Your classic division of labour. Works like a charm, isn't that right, love?"

Anya reached over to him and ran her hand down his arm. "That's right, Peter."

* * *

After dinner I was in the study tucked up in an ancient leather armchair. The downtown sky glittered in the velvety dark on the other side of the French windows. Quincy was sprawled across the Persian carpet gnawing on a dog treat bone. I snapped open my laptop and googled: *Valuation proven, probable, and possible reserves*. Ah yes, here it is. Proven reserves has a ninety percent chance of being extracted. Possible reserves, less than fifty percent. Probables, somewhere in the middle.

There was a ninety percent chance the GTX mine was worth $600 million and a less than fifty percent chance DreamStone's mine was worth a billion.

I'm not great at math but this didn't give me a warm and fuzzy feeling.

CHAPTER 24

EVACUATE

Louisa was still asleep when I left for work the next morning. She'd been at the hospital for sixteen hours straight, two people had called in sick and it was well past midnight when she staggered through the door. "You won't get a peep out of her until noon," I told Quincy as we jogged down by the river before breakfast. We splashed through the puddles, there were too many to dodge now, and made a godawful mess in the foyer when we got back to the house.

Bridget almost ran me down in the corridor as she charged out of AJ's office. "The Battle of the Thermostat, I presume?" It was the lumpy red sweater pulled tight across her chest that gave her away.

She nodded and said, "I look like my grandma and I don't care. It's mid June. I'm freezing."

"I feel your pain," I said as I settled behind my desk. Louisa and I used to have the same battles with my mom. She'd set the thermostat to 20°C from the end of May to the beginning of October. If either of us complained she'd tell us to jolly well—Dad's expression, when she said it, it sounded like *joolie vel*—put on a sweater. We'd huddle together under a crocheted throw and stare at her with huge, sad eyes. It never worked but it always made her laugh.

Madeline's pale blue trench coat flashed past my open door as she breezed down the hall. I called her name and she reappeared, untying the headscarf knotted Audrey-Hepburn-style under her chin and slipping it into her pocket. I handed her the DreamStone file. "Can you get yourself up to speed? I've got a few calls to make, you'll probably have to follow up."

"Be your nag in other words," she said.

"That too."

My first call was to the Tyrrell Museum. If they had no issues with the disposition certificate application, I'd have more leverage when I called Laura at the Department of Culture. Eventually I was put through to someone who could help me... except they couldn't. In fact, they were livid that DreamStone was pestering them again.

A peeved voice said, "How many times do I have to tell you people, this takes time. I am not a rubber stamp; I will not tick the box so you can turn priceless archeological artifacts into souvenirs."

Oh dear. In my best 'pretty please' voice I asked if there was anything I could do to speed up the process. I hate using my 'pretty please' voice but arguing with someone who can make your life miserable is pointless.

He began to rail against the government's process. In his opinion ammolite should not be allowed on the market without a Kimberley Process Certificate.

"Really? Ammolites aren't blood diamonds."

"They're an important part of our fossil record. They should be protected."

"Yes, but some aren't of that high a quality, right? Besides, you'd need governments all over the world to participate in the process to make it effective." *Why was I debating with this guy?* I switched back to my 'pretty please' voice and said I'd greatly appreciate whatever help he could give me. He harumphed, then relented, saying he'd get his report into the government's hands by the end of the day.

One down and one to go.

My conversation with Laura Bazin—mid-level government bureaucrat, single mom with three kids, in dire financial straits, none of which I should know—quickly took a bizarre turn.

When I said the Tyrrell Museum agreed to send its report to her by the end of the day she interrupted. "Those egg heads at the Tyrrell think they have all the power, but it's my call whether to issue a certificate or not."

"I'm sorry, what?"

"The Department of Culture; *that would be me*, determines whether that ammolite can leave the province."

"Um, Laura." I had to choose my words carefully. No one likes a smart-ass lawyer telling them how to do their job. "The regulations say officials, namely the Tyrrell guys, do the examination and make the call."

"Evie," Laura's tone was beyond condescending, "you're talking about words on a page. I'm talking about the real world." Wait, was she implying she could *hold up* the certificate as easily as she could approve it? "I'll call Juve, we'll sort it out." She hung up, leaving me with nothing but a dial tone buzzing in my ear.

"Good, you're off the phone." Madeline swept into my office.

I glanced up, struggling to shift gears. Laura had no need to call Juve, unless...

Madeline announced that Patrice was here for a meeting.

"With me?"

"No, with me. She wants to discuss Finn's DreamStone shares. Something to do with her role as executor of his estate. You may want to join us."

"I *may* want to join you?"

"You should join us."

When Madeline, the queen of client relations, suggests you join her in a client meeting, you do it. Even if you're worried sick that a government employee who's fallen on hard times is going to talk directly to your client who might be inclined to give her a helping hand in return for a favour.

I assured Madeline I'd join her right after I'd made a quick call. Then I left Juve a sharply worded message reminding him of our 'no bribes!' conversation and met Madeline and Patrice in the conference room.

I didn't know Patrice as well as I'd known Finn but I always thought they were a good match. Patrice was intelligent and shared Finn's interests, except for his abiding love of the outdoors. She preferred less out-there-in-the-raw-elements pursuits.

Years ago I'd let it slip to Finn that I liked birds and somehow, I still don't know how it happened, I became his birding partner. We go twitching at the Inglewood Bird Sanctuary or Bowness Park and bet coffee and a donut on who could rack up the most correctly identified birdcalls. It quickly became apparent he'd bankrupt me unless he gave me a handicap.

Patrice's eager smile fell away as she described her problem. "How am I supposed to administer Finn's estate if I can't find his assets?" She shot Madeline a worried glance. "Then there's Revenue Canada and the provincial government, their filings are incomprehensible." She sighed. "Why is coming into this world so easy and leaving it so hard?"

Madeline took her hand. "Patrice, let us help you. Give me whatever papers you have. We'll take care of the rest."

Patrice blinked back tears. "His files are a mess."

"Kind of like his office at the university?" I said.

That made her smile. "You wouldn't believe the junk he kept. Fleetwood Mac ticket stubs, Peter's old high school report cards, his expired passports. He was so young once. Everything is jammed higgly piggly into a shoe box, lots of shoe boxes."

I'd never thought of Finn as a sentimental man but we all have a secret stash of memories somewhere, don't we.

"There's one other—"

Madeline cut Patrice off. "Did you see that?" She was staring at the overhead lights. "Am I losing my mind or did the lights just flicker?" The conference room lights flickered twice, then died. The power was off. Silence, except for Keith's antique clock ticking next door.

Then the backup generator surged to life, the lights blinked on as electricity hummed through the sockets. Bridget rushed into the room, her cell phone was making a screeching noise. "We have to go!" she said. "Something's happened at the Springbank dam!"

I heard AJ coming down the hall. "What the hell is that infernal racket?"

Keith appeared in the doorway. "Let's go! It's an immediate evacuation order. Now!" We were all clustered in the hallway, staring at each other, confused.

Keith's voice rose in pitch. "For the love of God, people, let's go!" Nothing fazes this man, he births calves when it's so cold your lungs will freeze, but now he was rattled. I dashed into my office and grabbed my cell which was wailing and buzzing on my desk.

"Get out. Drive to higher ground!" Keith was behind us, arms spread wide, herding us like sheep into the lobby.

"Evie," Patrice looked stricken. "I Ubered over, I don't have a car."

"You're with me." I grabbed her arm and dragged her out into the parking lot.

We ran to our cars, our key fobs popping the doors open one by one. Gravel flew as we merged with the stream of cars flying through the flashing red lights at the intersection. Everyone was on the road, fleeing the flood.

Patrice clutched her phone, poking at it, trying to silence the alarm so she could call Peter.

"Text him," I said. "Tell him you're safe with me. I'm taking you home."

* * *

Thirty minutes later, after dodging speeding cars and pedestrians darting everywhere, I pulled up in front of Patrice's house, a pleasant bungalow in a hilly older neighbourhood on the north side of town. Our phones had finally stopped wailing and we sat in Patrice's driveway listening to the rain and the steady swish of the windshield wipers, left, right, left, right.

My heart was settling down. I wasn't aware it was racing until that moment. I glanced at my phone—no message from Louisa—and was about to call her when Patrice said she'd run into the house and fetch Finn's shoeboxes for me. I gave her an absentminded nod and sent Louisa a text:

Where are you? Are you OK?

Patrice returned a minute later, clutching four shoe-boxes, the one on top was starting to slide and she pressed her chin down to keep it from getting away. I flung the passenger-side door open; she leaned in and I grabbed the top box just before it opened and scattered bits of paper all over the wet road.

"Is that it?" I asked as I shifted the boxes out of the front seat and into the back.

She slipped into the car, her clothes and hair smelled damp, and nodded. "That's it for the house. There's a bunch of files at the university. They're sending them later this week."

Her phone pinged. A text from Peter. "Oh, thank goodness," she said, holding it up so I could see the message. Peter and Anya were at the mine, they were worried about their house and were driving back into town to check on it.

I glanced at my phone. Still no response from Louisa. My thumbs flew across the screen:

Are you home? Are you OK?

The thought of Louisa in a dead sleep with the river rising behind her made my blood run cold. I was about to roar out of the driveway when Patrice reached over and touched my hand. "Evie," she said, "Peter needs my help."

CHAPTER 25

THE PHOTO WALL

"What?" Maybe I hadn't heard her correctly.

"Peter needs my help." Patrice pushed a wet curl behind her ear. Her face was pale, even her eyes looked faded.

"What kind of help?" It had to be money, it's always money. But Peter had more money than Croesus. "Help for DreamStone or for himself?"

"Personally, they're fine. They're millionaires many times over, always jetting around the world to visit friends in Silicon Valley or Europe or Asia. They know people everywhere. They have more than enough money." Raindrops beat down on the roof of the car. The windshield wipers couldn't keep up and I turned them off. "It's the business. Now don't get me wrong, DreamStone's not in financial trouble or anything. It's just a timing issue. You know how it is in businesses."

"Not really, Patrice."

She rushed the words as if she just wanted to get them out of her mouth. "I'm going to put a mortgage on the house and lend Peter five-hundred thousand to tide him over until his share of the estate comes through. Can you do the paperwork?"

Of course I could do the paperwork, the big question was whether I wanted to do the paperwork. Five hundred thousand was more than half the value of Patrice's house.

"I don't understand, Patrice. If the business needs money Peter should put a mortgage on his own house. The mansion must be worth what, five, eight, million. A five hundred thousand mortgage on a multimillion-dollar house is a small risk to him but it's a huge risk to you."

She gave an impatient shake of her head. "Yes, but for business reasons it's easier for me to take a mortgage on this place than it is for him to take a mortgage on his." She glanced at her small house, the front door was wide open, she hadn't shut it properly and now rain was pouring into her foyer. "They'll pay it back quickly, it's just a stopgap measure."

I wondered whether she had any idea what she was talking about. "Patrice, DreamStone is a company. It has a line of credit or other financial arrangements with the bank that it could—" That's when the penny dropped. Peter and Anya had maxed out their borrowing lines and the banks refused to lend them any more money so now they were hitting up Patrice for a loan. Finn said 'don't let them push you' and now they were pushing Patrice. I had to stop them.

"You know, Patrice, probate can take a while. Peter might not get his share of the estate for months." Patrice was a military historian, her income was erratic, she might not be able to keep up with the monthly payments without draining her personal savings. "We don't even know the value of Finn's estate yet."

Patrice shot me an irritated look. "I'm well aware of that, Evie. I am the executor after all. But Peter needs an infusion of cash now"—that was Anya talking— "and a simple loan from me is the best way to tide the company over in the short term." More Anya-talk.

My phone pinged. It was Louisa telling me she and the dog were at home, they were safe.

Patrice clicked open the car door and flashed a bright smile. "How quickly can you draw up the paperwork?"

I don't really like corporate law, but I love litigation. This loan agreement would be bullet proof. It would include every conceivable clause to protect Patrice if DreamStone so much as hiccupped on its repayment schedule, Code of Conduct and my obligations to DreamStone be damned.

*　*　*

As we trickled back into the office, I felt almost guilty about abandoning our little building to the raging waters that failed to appear. Soon, short clips appeared in the online press with headlines like *Springbank Springs Back*. It turned out a mechanism that was supposed to divert the Bow, the bigger of the two rivers converging on the city, had failed to do its job, throwing the engineers into panic mode thinking the device they'd installed to save us would drown us all.

"A spring back mechanism? Any idea what they're talking about?" I asked Keith, who was the most mechanically inclined of the bunch of us.

"Not a clue."

My phone pinged. It was Hadiza wondering if I could join her for drinks later in the day.

I slipped out just after five o'clock and was soon striding

through Murray Fraser Hall, searching for the staircase to the third floor. Across from the stairwell was a slim figure in a black hoodie and khaki pants. He appeared to be mesmerized by the photo wall which displayed every graduating class since the law school's inception. The photos were arranged in an artsy way: instead of setting the pictures for each graduating class in a square frame, they were strung out in two long rows, like a photobooth strip running the length of the wall. All those young, fresh faces totally unprepared for the real world.

The man in the black hoodie traced his finger along the line of students in my graduating class, searching for someone. Then he stopped. Tentatively, I called his name.

"James?"

The hood slipped back onto his shoulders revealing James McQuinn, head chef at Banff Springs Hotel. His eyes lit up when he saw me. "Evie, hey."

"I thought that was you. What are you doing here?"

He tapped the line of photographs. "This would have been me, right here between Leveque and Macmillan... if I'd graduated."

"Yeah, but you'd have had better hair." Even back then Leveque's hairline was fading. Now he shaved his head and looked like a billiard ball with a beard.

"Macmillan's mustache isn't bad though."

"True. And he still has it. He's practising out of a strip mall in the northwest." I don't know why I added the bit about the strip mall, it sounded uncharitable.

We both turned at the sound of footsteps clicking down the hall. Hadiza, in a flowing red dress, bore down on us, majestic like a ship setting sail with foghorns blaring and streamers flying. "Hadiza, you remember—" she cut me off as she extended her hand.

"Of course. James, how nice to see you. What brings you to the city?"

James explained he came into town to meet with SAIT—the Southern Alberta Institute of Technology—about teaching a course in their culinary arts program.

"You're not leaving the Banff Springs, are you?" I asked.

He shook his head. "No, no, just looking for ways to beef up my resumé. It pays to be ready for any opportunity." He glanced at his phone, noted it was getting late, and disappeared down the hall. The heavy doors banged shut when he left, then banged a second time. Hadiza's hand shot out and she grabbed my wrist.

"Shit." She nudged me so we were both facing the photo wall. "Don't look now—damn, he's seen us."

"Who?"

"Doctor Death."

No sooner had she uttered the words than Gideon Gold's reedy voice hailed us. "Ladies!" Hadiza continued to stare at the wall as if she could ignore him into oblivion.

This was ridiculous. I turned and extended my hand. "What are you doing here Doc—er, Gideon?" I asked.

He took a moment to draw himself up to his full height, inhaling slowly as he realigned every skinny bone in his body, and said he was auditing a class. His mouth twitched and he looked like he was fighting the urge to laugh.

"Gideon." Hadiza sounded stern. "You have not been auditing a class." She turned to me. "My esteemed former colleague"—she hit the word 'former' extra hard—"likes to pop into my class now and then. You'd think he'd have better things to do with his time now that he's retired, but he's becoming a regular fixture around here."

Before I could tease Gideon about needing to get out more, he said, "I'm here for the 'edutainment'." Hadiza pursed her lips and looked past his shoulder into the empty corridor. "I keep telling her, she's letting them walk all over her."

Hadiza took a slow breath and looked at me. "Sadly, Gideon doesn't understand that the world has changed since he was a prof. Students need a little more hand holding now than they did back in his day."

He snorted, then pulled a crumpled handkerchief out of his jacket pocket and dabbed the tip of his nose. "There's teaching, Hadiza, and then"—here he made jazz hands—"there's edutainment." His milky eyes shone with malicious glee. "They're training for the bar, Hadiza. They're here to be educated, not amused."

By now Hadiza was bristling. Gideon tipped his head to one side and said, "Far be it from me to tell you how to do your job, but honestly Hadiza, when that kid complained you were going too fast and he couldn't keep up, poor dear, and told you, *he told you,* to redo your PowerPoints, that was too much."

"PowerPoints?" I asked.

She nodded. "We started using slides during the pandemic when we switched to online classes. We're back to in-person teaching now, but the kids got used to downloading the PowerPoints before each class. So we kind of have to keep doing them." She shot a brittle glance at Gideon. "That kid had a point, though. I could have made the lesson clearer."

"Hah!" Gideon started to cough. He clutched his handkerchief to his lips and made an awful noise. After he caught his breath he said, "It's a bloody admin law class, Hadiza, not rocket science. Finn would never have put up with it."

"Perhaps," she snapped, "but Finn's no longer here."

Gideon refused to let it go. He railed on about the

school's appalling decision to switch from a five grade system: A, B, C, D, and F, to an eleven grade system with pluses and minus. "Pure grade inflation, nothing more," he huffed.

"Grade inflation!" she repeated, her colour rising.

"Hadiza," I had to get her out of here before she throttled him. "We really must be on our way."

*   *   *

We settled on a couple of bar stools in a large, chilly room decorated in glittering glass and shiny steel. Not exactly a welcoming place, but Hadiza was a regular here. Still, she was impatient to the point of being rude to the bartender when he finally came back with our orders. Her whiskey sour was half gone in one large gulp. She thumped it down on the bar and asked, "What is it with these stupid old men?"

Slowly, I stirred my gin and tonic. "Are you referring to old men in general or one old man in particular?"

"Why don't they have the decency to step aside and go away quietly when they've become irrelevant?"

I had to deflect her or she'd go off on a rant about privileged old white guys; we'd beaten this topic to death many times. "How are you managing Finn's job on top of your teaching load?" The minute the words were out of my mouth I knew it was a mistake.

"Why does everyone keep calling it that? It's not *Finn's* job, it's *my* job." She downed the last of her whiskey and stared daggers at the back of the bartender's head until he turned around and met her eye. She waved her hand. *Again.*

I tried to reset the conversation, but she was in high dudgeon.

"Finn! Everyone keeps banging on about Finn." She glared at the bartender when he set down her drink. "Gideon and Finn. 'Rules are rules, Hadiza, rules are rules.'"

I had no idea which one she was talking about, Gideon or Finn. "What rules?"

"Are you kidding? Universities are nothing but rules. Rules on what to teach, how to teach, what to research, where to publish. It's a miracle anything meaningful gets done, ever."

I shivered, it was so bloody cold in here, and signaled the bartender, *coffee*. I'd prefer a hot chocolate but that would be juvenile. Turning to Hadiza I said, "We are talking about a law school, Hadiza, lawyers are hard-wired to respect rules. It's the only way to ensure fairness."

"Oh, don't you start," she scoffed. "Fairness, like beauty, exists in the eye of the beholder. If the dean likes you, you get to attend a conference in Copenhagen. If she doesn't, you stay home. The world isn't fair. We didn't need three years of a pandemic to figure that out."

Hadiza was gnawing on the tip of her stir stick. It was plastic, the bar must be using up the last of its supply. "Things happen much faster now. You have to work your ass off to keep up. You want to hear about my teaching load? Well, let me enlighten you. No one becomes an academic because they love to teach. Teaching is the price we pay for the freedom to do research." She slumped with disappointment as she stared into her empty highball glass. "Sometimes you have to take shortcuts, it's the only way to keep your head above water."

The bartender returned with another whiskey and my coffee which tasted like it was fresh out of the microwave. Hadiza was right about things happening faster now.

Sometimes I long for the days when a lawyer could send a client a letter, a real letter in an envelope with a stamp. It would take days to arrive and the client would take days to draft a response and mail it back. Now people fired off emails like a popcorn machine run amok and expected a reply the minute it hit your inbox.

"Look on the bright side, at least you work in a collegial environment." I was thinking back to my time with Gates, Case and White which was as collegial as a shark tank. Lawyers guarded their clients so jealously they'd work from a beach in Hawaii rather than let a colleague babysit their practice for ten days. They were more worried about losing a client than losing their spouses.

"Collegial environment?" Hadiza snorted through her nose. "Ow, that hurt! Don't make me laugh."

I passed her my napkin; she shook her head, she didn't need it.

The bartender was chatting to another customer and Hadiza leaned across the bar, waving her arm to catch his attention. Why, I didn't know, her drink was sitting right in front of her. He ignored her and she continued. "Law departments may have less hierarchy than other university departments, but they're just as fraught."

"Fraught?"

"Fraught. As in drama, drama, drama. Some of my esteemed colleagues aren't on speaking terms with each other. Makes for interesting staff meetings, let me tell you."

"Really?"

Hadiza swung around to face me in such a loose, sloppy way that she almost slid off her stool. "Yes, really. As if we don't have enough to do, teaching and hounding people to deliver what they promised in committees."

I assumed she was talking about her work with the

Consortium, but her face was so red, flushed with anger and alcohol, I didn't dare ask. I put a hand on her shoulder and was startled to feel a shudder. "Hadiza?" My tone was gentle.

She glanced up. She was on the verge of crying.

"I miss him, Evie." She said with a sad shake of her head. "Finn could be such an ass, but I really miss him."

"I miss him too."

"And the students miss him. Gideon is right, they'd never push Finn the way they're pushing me. Even when his PowerPoints were incomprehensible." I recalled Finn's weird shorthand where a triangle stood for 'person' and the yin and yang symbol meant 'the world' or 'the people'. She sniffed. "How can I possibly replace him?"

I pulled her into a side hug. "No one expects you to replace him. Just be yourself. Take it one step at a time. Finn wasn't brilliant from the outset." That last part wasn't true. From the first day I'd met him Finn's brilliance was undeniable. But Hadiza didn't need to hear that.

She pulled the serviette out from under her whiskey glass and dabbed her eyelids. "I said such horrible things to him that weekend in Banff. Why did I push it... Maybe in the fullness of time—"

Just then the bartender swooped in and asked if we'd like another round. She thought about it for a minute, then shook her head. I paid the tab and dropped her off at home.

As I sailed down the streets and avenues heading back to my sweet little house on the banks of the Elbow River, I thought about Hadiza, so critical of Finn one minute and utterly lost without him the next. What was the true nature of their relationship? All the while Doctor Death's words played on a loop in my brain: *Hadiza will be glad when Finn's finally in the ground.*

CHAPTER 26

ANYA'S WORLD

C an I see you a second?" Whenever Madeline says that I'm reminded of my dad's silly joke about placing bets at poker: I see your second and raise you a third. Usually it made me chuckle, but today I couldn't muster a smile.

"Look at that." I pointed at the swollen river carving a wide channel through the woods on the other side of my window. "It's wider, I swear it's wider."

"The ducks will be happy," she said, peering through the drizzling rain, "flooding means more food." If anyone would know about ducks it would be Madeline. Like Cinderella in the woods, she's been feeding the woodland creatures since the day we moved in.

"We need sandbags, Madeline. Where do we get sandbags?"

She patted my arm. "Don't fuss, I'll take care of it, now come with me." I followed her back to her office. Finn's shoeboxes were stacked on the small table by the window, ten rainbow-coloured files were lying on her desk like an oversized deck of cards.

"I've gone through everything," she said as I picked a shoebox off the table. Gently she took it out of my hands and placed it back on top of the stack. "Forget the shoeboxes, there's nothing in them except Finn's memorabilia. Patrice was right, the man was a packrat. I've winnowed out the relevant stuff. It's all here."

She sat down behind her desk and fanned out the file folders as if she was about to do a magic trick. *Pick a card, any card.* I took the chair across from her and waited.

"His important documents from his personal files and his university files." She rifled through the coloured folders and found the one she wanted. "Other than an RRSP and his university pension, the bulk of Finn's estate is made up of DreamStone shares. Patrice says they're worth close to five million."

"Which is why she's comfortable lending Peter five hundred thousand."

"Right, but here's the thing. I've combed through every scrap of paper and can't find anything that confirms Patrice's assumption. For all we know Finn's shares are worthless."

"So get a valuation done. Patrice is the executor; she can hire an accountant to run an independent valuation."

"We already tried that," Madeline said with a frown. "Anya told her not to waste her money on an independent evaluation. She says ammolite is such a rare commodity"—a hint of sarcasm crept into Madeline's voice— "that no one knows its value better than she does. Oh, and if Patrice would kindly light a fire under her lazy-ass lawyer and get that loan agreement signed, that would be greatly appreciated. God, that woman is worse than a telemarketer."

"Who's a telemarketer?" AJ popped his head in the door. He was across the floor and seated in the other visitor's chair before I had a chance to invite him in. Madeline explained our fear that Finn's shares might be worthless.

He leaned back and stretched his arms over his head. "How does DreamStone pay dividends to its shareholders? The shareholders are Finn, Anya, Peter, and Juve, right?"

"Not Juve," Madeline said, "he's on salary and bonuses, and hefty bonuses at that. Why?"

"Just wondered whether they pay dividends in cash or cryptocurrency, something like Bitcoin or Ethereum?"

"Why on earth would DreamStone pay dividends in Bitcoin?" If I were in court I would be jumping to my feet with an objection. This had nothing to do with getting an independent valuation of Finn's shares.

AJ gave me the look I used to give my mom when she talked about *The* Facebook and said, "I did some digging after you got back from your meeting with the Edmonton lawyer." He was referring to the Justice Department lawyer who grilled Finn about minerals and cryptocurrency.

"And?"

"And," he continued, "ammonite miners, companies like GTX, are deep into cryptocurrency. They'd have to be if they're flogging ammolite-backed tokens. They're big dreamers. They take big risks. This is Anya's world. She knows all about the crypto marketplace. She made a killing in crypto way back in 2016, 2017, right?"

That weekend in Banff came back to me. Hadiza and I had just arrived at the Banff Springs Hotel. I thought I was locked out of my room, the card reader kept beeping red. I was about to go downstairs and get a new card key when Anya floated down the corridor in a stunning black Mossimo dress; with her shiny black hair and full red lips she looked like a model. They'd arrived a couple of days earlier.

"We're celebrating our wedding anniversary," she'd said, her voice low and silky. "It's been seven amazing years."

She showed me a Qiviuk shopping bag; Qiviuk sells high-end, handcrafted clothing made of exotic materials like bison and muskox hair. "Seven is the copper and wool anniversary." She shuddered. "Copper goes green and wool is itchy, so that's absolutely out of the question. Look what I got Peter. He'll love this." *This* was carefully wrapped in tissue paper and tucked inside a box which was tucked inside a bag so she couldn't drag it out to show it to me. Instead, she described it as the softest, most beautiful cardigan she'd ever seen.

Peter and Anya were married in 2016 right after she'd graduated at the top of her class from Wharton, an Ivy League school that accepted less than six percent of its applicants. According to Finn it was Anya who got them into crypto, Peter was just along for the ride. And what a ride it was. They got in early, invested heavily and pulled out just before the crash. They invested their millions in DreamStone and used the rest to buy a beautiful mansion, expensive cars and holidays, all the accoutrements of an extravagant lifestyle.

"All this is very interesting, AJ," I said, "but let's focus on our immediate problem. Anya is blocking Patrice from independently valuing Finn's shares and I don't want Patrice to lend DreamStone five hundred thousand dollars if Finn's shares are worthless and the company can't pay her back."

As I said it out loud I finally understood why the alarm bells were ringing in my head. DreamStone didn't just have a cash flow problem, it was in financial crisis, but I couldn't prove it.

CHAPTER 27

THE JACKRABBIT

It took twenty minutes, but Quincy finally stopped slobbering on my shoulder and flopped down in the backseat of the Mini, his forehead wrinkled with concern.

"He thinks we're going to the vet," I said. "Why else would we be in the car at nine o'clock on a Saturday morning."

Louisa was slumped in the front seat next to me. She didn't look any happier than the dog. "When you said let's go for a drive in the country, you didn't say it was a work trip."

"Oh, stop grumbling," I down-shifted into third and swung through a tight cloverleaf onto the highway heading south. "It's a glorious day, the nicest weekend we've had in weeks. Sit back, relax, enjoy the ride."

She rolled her eyes at me. "You are not an airline pilot. We're not going on vacation, we're visiting a mine, Evie. A *mine*."

"You like to learn new things, it'll be fun." I'd finally convinced Peter to show me the DreamStone mine. He didn't understand why I wanted to see it, it was just a hole in the ground. I said I wouldn't bill him for my time, I just liked visiting the projects I'm working on. "Humour me, Peter." I'd said. Finally he'd agreed. Louisa on the other hand had little interest in humouring me so I tried a different tack.

"Louisa, darling, this is your chance to become one with the universe, they say all seven colours of ammolite have magical powers."

"I prefer diamonds, thank you very much." She tried to sound huffy but I could hear the smile in her voice.

We got caught behind a flatbed semi-trailer carrying a gigantic white blade for a wind turbine and the drive into the Foothills took almost two hours. By the time we were rattling down washboard roads and into a rudimentary parking lot, the sun was high in the hazy sky. Everyone, especially the dog who's prone to carsickness, was glad to get out of the car.

Louisa clipped Quincy into his harness while I texted Peter to say we'd arrived. Next to the parking lot was an enormous pit where massive yellow machines rumbled around on tank treads, lifting and lowering buckets that screeched as they scraped the rocky ground.

Quincy bounced around stiff-legged, yanking Louisa toward the pit. When we got close to the lip she said it looked like a gigantic archeological dig.

"Yes," I shouted over the noise, "except archeologists work with precision hand tools, not noisy machines." The regulations stipulated any excavation done near a fossil had to be performed with hand tools, but none were being used today.

A chilly dusty breeze blew grit into our eyes and we were debating the wisdom of getting closer to the edge of the mine when Quincy barked. Two sharp quick yips, his tiny black eyes focusing on something in the distance.

Then he bolted.

Louisa had clipped him into the long puppy training lead, it snaked out ahead of her. "Quincy!" she yelled. "Stop!"

He didn't stop but continued hurtling toward a long low warehouse in the distance. She clutched the lead tightly and braced herself but without her leather training gloves the cord shredded her palms and she lost her grip. The lead whipped through the air, snagging on thistle bushes in the long grass.

"Quincy!" we both screamed his name. He was so focused on something up ahead and the machines were so loud, he couldn't hear us.

We broke into a sprint. He was tearing up the slope at breakneck speed, zigzagging from left to the right and back again.

"It's a jackrabbit!" I yelled. We ran faster, getting closer to the low grey warehouse. "He's chasing a bloody jackrabbit."

"I see it!" Louisa's arms and legs were pumping as we fanned out, hoping to anticipate the jackrabbit's moves.

The rabbit, a brown dot in the brown field, was visible only in flashes of white tail and I prayed it wouldn't do an about-face and shoot between us straight back to the pit.

Quincy was barking wildly now. Dodging and weaving, his long lead flying behind him. My lungs burned and my legs ached. We had to catch him. He would never stop.

The jackrabbit hesitated, popped up its head, then raced straight for the warehouse door. Quincy was gaining on him. Twenty feet, fifteen feet, ten feet. He was on top of it.

No, the rabbit disappeared into a small dark hole under

the cement step. Quincy was moving so fast he couldn't stop. He crashed into the door. It banged open and he skittered inside, legs flailing across the concrete floor.

"Jesus, Quincy." Louisa flew through the door right behind him and tackled him, hooking her shredded hands under his collar. I charged through the door, tripped on the threshold, and crashed on top of them both.

That's when Quincy started to growl. A low guttural sound that raised the hairs on the back of my neck. I looked up. Into the barrel of a gun.

CHAPTER 28

REPLICA

Jesus Christ, Juve," I yelled, "put that damn thing away before you shoot someone" Quincy snarled, a frothy vicious sound, desperately trying to claw his way out from under Louisa.

"Control your dog." Juve's tone was harsh. I staggered to my feet and ran back to the door, slamming it shut so Quincy couldn't escape. Louisa was on her hands and knees crouching over the dog. I touched her shoulder. "I got it, he can't get out."

A second man appeared, shorter and stockier than Juve. He took one look at Quincy and grabbed a wrench off the workbench, bouncing it in his other hand. Ready.

"Control your fucking dog," Juve repeated, more slowly.

"For the love of god," I shouted, "what's wrong with you people?"

Louisa sat back on her heels, stroking Quincy's ears with a lacerated hand. As the dog relaxed she coiled the long lead until he had just five feet of running room. Slowly she rose to her feet and glared at Juve. "The fucking dog is fine." Quincy rumbled deep in his throat; not quite fine but getting there.

Juve pointed the gun at the floor. "You're damned lucky I thought you were Evie."

Louisa's eyes grew wide. "What? You'd have shot me if I wasn't?"

Juve turned his back on her and set the gun on the workbench. The man with the wrench asked if Juve had everything under control. Juve nodded and the man disappeared back down a narrow corridor in the back.

"Yeah, sorry about that." Juve grinned at me, the cold glint gone from his eye, limbs loose and relaxed. "We've got a coyote problem. So, Evie, what brings you to my neck of the woods?"

The hissing in my ears subsided as my heartbeat dropped back into normal range. "Where's Peter?" I asked. "He promised us a tour of the mine."

I glanced around the long room. It looked like an apothecary shop and smelled of dust and metal shavings. There were no windows but it was filled with light from the overhead lamps and goosenecks spaced at regular intervals along a long wooden bench that was scattered with lathes and strangely shaped tools. Shelves along one wall were stacked with boxes of all shapes and sizes. Wooden crates bursting with straw-like packing material lined the wall on the opposite side. Dead centre on the bench behind Juve rested a heavy nautilus shell. No, not a nautilus, an iridescent ammonite shell. The biggest I'd ever seen.

"Wow." I moved closer. "This must be worth a fortune." It was four times the size of the one stolen in the smash and grab in Vancouver; the one that was valued at $500,000.

"Don't touch it." Juve's tone was sharp.

"Don't worry about it. It's fake." Peter appeared out of

the shadow of the narrow hall. He walked over to Louisa and reached down to stroke the dog's head. "Touch it all you want." Louisa asked if there was somewhere she could wash up. Her hands were a mess of dirt and dried blood. She passed me Quincy's lead and followed Peter down a corridor to a bathroom in the back.

I turned to Juve. "This one's fake too, like the one you had on display in Banff?"

Juve nodded. "Yeah, but I don't want that damn dog scratching it or knocking it down."

Peter returned. "Juve, lighten up. What harm could it do?" I shuddered at the thought of Quincy knocking the replica off the bench and smashing it into a million pieces. Clutching his lead tightly I stepped closer to the piece. It was so beautiful, glistening with flashes of deep blue and violet. As I reached out to touch it Juve said something to Peter but his words were swallowed by the hum of the air filtration system overhead.

Quincy broke free when Louisa returned. She caught his lead with a bandaged hand and made him sit quietly while Peter explained how the piece had been made. Something to do with filling a mold with resin and adding mica flakes and chips of real ammolite to make it look authentic. "The trickiest part is getting the damn thing out of the mold without breaking it," Peter said.

"It's really remarkable," Louisa said, running the side of her hand along the edge of the coiled chambers; her white bandaged palm glowed with reflected blue and violet light.

Peter patted Juve's shoulder. "Yeah, Juve here does a really fine job." Juve laughed and said with all this fancy equipment it was child's play.

After a few minutes Peter said we had to let Juve get back to work. Quincy trotted calmly beside us as we crossed the field between the warehouse and the parking lot, lifting his head every so often, scouting the horizon for the jackrabbit. I gripped his lead tightly, it was stained with Louisa's blood.

"Peter, what is that place? A staging area?"

He said something about gem production but the rest of his answer was swallowed by the roar of the diggers down in the pit. When we reached the Mini, Peter asked whether we'd like to go down into the mine, maybe to the first level. Louisa said absolutely not, the dog had had enough excitement for one day.

As we trundled back down the narrow washboard road, Louisa pulled a box of handi-wipes out of the glove compartment and daubed the dust off her bandaged hand. "Well, that was quite the fuss."

"We have to get Quincy back into puppy training. He could have killed you, or himself, if that jackrabbit bolted for the mine."

"I'm talking about the warehouse. Juve had a gun. And that other guy was waving a wrench around. Since when do coyotes break into warehouses and terrorize the people inside?"

"Juve is a miner, Louisa, a throwback to the Klondike Gold Rush—"

"I don't like him," she said firmly. "Neither does Quincy, and he's a good judge of character."

I glanced into the rear view mirror. Quincy was sprawled on his back, his legs in the air, snoring like a buzz saw. The dog may be uncouth, but Louisa was right, he is a good judge of character.

CHAPTER 29

THE DARK WEB

Monday morning I hustled into the garage in my brand new Ferragamo heels and stylish wide leg slacks and stepped smack into a puddle. *Inside the garage?* Rain hammered the metal garage door, sheets of water rippled in under the rubber seal. Not good. I pressed the door opener—a mistake as it turned out—and more water sluiced down the driveway sloping into the garage. I cinched my raincoat tighter and ran outside and discovered the storm drain at the top of our driveway was clogged with leaves and twigs and a random sock. By then my slacks were soaked to the knees and my shoes had lost their glossy shine. When I'd cleared enough debris to slow the flood down my driveway, I returned to the house and changed from head to toe. Then started the morning all over again.

I arrived at the office thirty minutes late for our Monday morning debrief. Hanging my limp raincoat on the hook behind my door, I rushed down the hall and joined the others in the conference room.

"Ah, there you are," said Keith. He was sitting in his

usual place at the head of the table, AJ, Madeline, and Bridget were clustered around him.

"Wow, what happened to you?" AJ, ever so tactful, stared at my damp hair. Usually poker straight, it was starting to go wavy. I muttered something about the storm drain and the garage and flooding, and the grins on their faces faded.

"You've got to get out of there," Bridget pronounced. I told her not to panic, by all accounts the river would not breach its banks, this was just overflow from culverts unable to keep up with the heavy rain.

Then everyone let loose with their own will-this-infernal-rain-ever-end stories. Bridget's garden was covered with drowned worms— "they're all over the place, even the flagstones, it's so sad"—Madeline was going mad cleaning her dog's muddy paw prints out of her Persian rug, I complained about my ruined Ferragamos, saying at this rate I'd need hip waders to get to the car. AJ smiled smugly saying he was safe and dry up there in his fifth-floor condo; his smile faded when Madeline reminded him that his car, parked in the basement, was toast.

Keith pulled his gaze from the rain-soaked poplars shuddering in the wind outside and said, "All kidding aside, we have to take this seriously. Does everyone have an emergency plan?"

"A what plan?" Bridget frowned.

Madeline said, "He means are you ready to run for your life if the river overflows and floods your house and destroys everything you own."

Bridget shot Madeline a horrified look. "I prefer the way Keith said it."

"I know, Bridget," Madeline's tone softened, "so do I." It struck me that she may be more worried than she was letting on. This was disconcerting. Madeline sailed through the 2013 flood with her usual aplomb despite being dragged out of bed at two A.M. by a police officer who said her neighbourhood was under mandatory evacuation and she had thirty minutes to get out. She lived alone with a menagerie of animals, two street cats, a small yappy dog, a cockatiel named Rupert, and a tank full of expensive saltwater fish.

Ever resourceful, she'd called Bridget who had a large van, and Bridget called me—Lord knows why, I drove a Honda Civic at the time. The three of us plus a random firefighter we later discovered had been Madeline's overnight guest packed the animals and Rupert into travel cages and transported them with great big bags of pet food across town to Bridget's place. The firefighter told Madeline to leave the fish; the tank was four feet off the ground and they should be safe. Madeline said if the flood waters topped the tank, the fish were on their own. As it was, all the critters survived, but a year later Madeline sold her place and moved to higher ground.

I glanced around the table. "Seems to me the only ones who are really at risk here are AJ and me. Louisa and I have an emergency plan."

"I'm fine in the condo," AJ said.

"Assuming the bridge isn't washed out and you can't get home... or, you're at home and can't get out," I said.

"I'll cope, but I need somewhere safe to park the car."

Madeline volunteered to take his MGB off his hands. He said he'd release it to her over his drowned dead body.

"Guys, this is serious," Keith flicked his eyes around the room. "I was talking about an emergency plan for the office." He was right. Braxton, Lawson, Valentine was in a low building a mere fifty feet from the river's edge. Every morning for the last week we'd stood at our windows watching helplessly as the Elbow River rose higher and higher. I suggested our first priority was to protect the sensitive files in our vault. We could raise everything off the floor, but no one knew how high was high enough.

Madeline said, "We have to sandbag the entire building."

Keith shook his head. "Too late, there isn't a sandbag to be found in the city."

Madeline looked affronted. "I'm telling you, I've got this."

Keith threw her a skeptical look. "You've got this?"

"Madeline knows a guy," I said. In my experience Madeline always knows a guy.

Keith wasn't convinced. "This better not be a guy who just happens to be standing on the side of the road when a load of sandbags falls off the truck."

"No," Madeline said primly. "It's a guy who owns a company that makes sandbags." She named the CEO of a large concrete and excavation company. "I talked to him. He'll deliver as many sandbags as we want." She gave Keith a smug look. "And he'll supply the crew to lay them down properly, too." You could almost hear the words *So there!* At the end of her sentence.

Keith tipped his head in a deferential nod and stressed that BLV would pay the going rate for sandbags and installation. If he was worried about the allegations that Madeline's friend may have been involved in a price-fixing scandal last year, he had the good sense not to mention it.

After the meeting, I followed AJ back to his office. "Have you got a minute?" I asked.

He grinned and said, "You can't have my car either, I've seen the way you drive."

"Hah. I don't want your silly old car." He pretended to be offended. "I want to pick your brain about cryptocurrency."

The thought that Finn's shares might be worthless and Patrice would not be able to pay off her mortgage kept me up half the night.

We sat at his small round table by the window and for the next hour he took me down a rabbit hole of charismatic crypto CEOs: one who mysteriously died in the Pink City taking key passwords with him to the grave, and another who convinced luminaries like Tony Blair and Bill Clinton to promote his magical reality then got indicted for fraud and money laundering.

"Hold on," I said, "How did we go from legal to illegal activity, from cryptocurrency to fraud and money laundering?"

"Are you kidding?" he said, "Crypto and the dark web are a goldmine for money launderers."

"Why?"

He cocked his head and said, "Here's the Coles Notes version. Imagine you're a drug lord; your dealers sell your drugs for cash and shuffle that cash to a broker who converts it into anonymized cryptocurrency—which incidentally is extremely difficult to trace—then converts it back into Bitcoin or hard cash and sends it to your illicit address. Once you've got your hands on it, you can use it to buy whatever you want."

I blinked and he smiled. "Okay, it's lot more complicated than that, but you get the drift. Over the last three years, eight to ten billion dollars, *billion,* have been laundered through crypto."

"I'll take your word for it, AJ. So tell me, why do you know so much about illicit cryptocurrency markets?"

"Why are you so interested?" he countered. "Has this got something to do with DreamStone?"

I shrugged. "I wish I knew, AJ. I wish I knew."

CHAPTER 30

A BROKEN CAMERA

An excitable man on the car radio was rabbiting on about the jet stream stalled over the Foothills, it was sucking moisture out of Saskatchewan, the U.S., and the Gulf of Mexico like a giant vacuum cleaner and dumping it on us. I turned down the volume and peeked up through the rain-specked windscreen: should we be bracing for the deluge?

I had to clear my mind. I was on my way to Patrice's place with the loan documents.

Earlier today Madeline marched into my office and thumped the DreamStone minute book on my desk. "You have to have a come-to-Jesus talk with Patrice."

"Now what?"

Her face was unusually pale against the robin's egg blue of her dress. "Five words: DreamStone is circling the drain."

Bloody hell.

Madeline tapped the minute book. "We finally got the documentation we needed from the banks. The company is in financial crisis."

"Take me through it."

The colour returned to her cheeks as she sat down and flipped open the minute book. I held up my hands and asked for the Coles Notes abbreviated version. I've been getting the Coles Notes version of a lot of things lately.

She flipped the minute book closed again, took a deep breath and said, "Long story short, DreamStone owes the banks fifty million dollars and the banks want it back. Peter and Anya mortgaged their house for eight million, gave the funds to DreamStone which repaid a part of the bank loan, but it's nowhere near enough. The banks want another twenty-five million or they'll start seizing DreamStone assets."

"Like the mine."

"Yes, the mine."

"Anya is trying to keep the banks at bay by dribbling some money, like Patrice's five hundred thousand and the profits from sales, back to them. It's a stall tactic. No wonder they're desperate for those disposition certificates. If they can't get the money out of Asia fast enough they'll lose everything. The mine, the business, their house, their personal fortune. All of it will collapse." Madeline's eyes met mine. "Right on top of Patrice."

* * *

Patrice's house was in a quiet inner-city neighbourhood close to the university. Finn was one of those fanatics who biked to work all year round. Today he'd have been zipping down the road, hunched over the handlebars in his red bug-eye goggles and a slick white helmet, his fluorescent yellow rain slicker flapping behind him.

Patrice answered the door before the bell stopped

chiming and led me through to the airy kitchen at the back of the house. She was casually dressed in khaki slacks and an oversized black sweater and looked happy and relaxed.

She put the kettle on for mint tea and popped open a Tupperware container. A hint of banana oatmeal cookies filled the air.

"If it wasn't raining so hard, I'd show you Finn's garden," she said, pulling two small plates out of the cupboard.

I asked if Finn was growing asparagus back there and she laughed and said no, Finn would never *grow* asparagus, not when he could forage for it in the wild.

"He refused to divulge his secret harvesting spots, you know," I said with a smile.

"You should have seen his face when he returned home with an exceptional haul. You'd think he'd been panning for gold and found the motherlode."

The kettle whistled and the tea was steeping when I told Patrice the purpose of my visit: DreamStone was fifty million in debt, it was financially unstable, and I had to be absolutely certain she understood the risks before she went ahead with the five-hundred-thousand dollar loan.

"Patrice, you may never get that money back. It could be gone forever."

Something flickered in her eyes, uncertainty, then a flash of stubborn irritation. "That's silly, Evie. The company is doing very well financially."

"Then why do they need your money?"

She waved one hand impatiently in front of her face as if she were batting away a fly. "It's just a timing issue, the delay with the Asian transactions is impeding cash flow."

I was certain she had no idea what she was talking about. I said she'd lose the house if DreamStone collapsed.

This little house was all she had. "Finn wouldn't want you thrown out into the street, Patrice."

"Oh, for the love of God." Two red spots appeared on her cheekbones. "I've got more than this house. I'll have Finn's DreamStone shares once probate issues."

I'd have to spell it out for her. "Patrice, the shares haven't been independently valued since 2017. All you've got is Anya's word for it. What if they're not worth as much as she says they're worth?"

Her eyes sparked at me over the rim of her teacup. "You sound just like Finn."

"Finn was a very smart man. He'd want me to do my best to protect you. Patrice, you must understand, you're taking a huge risk. You could lose everything."

She glanced out the window, it was pouring so hard the rain sluiced out of the gutters, then she turned to me and said she wanted to sign the documents.

"Fine." I reached into my briefcase and placed four copies of the loan agreement down on the table with more force than was really necessary.

After she'd scribbled her signature on the last page, her mood lightened. She went to the sink, ran more water into the kettle and set it to boil. "Finn hated the rain. What's it been, two weeks or more?" The kettle whistled, she warmed the tea remaining in the teapot and topped up my cup. "But he wouldn't let it stop him. He'd be out there, walking, biking, hiking, rain or shine. He loved the outdoors," When they were first married, they travelled the world, going on grueling multi-day hikes. "We did Rainbow Mountain in Peru and the Dolomites in Italy." She tilted her head sadly. "Then my knees gave out and I couldn't keep up with him anymore."

She glanced over her shoulder into the dim light of

Finn's study, "I have to show you something," and darted into the other room, returning with a camera in her hand. "Finn took photos everywhere he went. For me. It was his way of including me in the experience. We'd spend hours looking at the pictures when he came home, what he'd seen, who he talked to; honestly Evie, it was like being there with him every step of the way."

She handled the camera reverently, placing it on the table. The lens was gouged with a deep, nasty scratch. Her eyes filled with pain when she spotted it.

"You were his birding buddy," she said, "recognize this?"

Patrice picked up the camera and clicked through the digital images. "These are the last photos he took." She turned the camera to show me the LCD display.

There were four shots at the end of the reel. The first two were blurry, the bird was bobbing around in the branches of a pine tree. In the last shot it was flying out of the frame. But the third shot was perfect. The distinctive black-crested head and rich blue body, bright in the sunlight. Its pointy little claws gripped the gnarled grey branch.

"Wow! That's a Steller's Jay. It's been on Finn's list for years."

Patrice chuckled. "That's what I thought, but I couldn't confirm it, he didn't enter it in his Merlin app."

Despite the warmth of the room, I felt a chill. This was it. This was what Finn wanted to show me on that last day when he was racing to his room to fetch his camera. I'd begged off, I had too many last-minute details to attend to before his celebratory dinner. The camera was a clunky thing, heavy around his neck. Did he lean out too far? Did it drag him off the balcony? If I had been there, could I have saved him?

I heard Patrice's voice through the haze of my pain

and forced myself to focus on what she was saying. "The EMT people found his camera in the ambulance. They tracked me down and sent it back. FedEx delivered it this morning." She glanced at the bright-eyed bird one last time, then her smile faded.

"Patrice," I put my hand on her sleeve. "Did Finn ever talk to you about any issues he might have had with the Environmental Consortium... or at the university, perhaps with Hadiza?" I didn't dare mention DreamStone again for fear she'd shut me down completely.

She looked puzzled. "Issues? No, not that I can think of. Why?"

I didn't have an answer. But something was niggling in my brain and I was desperate to figure it out.

The doorbell rang, a brittle jangly sound, and the rain-soaked front door squeaked open. "Mom?" It was Peter.

She grabbed the camera, hustled back into Finn's study and shoved it into a deep drawer in the filing cabinet. Returning to the kitchen her voice was artificially bright. "Peter, honey, we're in here."

Peter shouted hello and came around the corner into the kitchen, when he saw me he hesitated in the doorway. "Evie." It came out slowly, almost a drawl. "To what do we owe the pleasure?"

I gestured at the thin stack of paper lying on the kitchen table and said I'd dropped off the loan agreements for Patrice's signature. "If you'd like to sign on behalf of DreamStone, that will save me a trip out to your place."

"Delighted." Peter sat down next to his mother and slipped a Montblanc fountain pen out of his jacket pocket, popping off the cap. The gold nib made a skritching sound as he scratched his signature across the page.

"Peter, what's the purpose of the loan?" Patrice's question sounded casual, as if the answer didn't matter.

His eyes tracked the words on the first page of the agreement. "Well, as it says here, Mom, the funds are required to operate DreamStone's business."

"Peter, dear," she said, "I can read that for myself. What specifically do you need the funds for? It is a lot of money." *Well done, Patrice.* An hour ago she'd snapped at me for suggesting she should think twice about parting with this much cash, now she was grilling Peter like a lawyer conducting due diligence. Maybe something I'd said was finally sinking in.

Peter flashed a lopsided grin. "You'll have to ask Anya, she's the CFO. I'm just the marketing guy." I was dumbfounded. He was asking his mother to put her house on the line and he had no idea why. Patrice looked puzzled but let it drop.

"Speaking of marketing," he said, leaning over to kiss his mother on the cheek, "I have to get going. Just wanted to check in and make sure you're okay."

I said I had to get going as well. Soon Peter and I were outside, darting through the heavy rain to get to our cars. He held my door open and I slid in behind the wheel. The rain poured down the back of his neck and he flipped up his collar, then leaned closer and asked, "Evie, is there a concern about DreamStone's financing?"

"Peter, you'd know the answer to that question better than I would."

As it turned out I was wrong.

CHAPTER 31

DOCTOR DEATH'S PIZZA

"Did we get an alert?" I called out to Louisa as I ran down the driveway to our garage. She was just inside the open door, taping down the flaps on a two-cube cardboard box.

She jumped and the roll of translucent moving tape flew out of her hand and rolled under the work bench. "Jeez, you almost gave me a heart attack! You can't be sneaking up on people like that." She dropped to her knees and crawled around on the cement floor trying to fish the tape out from under the bench.

"Sorry, it's just that everywhere I go people are preparing for The Deluge." I glanced around the garage and asked, "How long have you been at it?" Anything that could be lifted off the floor was stacked on top of the work bench or jammed into boxes and stowed on the utility shelves. "Dad said these shelves would come in handy one day." He'd spent the weeks after Mom died at our place, hammering and sawing heavy planks into a sturdy set of shelves that filled every square inch of wall space in the garage. We were afraid he'd lose a thumb but he was bereft and desperately needed something to fill his days.

"How long have I been at it?" Louisa dragged a dusty hand across her brow. "I dropped Quincy off at doggy daycare and have been preparing for The Deluge, as you so aptly put it, ever since. They say the rivers will peak in the next twenty-four to forty-eight hours." Both the Elbow and the Bow rivers were running abnormally high. "All we can do is batten down the hatches and be ready to run."

For some reason the thought of being at the mercy of the elements reminded me of Doctor Death being buffeted about on the sidewalk outside the coffee shop. A frail old man with too much bravado for his own good. I had to check on him.

Louisa trudged up the driveway and into her car to pick up the dog while I checked the contacts in my phone looking for Doctor Death's phone number. Nothing. Damn it. I'd have to drive over there. I'd have just enough time to check on him before dinner, assuming I could find his place.

After one wrong turn I pulled up in front of Gideon Gold's condo building and parked the car. It was in the same inner-city neighbourhood as AJ's building—one of the many neighbourhoods under an evacuation notice. I found Gideon's name on the lobby directory and pressed his buzzer. Without even checking who it was he buzzed me in. When I reached the third floor I was surprised to find his door wide open.

"Hello?" I stood on the threshold and rapped on the doorframe. "Doctor Gold? Gideon? Are you here?"

He came out of the kitchen, a thin, rumpled man clutching a twenty-dollar bill in his hand. "Of course I'm here," he said gruffly. "Where's the pizza?" Then he stopped short and blinked a couple of times.

"It's me," I said. "Evie Valentine."

He opened his mouth and the buzzer on the wall made a loud burring noise.

"Jesus wept," he muttered as he picked up the receiver. He nodded and pressed the button to release the lobby door. Then he turned, watching me carefully with his watery grey eyes. "I know who you are. What are you doing here?"

The elevator dinged behind me and a pizza delivery guy, a young fresh-faced kid, strode down the corridor as if he owned the place. He nodded at us. "Doctor G. How's it going?"

Gideon said he had no complaints and thrust the twenty-dollar bill into the delivery boy's hand. The kid flashed a toothy grin and disappeared back into the elevator. Gideon fixed his gaze on me and asked again what I was doing here.

Good question. I thought I was rushing over to check on a helpless old man and found myself being grilled by a crank pot who seemed to have everything under control. "Well," I said, making it up as I went along, "I was in the neighbourhood and thought I'd pop by to see how you were doing."

He tilted his head in the direction of the elevator. "As you heard me tell young Jacob there, I've got no complaints." He shifted the pizza box from one hand to the other and his eyes brightened. "You're staying for supper?" He lifted the pizza box to his nose and sniffed. "It's Extravaganzza," then he clicked his teeth together like one of those chattering false teeth toys.

He's such a weird old man, I have no idea why I said yes, but five minutes later I was sitting at a small wooden table watching Gideon hack the pizza to bits with a butcher knife. He handed me a stack of serviettes, "Not dirtying plates for this," and wrenched a ragged hunk of pizza out of the box. As he handed it to me, chunks of olive and beef crumble bounced off the table and onto the floor. I'd never eaten a pizza loaded with so much meat; it tasted surprisingly good.

"How's Hadiza?" he asked. "I understand her faction is getting antsy."

Did he mean faculty? No, that didn't fit the context. "Gideon, I'm not following you. Hadiza has a faction?"

He chortled, then stood up and asked if I'd like a coffee. *Sure,* I thought, *what better way to wash down two pounds of animal fat.* I nodded and continued eating. He pulled a jar of Nescafé out of a cupboard and put the kettle on boil. Soon he was back at the table, clutching two boiling hot mugs and a small bag of miniature marshmallows. "Tastes better this way." The marshmallow bag slipped from his fingers and landed on the table with a soft plop.

"You've heard the saying, 'universities are so ruthless because the stakes are so trivial'?" Of course I had, he'd told it to me. "When Finn announced he was resigning his post as Chair of the Consortium, the place turned into *West Side Story.* The Jets and the Sharks—you know the musical? Fantastic. I saw it in New York, music and lyrics by Bernstein and Sondheim. Now that was talent, not this—"

"Gideon," I cut in, "you were talking about Finn stepping down...?"

Gideon reached into the marshmallow bag and peeled five marshmallows off what appeared to be one large stale marshmallow. "When Finn threw his support behind Hadiza, the Sharks, the anti-Hadiza crowd, deflated. That included the dean, by the way. When it became apparent Finn had had a change of heart—"

"Wait, how did it become apparent?"

He smiled a thin-lipped smile. "The usual ways. Finn was aloof, abrupt with her at staff meetings, veiled attacks in email strings, it all signaled one thing: Finn and Hadiza were on the outs."

I dropped two marshmallows into my instant coffee, took a sip, and dropped in two more. "You'd never get away with that nonsense in the corporate world, you know. They'd send everyone down to HR for a facilitated mediation."

Gideon snorted and continued. "Be that as it may, the more Finn pulled away from Hadiza, the more rabid the anti-Hadiza faction became. And the Jets, her people, fell back, leaving her vulnerable."

"Rabid? Surely that's an exaggeration. How?"

He looked at me as if I were a two-year-old. "Whisper campaigns, questioning her qualifications for the role, anything to denigrate her ability. She was livid. This kind of thing can destroy one's reputation if it goes on long enough." He picked up a small teaspoon and scooped the stale, melted marshmallows into his mouth one by one.

Hadiza had given me the impression Finn's wavering support was a relatively recent development, but Gideon made it sound like their rift had been bubbling for weeks.

"Why did Finn change his mind?"

"Because she stole her student's work."

"No," I said firmly, "it was *alleged* she stole her student's work."

He lifted a bushy grey eyebrow but didn't debate the point, saying instead, "Then Finn had the good grace to croak before he could formally revoke his support and Bob's your uncle, Fanny's your aunt, Hadiza was crowned his successor."

"And the Sharks faded into the background?"

"Hah." He sat back in his chair. "The Sharks will always be there lurking in the shadows, ready to rumble. They can't dethrone Hadiza, but they'll continue to undermine her."

"How?"

"The dean, who didn't support her in the first place, can give her the worst class hours, thereby reducing attendance. They can undermine her committee work. Anything that reflects badly on Hadiza and makes her job more arduous."

I finished my coffee, he was right, the marshmallows helped, and set my mug down on the table. "I gotta say, Gideon, I'm really glad I didn't decide to become an academic."

"You wouldn't be happy in academia. Much too rigorous for you, Evie."

"Much too juvenile, Gideon."

* * *

It took me a long time to get home. My usual route was blocked, a sinkhole big enough to swallow a car had opened up on the side of the road and traffic was being rerouted. Then I ran into a detour to avoid an underpass submerged under four feet of water. The wind was howling through the trees and the power lines fluttered, ready to rip loose at any moment.

When I asked Louisa about the nutritional value of an all-meat pizza, she shuddered and said, "You don't want to know."

CHAPTER 32

WE HAVE A PROBLEM

For one day, one full day, the weather gurus declared we'd be safe. The rain had stopped, the snow melt was manageable, the crisis had been averted. But the river behind the office still roiled its muddy banks and the wolf willows continued to slide into the water.

Bridget was cheery, ready to take the weather forecasters at their word. She was warbling about raindrops on roses and whiskers on kittens when AJ and I arrived. We gave her a hearty round of applause and the poor girl flushed and disappeared behind her computer.

AJ and I went straight down to the coffee room. His hair was wavy with the extra humidity and his eyes were sparkling as if he had a secret.

"Right, what's going on?" I asked, pouring out two coffees, one for him and one for me.

"My baby is safe."

I gulped. "You're talking about your car, right?"

"Damn right, my car! There's nothing but sunshine

and blue skies in the forecast." He spun around and almost hugged me before he caught himself.

I laughed and went to my office and swung my feet up onto the windowsill. Clasping my hands behind my head, I took a moment to watch the warm light dance through the glistening trees by the river.

A few minutes later my phone rang: Laura Bazin, the government employee who issued disposition certificates for DreamStone. "Laura, how can I help you?"

"We have a problem." Her voice was flat.

I swivelled around in my chair and grabbed a note pad. The last I'd heard the disposition certificates had been issued, the crates were packed and the ammolite was on a cargo ship heading to China. In my imagination the ship wasn't a drab freighter stacked high with C-cans but the Queen Mary, sounding its horn and belching smoke out of tall red smokestacks.

"We need to talk," Laura said, "but not on the phone." Did she want me to set up a meeting with her and the DreamStone team, I asked. She snorted. She'd been trying to reach the DreamStone team for days.

"They're ghosting me, Evie," she said, her voice rising. "I will not be treated this way."

Clearly she was angry but she wouldn't tell me why. She demanded we meet, just the two of us, outside of the office. "Noon, tomorrow at the food court in Kingsway Mall, next to Manchu Wok."

"What? In Edmonton?" A couple of weeks ago I'd blown most of a day going to Edmonton to meet with the Justice Department lawyer, I really didn't want to go back up there again.

"Damn right, in Edmonton. You'll be there if you know

what's good for you and your clients." Against my better judgement I agreed.

* * *

The next day it started to rain. Just a light sprinkle, not enough to stop me from driving three hours up to Edmonton. I called Peter and Anya who ghosted me just like they ghosted Laura. They travelled a lot for business but this was ridiculous, surely someone was checking their voicemails.

I pulled into Kingsway early, parked at the wrong end of the mall and wandered past the jewelry stores, clothing stores, and liquor stores, killing time before I found the food court. It was almost noon. The place was packed with tired moms feeding chicken nuggets to screaming toddlers and old people glaring at rowdy teenagers. I had no idea what Laura looked like but figured she'd find me based on my photo on the BLV website.

My coffee from the burger joint was stale and there were no messages or emails on my phone so I watched the milling crowd. Eventually someone called my name. A woman in her early forties approached my table. Her tan raincoat was creased and her hair was flat from the humidity but her lipstick had been freshly applied.

She reached out a hand and introduced herself as she sat down. Laura Bazin.

"I hope you haven't been waiting long." It was an oddly polite thing to say under the circumstances; we weren't a couple of friends meeting up for lunch.

I said something about the traffic being lighter than expected. Then waited. The silence between us filled with the squeal of children's voices. After a beat she picked up where she'd left off yesterday. "We have a serious problem."

"Laura, as I told you yesterday, I have no idea what you're talking about. Is there a problem with the disposition certificates?"

"Not yet, but there will be. It's up to your guys."

The teenaged girl at the next table screamed, startling everyone within a ten-foot radius. A couple of teenaged boys were sliding her phone back and forth across the table between them. She lunged and tried to pry the phone out of their fingers, but it was all for show.

I raised my hands in a helpless gesture. "I can't help you if I don't know what you're talking about."

And that's when she explained the whole sordid mess.

CHAPTER 33

WHAT LAURA SAID

An hour later I was back in the car, windows rolled down, a cool damp breeze playing with my hair. Behind me Edmonton gleamed in the sunlight, fresh and green. It had rained on and off all morning, the wild strawberries and black currants in the river valley would be off to a good start. I inhaled deeply, but I couldn't get enough air.

What a godawful mess. After I spoke with Laura, I called Bridget and told her I had to meet with Keith and AJ as soon as I got back.

"Keith is leaving early," Bridget said, "his wife called, something about too much water pooling somewhere on the acreage..."

"Ask him to wait, please. It's important."

"What about AJ? It's bucketing down here."

"Yeah, him too."

My hands trembled as I clutched the steering wheel. Static fizzed on the radio and I turned if off. With each kilometre the air grew heavier. It was pouring by the time I got back to the city. Fat raindrops splashed across the windshield. Rush hour was building, traffic crawled down the major north-south and east-west roads. I cruised past houses, strip malls, churches, everything was fine until I entered the CP rail underpass.

The road was gone. Vanished under a foot of water. I braked hard. Sliding sideways. Almost rear-ending the car ahead. Great, I was boxed in by cars and concrete walls. The moron behind me leaned on his horn while the cars ahead inched forward. The only way out was through the small lake ahead of me.

I slipped the Mini into first gear and crept down the slope. The Mazda ahead was slowly grinding through the bubbling black water, inching up the slope on the other side. *If he can do it, we can do it.* I was talking to the car. The Mini made an odd noise but moved doggedly forward. And then we were safe on the other side. I patted the dashboard, half expecting the car to give itself a mighty wet-dog shake.

I wheeled into our muddy parking lot and was barely through the door when Bridget called down the corridor, "She's here." Keith and AJ met me at the door to the conference room.

"What's up?" Keith's expression reflected concern, whether it was because of the flooding on his property or me wanting an urgent meeting, it was hard to tell. He leaned against the watery grey windows, arms crossed and legs crossed; he couldn't look more tense if he tried. AJ and I sat at the table and turned our chairs to face him.

Where to start? God, I was sick of clients who pulled stunts that could get me disbarred.

I let out a big sigh and said, "Juve may have crossed the line." Keith inhaled sharply. "What I mean is, Laura Bazin says she 'expedited' DreamStone's disposition certificate application."

Keith's eye twitched. "In return for what? He bribed her?"

I pursed my lips and said, "Not a bribe, per se. But… it's a little complicated."

"What else is new," AJ said.

Keith pushed away from the window and began to pace. His neck was red and blotchy. He's a level-headed guy who rarely loses his temper, but when he does it starts like this.

This wasn't my fault. Why did I feel like it was my fault?

"According to Laura, she felt sorry for Peter and Anya. She knew they'd default on the Asia contract if they didn't get their certificate within a week. Normally, it's a three-week process, but—"

Keith stopped pacing and leaned forward, clutching the back of the chair next to me. "Cut to the chase. What did they give her?"

"That's the tricky part." I pulled back in my chair, he was so close. "Juve told Laura if she bought ammolite-backed crypto tokens she'd make a thirty percent profit overnight. She cashed out her RRSPs and emptied her savings account and gave it all to Juve to invest."

Keith was breathing in shallow puffs. "And he stole it?"

"No, he didn't steal it. He invested it and the tokens crashed."

Now AJ was on his feet and pacing on my other side. "Just so I'm clear here, Laura gave all her money to a guy she barely knows to invest in something she doesn't understand."

"Yeah, that's the long and the short of it." Was it greed or gullibility? Probably a bit of both. "She's lost everything.

And she wants it back. All of it, plus the thirty percent profit Juve promised her."

Keith sat down heavily beside me. "So, it could be a bribe or it could be crappy investment advice."

"Or insider information, depending on which token he told her to buy."

"Shit," said Keith, the man who never swears. "Thirty percent profit overnight. No wonder the Justice Department lawyer was all over Finn about ammolite-backed crypto."

"Laura says unless she's made whole, she'll hold up all of DreamStone's disposition certificates forever."

"That's extortion!" AJ said.

"Be that as it may, by the time DreamStone gets this into court, they'll be bankrupt."

AJ grabbed a chair, spun it around and straddled it. "I don't get it. Why did Laura contact you?"

"DreamStone is ghosting her and she thinks I can force them to pay her back."

"That's never going to happen," Keith's voice was tight. "We're done with this file. I don't care what you promised Finn, BLV's relationship with DreamStone is over. Right now. Today."

"Agreed," I said. "But as you've pointed out, we can't summarily fire them without talking to them first. That would be unethical." For once I was waving the Code of Conduct in Keith's face, usually it's the other way around. "We owe it to them—and to Patrice, who just loaned them five hundred thousand dollars—to get their side of the story. If they have no reasonable explanation, we'll cut them loose."

At that precise moment Madeline steamed down the corridor, a phone pressed to her ear. "I don't care... No, don't interrupt me, I said *I don't care*." She slammed her door, it caught on the sleeve of her coat hanging on the back of the door and bounced open again. "I don't care about your supply chain problems. I don't care about the price of woven polypropylene. You tell your boss he promised me sandbags and the crew to lay them and he damn well better deliver sandbags and the crew to lay them, or so help me God."

There was a short silence. "Good!" She glanced into the hall and saw us staring at her through the conference room door. Without a word she marched to her door and slammed it shut.

"I'll check in on her," I said.

"Is that wise?" Keith asked.

AJ glanced at her door and said, "Abandon all hope, ye who enter here."

*　*　*

I rapped on Madeline's door, then barged in before she could tell me to go away. When she gets like this, a firm hand is required.

She was at her desk, elbows resting on the arms of her chair, hands clasped under her chin, tracking every step I made with those bright green eyes. I raised my eyebrows. She blinked a couple of times. Had she been crying? I sat down, casually crossing one leg over the other.

"So, what's going on?"

She took a deep breath. "There was a problem with the sandbags. It's sorted now."

"I gathered that." I narrowed my eyes. "But that's not what I meant. Are you all right? You sound very angry."

No response.

"Madeline, forget about the sandbags. We'll manage.

If the river floods, it might not reach the office. And if it reaches the office and the place fills with mud to the rafters, we've got flood insurance." That was one nasty lesson we all learned coming out of the 2013 flood. Too many homes and businesses did not carry flood insurance. It costs a fortune, but you'd be nuts to live this close to the river without it.

Madeline spoke slowly as if she were forced to say the words. "It's not the office. I don't give a flying fuck about the office."

Since the first day I'd met her, Madeline's been an enigma. One of those cool, competent people who doesn't need anyone and yet draws people into her orbit. She's in her mid forties, financially secure, and owns a beautiful house in a toney neighbourhood. She has more male admirers than a Hollywood starlet and her friends were loyal to a fault. What was going on with her?

Then I had it.

"Is it the animals? The Menagerie will be fine. You've got a plan, right?" Madeline loved her pets more than she loved people. Other than me and the BLV gang.

"Don't be ridiculous. Of course I have a plan. I packed up and moved to higher ground, remember? No one is going to bang down my door in the middle of the night and tell me I have to get out or drown."

"Well, what is it then?"

Surreptitiously she brushed the corner of one eye; she *had* been crying. Her voice was low. "It's not *my* animals, it's all animals. You know what happened at the zoo the last time."

In 2013 both of Calgary's rivers breached their banks. The Elbow flooded twenty-six neighbourhoods and all of downtown while the Bow swept across St. George's Island, engulfing the zoo. Staff members, many of whom were being flooded out of their own homes, had ten hours or less to evacuate the animals before they drowned in their enclosures. Porcupines, meercats, zebras, lions, tigers, elk, musk ox, all crated. The smaller ones jammed nose to tail in cages stacked up in the admin buildings, the larger ones evacuated to a ranch outside the city limits.

Madeline stared into the corner of the office, not seeing the files neatly stacked on her credenza. "Remember the giraffes? They were shivering in murky water up to their bellies. That's as tall as me. For three days their keepers did everything they could to lure them to higher ground but they wouldn't budge. It's a miracle they survived. And the hippos; the water rose so high they swam right out of their pens. They would have been shot dead if they'd escaped."

She inhaled deeply. "That photo of the gibbon reaching through the bars of his cage to touch his keeper's hand. It broke my heart. What if it happens again and they aren't so lucky this time? What if it's worse?"

"Oh, Madeline." I dared not touch her for fear she'd break down completely. "Things are different now. Back then no one believed it could happen. Now we know better. The zoo has better protocols now. They're ready."

As I said it, I thought about all the people who'd been impacted by the 2013 flood, not just in Calgary but all over southern Alberta. Five died, and over 100,000 were evacuated in the space of twenty-four hours.

"We learned our lesson, Madeline. We're ready this time."

She blinked rapidly, then straightened in her chair and looked at me. "Don't be too sure about that. The Springbank reservoir isn't finished yet. The river doesn't care if the zoo, or the city for that matter, has protocols. the rivers can go from safe to deadly in a day. When that cold, filthy water bursts its banks, all the sandbags in the world won't make the slightest bit of difference."

There was nothing more I could say. She was right. The Springbank reservoir wasn't finished and even it if were, it only protected us from the Elbow River, not the Bow which was just as dangerous if not more so.

* * *

By the time I crossed the hall back to my office the rest had gone home. I threw some files into my briefcase, Lord knows why, I was in no mood to read them, and was almost out the door when my phone pinged with a text.

It was Hadiza asking if I was going to Finn's celebration of life service tomorrow. I'd barely read her text when three more texts came in rapid succession. All from Doctor Death:

Finn is with the invisible choir.
Are you going to his death ceremony?
I need a lift.

I groaned and called out to Madeline. "Can I foist Doctor Death off on AJ? They live in the same neighbourhood."

"No," she shouted back across the hall.

I texted Hadiza to say yes, I was going to Finn's memorial and would be picking up Doctor Death on the way, would she care to join us?

She replied with a terse:

Not a chance!

CHAPTER 34

FINN'S FUNERAL

The guidebooks describe Kananaskis as Alberta's year-round playground. That's not bloated hyperbole, it's fact. Hiking, cross country skiing, dogsledding, it's all there with plenty of room to breathe under wide open skies, although today the sun was hidden by fat grey clouds that thickened with every passing mile.

"I told you it was going to rain," Madeline said with satisfaction from the backseat of the Mini.

Doctor Death didn't care about the weather. He rubbed his hands in anticipation as we pulled into the meeting place, an information centre in Peter Lougheed park. He'd pestered me with texts all day yesterday telling me where to pick him up, what time to arrive, and asking whether he should bring something, scotch perhaps, to give Finn a righteous send-off. When he asked what he should wear to the 'casting ceremony' I was tempted to say a toga.

We joined Keith and Bridget who were standing slightly off to one side of the family, they were having a hushed conversation with some people I recognized from the university. Last night when I called Patrice to tell her Doctor Death was determined to make an appearance, she graciously replied that Finn would have wanted his good friend Gideon to be there, then she asked me to keep an eye on him, "that man has no filter!" I promised to do my best.

Gideon trailed behind me as I approached Patrice. She gave me a brave smile and I hugged her and reintroduced her to Doctor Death.

"Doctor Gold," she said, "it's been a while." Thankfully Gideon refrained from saying Finn had 'pegged it' or any of the other euphemisms—bought the farm, pushing up daisies, left the building—he'd peppered me with over the last few days.

AJ parked his MGB behind Hadiza's Mazda and they both greeted us as we joined the small crowd clustered around Patrice. She gave a tremulous smile, thanked everyone for coming and said she'd take us up the paved path to Finn's favourite birding spot. We walked slowly behind her. A pine-scented breeze drifted through the darkening forest and the sky turned a shimmering pearl grey.

Patrice, Peter, and Anya, all clad in inky black and somber grey, led the way. Patrice carried a tube, about a foot long and decorated with orange and red leaves. Juve walked slightly behind them, looking fidgety and out of place in a creased navy jacket.

The university profs, decked out in blue, green, and violet, chatted quietly as we made our way up the hill. I glanced behind me and saw Gideon walking with Hadiza. He'd hooked his arm through hers; she didn't seem to mind. Hadiza was majestic in a flowing red dress shot through with gold and silver while Gideon trudged along on creaking knees. His outfit was outlandish—a wine-coloured jacket, yellow cardigan and houndstooth-checked trousers—and on his head was a straw boater. Clearly the rule that mourners must wear black no longer applied; most of us looked like we were heading to a cocktail party.

The paved path veered off to the right and we climbed higher and higher until we reached a small clearing that opened up to sweeping panoramic views of snow-capped mountains and a glittering green lake.

Patrice held the tube close to her chest and made a short speech, a sad echo of the one Hadiza had given at Finn's gala dinner just two weeks before. I knew the speech by heart, having helped Hadiza write it. Tears welled up in my eyes when Patrice skipped the bit about Finn's plans for the future, his future having vapourized in the blink of an eye.

Patrice was choking back sobs by the time Peter stepped up and handed her off to Anya. His speech was detached to the point of being clinical. He described Finn's achieve-ments as if he were reading Finn's resumé. Other than a few closing comments about Finn being a good husband and father, one would never have known Peter was Finn's flesh and blood. But as Louisa always says, everyone deals with grief in their own unique way.

Then it was Anya's turn. She stood by Peter's side, the breeze playing in her shiny black hair, and began to speak in a solemn, clear voice. Her eulogy, unlike Peter's, was filled with affectionate anecdotes. She'd met Finn early in her relationship with Peter when he invited her back to the house for Sunday dinner. It was a spur of the moment thing. Her eyes shone as she described the evening. "Patrice served falafel; when Finn and I both speared the last one he lifted his hand in surrender and said, 'To the victor go the spoils.' I felt like the Queen of Sheba as I made off with it. Finn was such a magnanimous and loving man, he welcomed me into the family and always made me feel at home. He was my second dad, really."

Her voice cracked as she described Finn's last days. "We ran him ragged at Banff, pestering him with tiny details, so insignificant in retrospect, and yet he was generous with his time," she paused and arched an eyebrow, "provided we gave him space to go hiking and to take pictures of the elk and blue jays and that tiny little snail. Wildlife fascinated him." Here she allowed herself a brief, sad smile and some people in the crowd whispered yes, that was our Finn.

She pulled a Kleenex out of her pocket but didn't use it. "It's heartbreaking that Finn's greatest moment, where he would have been honoured by those he loved and respected, was stolen from him." Here she faltered. "But he died doing what he loved." Tears rolled down her cheeks and Peter stepped forward to cradle her in his arms.

Patrice hugged them both, then turned her stricken face to us and asked whether anyone else had anything they'd like to share about Finn. When no one stepped forward she finished the ceremony by reading "O Moon", a poem by William Wordsworth. By this point I was counting backwards from one hundred to stop myself from completely breaking down.

Patrice raised her head and, clutching the orange and red tube, walked alone to the edge of the clearing. With the breeze at her back she popped the lid off the tube and shook it gently at the base of a massive pine tree; Finn's ashes floated up, mingling with the pinecones high overhead. She placed the tube at the base of the tree, later I learned it was biodegradable, and we straggled back down the path to the parking lot where everyone said their goodbyes.

Patrice caught my hands, urging me to come back to the house where she was hosting a small reception.

"Oh no, Patrice, there will be so many people there." Many of Finn's friends and colleagues chose not to make the journey to Kananaskis, opting to pay their respects at the house. "You'll be run off your feet as it is."

She gripped my hands more tightly and looked up at Keith, who'd caught up to us by then and said, "Keith, please come, it would mean so much to the family." He glanced at me, his eyes signaling we really should attend, then turned to Patrice and said we'd be there.

She turned to greet another mourner and I glanced up at Keith, whispering, "God, I don't want to go. I don't think I can bear another moment of this." Funerals, all funerals, have become excruciatingly painful ever since my parents died.

Inclining his head, he said, "Come for an hour. Look at her." We watched Patrice embrace the few remaining mourners. "It'll mean so much to her."

Gideon sidled up beside us and said to Keith, "Of course we're going to the reception. It's the least we can do to honour Finn."

Keith thanked him and I took Gideon's elbow and led him back to the car.

"Gideon," I said as I unlocked the Mini and pulled the seat forward to let Madeline climb into the back, "you're only going for the food and the booze, and you know it."

He chuckled and said, "That's what Finn would have wanted."

As I helped Gideon with his seatbelt, I noticed a figure moving toward a car at the far end of the parking lot. Cedar James McQuinn was the last person I expected to see at Finn's funeral.

THE RECEPTION

Gideon Gold and I followed the murmur of voices down the narrow corridor toward the kitchen. A few years ago Finn and Patrice decided to modernize their unassuming little bungalow by bumping out the back to expand the kitchen and dining room. It was a major renovation that turned their lives upside down for five months, but in the end it was worth it. The heavy kitchen cabinets were ripped out and replaced by a large window that opened onto Finn's splendid garden. His cold frames stood open in front of the shed; Patrice and Peter had moved the tender tomatoes, bell peppers, and sweet corn into the vegetable garden where everything was growing in a lush green tangle.

Patrice edged her way through the crowd of academics and government officials clustered around the plates of charcuterie artfully arranged on the dining table. "Evie." She took my face in her hands and looked me in the eye. "I'm so glad you're here."

Gideon veered off in the direction of the drinks cart

and I didn't stop him. All the way here he complained about the stupid things people say at funerals. *He died doing what he loved? Falling off a balcony? What rubbish!*

Madeline disappeared out the back door and into the garden to join a clutch of women wobbling around on high heels peering at Finn's perennials.

I was about to pay my respects to Peter and Anya who were squashed together at one end of a crowded sofa when Hadiza materialized at my side and thrust a large glass of wine into my hand. Glancing at the two on the couch she said, "I'd leave them be if I were you."

As we were elbowed back into the hallway I asked, "Why? I'm not here to pick a fight." I may be impatient, but even I wouldn't ruin Finn's funeral by demanding to know whether DreamStone's chief geologist was in the habit of giving investment tips to government officials.

"Pick a fight?" She shot me a puzzled glance and I realized we were talking about two different things.

"Sorry, Hadiza, what were you saying?"

She lifted her glass and took a deep drink. "They've been testy with each other since I got here."

"Probably the stress—"

Patrice reappeared, urged us to eat something and disappeared again, swallowed up in the crowd. Gideon passed us carrying a very large tumbler of scotch into the living room. He hovered over a woman sitting in an armchair until she stood up and let him have her seat. Plumping the back cushions, he settled in with a sigh. AJ was at the opposite end of the room chatting to a woman I didn't recognize and Keith and Bridget had vanished.

"Hadiza, I've got to get some food into him"—I nodded in Gideon's direction— "before he says something horrible," and made my way back into the dining room where I found Madeline huddled next to a well-dressed man with a trim white beard. I threw a few samosas and vegetable rolls onto a small plate and returned to the living room where Gideon was staring glassy-eyed at Anya. He started when I draped a large napkin in his lap, then recovered, giving me a quick smile and shoving half a vegetable roll into his mouth.

Anya watched us from the sofa, her fingers holding her pendant, sliding the gemstone back and forth along its gold chain. "Oh, how nice," her voice was cool and sarcastic. "You're taking care of Gideon."

Before I could respond, Gideon mumbled through a mouthful of samosa that it was too damn spicy and if he didn't get another scotch immediately, he'd perish.

"I'll get it for you," I said, wondering if he'd notice if I switched him to water.

Laughter floated out of the kitchen. Madeline and the bearded guy, he looked like a big firm lawyer, were standing in front of the refrigerator pointing at photographs pinned up with coloured magnets.

"Evie, look," she said when she spotted me. "Carlos and I have been to every one of these places." The photographs were a combination of happy vacation shots, Finn and Patrice grinning in the hot sun at the entrance to the Colosseum and the Louvre, and somber shots of Patrice, alone gazing thoughtfully at war memorials in places like Vimy Ridge and Passchendaele.

"You've been to Groesbeek Cemetery?" I pointed at a photo of the Dutch cemetery for Canadian soldiers who'd died in the Second World War.

She shook her head. "Amsterdam, not the cemetery per se. I meant we've both visited every one of these places. Small world, eh?"

All this talk about cemeteries sent a prickle down my spine. Gideon had had enough scotch, I was getting a headache. It was time to go home.

An hour later, after I'd finally managed to pry Gideon out of his chair, we were in the car heading across town to his condo. The main elevator was, in Gideon's words, "on the fritz". He insisted he could climb up the three flights of stairs without any assistance, thank you very much. I didn't believe him and parked the Mini and ran around to his side of the car. He popped the door open and batted my hand away when I reached in to help him out of the seat. Then he rose slowly to his feet, his knees popping, and blinked in the sunlight.

"Here," I said, offering an elbow, "take my arm." Much to my relief, he did.

His puckish sense of humour returned by the time he unlocked the back door and we stood in the stairwell contemplating the long flights of stairs scissoring back and forth over our heads. "I'd take it slow if I were you," he said, "you're not in great shape."

I raised my eyebrows and we started off. The air was thick and close, reminding me of gritty stairwells in crumbling old parkades. Somewhere an industrial fan was whirring. Not that it did much good.

Gideon prattled on about the events of the day. As far as he was concerned throwing ashes at trees was not an appropriate send-off, but the reception, well, that was something else. "That Peter knows how to put on a good spread." It turned out Peter had paid for the catering and in Gideon's estimation the genoa salami was the best he'd ever had.

"Even better than in Genoa." He paused. "Nevertheless, they could have shown more decorum."

"Who? When?"

"Peter and Anya. Going at it, right there on the sofa. That was tasteless."

We'd stopped on the landing halfway between the first and second floors. He was panting and so was I.

"What on earth are you talking about, Gideon?" I recalled Anya's cold blue eyes assessing me from under thick black lashes when I flipped a napkin across Gideon's lap. Her comment, I couldn't remember it exactly, sounded innocuous and yet critical at the same time. But there had been no inappropriate displays of affection that I could see.

Gideon looked puzzled for a moment as if he'd lost his train of thought. Then looked down at his feet and said with grim determination, "Come along, no more lollygagging."

We set off again and I repeated my question. "Gideon, they were going at it...?"

"What? Oh yes, Peter was all over Anya, cooing at her like a lovesick pigeon. Not a shred of decorum for the solemnity of the occasion."

"Get a room? Is that what you're saying?"

"Harr," he gave a barking laugh. "Get your mind out of the gutter. He wasn't being amorous, he was trying to calm her down."

"Well, I'm sure she was upset, her father-in-law had just died."

"She's an odd woman," Gideon said, wheezing softly. "Peter thanked her for her eulogy; he especially liked the bit about Finn being like her second dad. And she bit his head off. They started quarreling about her father."

"*Her* father, not Finn?"

Gideon frowned, glanced up at me, then down again, focusing on lifting his thick-soled shoe up to the next stair, he'd just stumbled on the riser. "Yes, her father. Pay attention, Evie," he puffed. "Peter told her to let it go. They didn't need her dad's money. She flared like a harridan, teeth bared, eyes blazing; and Peter, ever the dutiful husband, starting the cooing and the patting."

"That's a little over the top, Gideon." Surely his judgment was clouded by all the scotch he'd belted down.

Red-faced, he stopped and we took a moment to catch our breath. As we set off he mumbled quietly, "I stand by my assessment: she's a silly woman. That eulogy. What bathos. *Finn died doing what he loved?* For Christ's sake, the man didn't fall off a mountain, he dropped off a balcony and died behind a dumpster... Where's my hat?" His hand flew to the top of his head, reaching for his straw boater which wasn't there.

"It must be in the car; I'll get it for you later." I prayed it was in the car or he'd have me tearing all over town searching for it.

Gideon was wheezing harder now. "Then she said—"

"No, that's enough talk about Peter and Anya." If he didn't shut up, he'd have a heart attack. He nodded and we stopped for another short break when we reached the third floor.

I got him down the hall and into his unit. "You're sure you'll be all right?" I asked.

He nodded and waved me away with a flick of his hand. I told him to call me if he needed anything and trotted back down the stairs and out to the car. Despite his cantankerous personality I was beginning to like Gideon, which was worrisome.

CHAPTER 36

HADIZA'S VERSION

Think of it as an entremente," James said when he called to invite me to dinner. I'd gone back to the office after dropping Gideon off, desperate to work on something that didn't involve grieving widows and cranky old men.

"Oh, James, I don't know. I'm exhausted." Then I remembered. "Was that you I saw at Finn's funeral?" I didn't add what I was really thinking: you despised the man, why did you bother to come?

James avoided the question, saying, "Patrice did a nice job, didn't she?" His tone softened. "Trust me when I say what you need right now is a palate cleanser, to clear your mind as it were."

He talked me into it and we agreed to meet at Regrub, a quirky little hole in the wall that served huge burgers and the kinds of desserts you'd find at Hogwarts. Food so different from the high-end cuisine James prepared at the Banff Springs Hotel I felt safe recommending it.

An hour later we were squashed into a plywood booth, we'd demolished our burgers and were sizing up our desserts. "Why are you staring at me like that?" James asked.

"Just waiting to see how the master chef is going to eat that thing." I nodded at his strawberry shake which came in a mason jar sporting a black handlebar mustache. A slice of cheesecake smothered in whipped cream perched precariously on top.

He laughed. "You first." I eyed my chocolate shake, picked up the ice cream sandwich, also smothered in whipped cream, and bit into it. The ice cream squished out onto my fingers and I nibbled quickly around the edges trying to catch it all before it hit the table. I looked up at him. "God, I love these things."

He laughed and I said, "You seem to be in a better place now, when it comes to Finn I mean." Over dinner the bitter, angry James of a couple of weeks ago had yielded to the charming James I remembered from law school.

He slurped his straw around the bottom of the mason jar one last time and said, "I've had time to think about it. If I'm completely honest, me leaving law school wasn't entirely Finn's fault. I could have asked for a deferral, special circumstances, like that woman who had a baby over reading break."

"Why didn't you?" As far as I was concerned James leaving law school was not even remotely Finn's fault.

He cast his eyes down, the table was sticky with smears of whipped cream and the maraschino cherry that had fallen off my shake. "Pride, arrogance, call it what you will. I thought I could pull it off. Law school during the day, the restaurant at night. Turns out I wasn't as smart as I thought I was."

He lifted his eyes to mine. "Everyone knew Finn was

a stickler for rules. I was nuts to think he'd bend them for me."

There was an awkward silence, then briskly he said, "Right, enough of that. I've gotta say, you guys drove my staff nuts changing your minds every two minutes."

"Hey, it wasn't our fault you promised wild asparagus then failed to deliver. Hadiza had that dinner planned down to the last microsecond. If there's one thing Hadiza likes, it's sticking to the plan."

He gave a gentle laugh. "Maybe so, but Anya's the queen of the flip flop. Every day it was a new edict. The sommelier almost strangled her when she downgraded the wine for the third time. We'd just tracked down enough crates of Sassicaia when she switched to Carménère."

He could see by the puzzled look on my face that I wasn't familiar with either wine and said, "Sassicaia is pretty expensive; we're stuck with ten crates and it'll take a while to move." Then he offered a gentle smile and said, "That's enough shop talk, let me drive you home."

"Your hotel is ten blocks in the other direction," I scoffed. The sun was warm and the air was golden. "Really, it's a perfect evening. Besides, the walk will do me good." I puffed out my cheeks and made my face round. "I could use the exercise."

"Then I'll walk you to the crosswalk." He crooked his elbow when we got outside. I took his arm and we strolled down to the end of the block. He crossed over to my side of the street, took me in his arms in something that was more than a hug and said, "It was great to see you again, Evie Valentine."

Suddenly I felt awkward and the best I could muster in response was, "Likewise."

Likewise? My face felt hot, but James had the good

grace not to tease me about it. He just smiled and waved over his shoulder as he crossed the intersection back to his side of the street.

When I got home, Quincy and I went up to Nose Hill Park for a long jog. It's an environmental park to the north of our place, we don't usually come here during the week but the riverbank behind our house was so unstable it was not safe and I needed to some air to clear my head.

"I had such a lovely time tonight, Quincy," I puffed as we set off up the hill.

He cocked a brindle-coloured ear at me but didn't break stride, he's used to me prattling at him when we run.

"I think you'd like James." I pulled Quincy to a stop, both of us panting as we gazed down across the tightly-packed neighbourhoods and farther south to the office towers winking reddish in the sun. A child's squeal in the distance caught our attention. Something was moving in the coulees below. Probably a deer or coyote. I tightened my grip on Quincy's leash and told him it was time to go home. "We'll have none of those jackrabbit hijinks tonight, bud."

Reluctantly he allowed me to take him back down the hill to the car. As we swung onto John Laurie Boulevard I thought about it some more: James spent fifteen years blaming Finn for ruining his life and now, as if someone had flipped a switch, all was forgiven.

"What do you think, Quincy? Is James being sincere? He's not doing it for my benefit, is he?" The dog wasn't sure.

Quincy and I were dozing in front of the TV waiting for Louisa to get home when we were jolted awake by an annoying buzz-buzz. My phone vibrated in the pocket of my bathrobe; I'd taken a hot shower and had just enough energy left to tell Netflix that yes, I was still watching the show.

Caller ID. *Hadiza*. 11:10 P.M. I groaned and picked up. The woman was babbling, her words coming so fast, her diction so sloppy, I demanded to know if she'd been drinking.

"No." Her voice was sullen.

I made her slow down and repeat everything she'd just said. Then I threw on some clothes and raced over to her place.

* * *

There was one parking space left in the tiny visitors lot across from her unit. I parked and flew up the cement steps to her house. It was one of twelve in a long row of townhouses built on a ridge on the west side of town. Hadiza flung open the door before I could press the bell and dragged me into the kitchen. I tossed my jacket on a chair and slid onto a stool at the island while she paced back and forth in the small kitchen, repeating what she'd told me on the phone.

"The cops called. They asked me about Finn's death."

"What would you know about Finn's death?"

"That's my point!" She sounded shrill. "Some nosy parker saw me arguing with him the day before he died. Evie, I can't afford to get dragged into this."

"Hadiza, I still don't know what *this* is. What did the cops say?"

Her hands flew to her hair, clutching little fistfuls, and I began to wonder whether my strong-willed, rational friend was going to have a full-blown breakdown right before my eyes. I went over to her and cupped her face in my hands, trying to calm her. "Hadiza, I know you've been under a lot of pressure lately, what with the new job and all, but you have to slow down. Take a deep breath, tell me exactly what the cops said."

Her eyes darted around the kitchen, she swayed a little and began to sob. Quietly at first then with such heart-breaking intensity I thought she'd never stop. I rubbed her back and led her to a stool at the island, then found a napkin and dabbed her cheeks.

"I'll make some tea," I said.

She shook her head and asked for a drink.

"Hadiza, tea is best." She gave me a weak smile and watched as I banged through her cupboards until I found the kettle and a metal canister of loose tea. When I sprinkled it into the teapot the spoon caught on the spout and some leaves fluttered onto the granite like green snowflakes.

"Top right-hand drawer for the tea strainer." Her mundane statement seemed to settle her nerves and she smiled again. The tea boiled; hot steam rose from our cups. I sat down beside her and we waited for it to cool. She found another napkin and blew her nose. "Sorry, I don't know what got into me. I shouldn't have fallen apart like that."

"Forget it." I squeezed her hand and glanced around her house. How strange, I thought, she's lived here for five years and everything looks brand new: white sofas, wheat-coloured carpets, shiny glass end tables. No pictures of her husband, also a professor, although that was understandable, he was long gone, but where were the photos of her children? The boy was in second year Engineering at McGill. The girl just graduated from high school. There was nothing personal reflecting Hadiza's life or her tastes to soften this sterile room.

"Work is crazy busy." The surface of her tea rippled as she blew on it. "I haven't been sleeping. I'm exhausted."

No, I thought, *this isn't about work*. Hadiza's an

ambitious woman, and a minority to boot, she's always worked harder than most. There had to be more to it than that. We stared out her large front window. It was late, the city was quiet, glittering in the darkness like a sparkly blanket.

"Hadiza, what did the cops say?"

"They were, how did they put it, *inquiring* into my relationship with Finn. Was it cordial? That kind of thing."

"Um hmm."

"Somehow the RCMP got it into their heads that Finn and I were enemies. Someone said they'd seen Finn arguing with a largish Asian lady." She rolled her eyes. "After they heard that Finn died they thought it was their civic duty to come forward and report it. The bloody busybodies."

"Hold on. You argued with Finn? When?"

"The day before he died."

"Christ, about what?"

Her face stiffened. "I've already told you. Finn was having second thoughts about me—"

"Finn thought you were eminently qualified. He certainly didn't express any doubts to me." Why was she still going on about this? Was she really this insecure?

She pursed her lips and stared at me for a moment, then took a deep breath and told me her version of Gideon Gold's story, the one where she wasn't a fraud but the victim of a malicious blackmailer who threatened to expose her "with a bogus grievance" unless she pulled strings to get him a junior position at the law school.

"Are you kidding me? A blackmailer?"

"Damn right. I said he could go fuck himself. Never give in, right? That's how you're supposed to handle blackmailers or they'll suck you dry. That bastard went straight to Finn with his cock and bull story." She blinked, as if in disbelief. "And Finn believed him."

"Hadiza, this makes no sense. I've known Finn since law school, he'd never accept an outrageous allegation like that. Not without proof."

Hadiza's shoulders curled in and she stared into her mug. "That bastard, he gave Finn some emails, correspondence between the two of us from a long time ago." She tightened her grip on the mug. "They were doctored, Evie. it's easy enough to do these days, but they looked convincing. And incriminating."

"But you'd have the originals. You could prove that bastard was a liar."

She sank lower in her chair. "It was years ago. I moved from Johannesburg to Toronto to here, It was a Joburg university account. I stopped using it eons ago."

"You didn't keep your emails? You didn't back them up? Hadiza, we're lawyers, we save everything." The image of Bridget lecturing me on Purge Day flashed into my head. Every scrap of correspondence, hard copy or electronic, had to be filed or purged. If I didn't do it, she'd do it for me. Which meant I'd never find it again.

Hadiza let out a long sigh and said, "Yeah, well, he'd been moody for days. Something was wrong and I decided to have it out with him."

My heart sank. Hadiza is not known for her tact. She'll confront any problem the minute it rears its ugly head and bludgeon it into the ground. Finn is the exact opposite. When something goes awry, he needs time to gather the facts and formulate his position; only then when he's good and ready will he address it. Rushing him was tantamount to an ambush in his eyes.

"Just where did this argument take place?"

"Outside the restaurant, the Vermillion Room, when we were waiting for the elevator."

"When?"

"The day before he died."

Oh God. "What happened?"

She squirmed in her chair as she related the details. The elevator was stuck on the eighth floor. She jabbed the button a few times, then her impatience bubbled over, she grabbed his arm and pulled him aside. "I said we needed to talk. He blew me off, saying this was neither the time nor the place. I, ah, insisted... I may have raised my voice... a little." More likely she was yelling and creating a scene. "He became stiff and formal. Then as cold as cold can be, he said that as soon as Peter's ridiculous celebration was over, he'd tell the Consortium people he could no longer, in good faith, support me as his successor."

Her eyes darted around the room, glistening with tears and indignation. "He had no right, absolutely *no right*, to pull his support so late in the game. I said he was being petty and spiteful and extremely unprofessional. He said I had a lot of nerve calling him unprofessional when I was the one who'd stolen a student's research and passed it off as my own. And he had the emails to prove it."

"Christ, Hadiza."

"That's when I knew what this was all about. I said the kid was a fucking blackmailer getting his revenge because I refused to break the rules to get him on staff."

Her lips moved soundlessly as she struggled to form the words. "Do you know what he said? That bloody hypocrite. He said he had to follow the evidence and since I couldn't refute these allegations, I was finished... as his successor and perhaps even as a prof. Evie, he threatened my reputation, my job, my very livelihood!" Her voice broke. "I've always been by his side, you know that, and this, this, is how he repays my loyalty, by threatening to get me fired!"

She was vibrating with fury, maybe I should have poured her that drink after all. She straightened her shoulders and lifted her heavy black hair off her neck. "Then Finn falls off that fucking balcony. And the cops want to talk to me, to *me*, about a stupid argument I had with him the day before." She made a little huff sound as she exhaled and said, "I'm not doing it. I'm not telling them a thing."

I shook my head. "Hadiza, they're just gathering the facts. It's usually a good idea to cooperate—"

"No, I'm done with Finn Tanberg, if the cops think I did something to him they can damn well prove it."

In the end I left her sitting on the squishy white sofa staring out the window at the heavy black sky, a mug of green tea growing cold beside her.

Finn was gone. Hadiza was losing her grip. I couldn't fathom it anymore.

CHAPTER 37

THE CHRISTIE'S AUCTION

The first thing Keith said when I got into the office the next day was, "It's breached its banks." He and AJ were in the conference room staring out the window, hands on hips, legs slightly apart, in what Mom would have called the 'manly man' pose, They were glowering at the river as if a display of ferocious masculinity would force the pooling water back into the riverbed where it belonged.

Before I could say anything Bridget appeared in the doorway. "Madeline's sandbag guys just called. They want her to stop haranguing them."

As if that was ever going to happen.

Then she grinned. "The good news is it worked. They're coming tomorrow to sandbag the place."

"Where are you off to?" AJ shot a curious glance at my khaki slacks, flats, and oversized white shirt, casual but dressy enough for a client meeting outside the office.

"I'm meeting with Peter and Anya at their place."

"Ah, yes, the come-to-Jesus meeting." Keith intended

it as a statement but it sounded like a question. He hates conflict, even when he's convinced it's necessary.

"Damn right," I said. "Today they get a chance to explain the purpose of Juve's crypto tip to Laura. I couldn't raise it yesterday, not at Finn's funeral. If I don't like what I hear, I'm terminating our relationship."

AJ glanced out at the river, then back at me. "No way you're going in the Mini. Peter's place is on the other side of the river. They're even more inundated with flood water than we are. Your car will stall out."

Keith pulled his key fob out of his pocket and pressed it into my hand. An hour later I was perched in the front seat of his suv plowing through gritty pools that rippled under the churning tires. I parked in front of their house and passed through the gates just as the sun emerged. A breeze rippled through the Japanese maple, showering me with tiny water droplets that glittered like diamonds.

Peter greeted me at the door with a rattling coffee tray in his hands. Anya was waiting in the office at the back of the house. We settled in ultra-modern armchairs arranged in a U in the buffer space between their two desks. The garden on the other side of the glass wall was so green it vibrated and I congratulated them on having the wisdom to construct a flood barrier when they moved in.

Anna wrinkled her nose, looking elegant and endearing at the same time. "Yes, well that didn't happen. I had to cancel the project; the landscaper and I couldn't agree on a design."

"Never mind that," Peter flashed a quick smile. "We've got great news, but you first. What brings you out here on this soggy sunny day?"

"Your chief geologist is an idiot." *Yikes, not quite the*

professional tone I was striving for. "What I mean is, Juve's gotten you and DreamStone into deep trouble."

"What's he done now?" Peter sounded as if he were talking about a rumbunctious ten-year-old who'd thrown a baseball through the neighbour's window.

When I said Laura Bazin dragged me up to Edmonton for a meeting, a thin line appeared between Anya's eyes. "Laura Bazin? The woman who issues our disposition certificates. Is there a problem?"

"That would be an understatement."

She looked mildly interested as I summarized Laura's accusation, then rose to her feet—she moved with the grace of a ballerina—and crossed to the window wall overlooking the garden. When I was finished telling them that Laura had lost everything on ammolite-backed tokens, Anya turned to me and said, "Only an idiot would believe anything Juve says."

Peter crossed one knee over the other, relaxing deeper into his chair. "That is unfortunate, but Laura's poor investment decisions have nothing to do with us."

"Are you saying she's lying? That Juve wouldn't pass along an investor tip, which incidentally might be insider information, in return for expedited service?"

Anya waved an impatient hand in the air. "Who knows what Juve tells people, we're his business partners, not his keepers."

"Peter?" He turned his head to face me. "Juve's your college buddy. Would he do this?"

He winced and rubbed the back of his neck, not making eye contact.

"Look, if Juve is shooting off his mouth about ammolite-backed cryptocurrency, you have to make him stop."

"Yeah, yeah, I get it. But Juve's not easy to control."

"Well, get him under control before he destroys every-one including your mother who, need I remind you, took out a half-million-dollar mortgage to help you out." Peter glanced at Anya who was staring into the garden with a detached, almost dreamy expression. "I can't stress hard enough how bloody serious this is." Something in my tone caught their attention.

Anya was unreadable, but Peter looked uncomfortable. Finally he laughed, a sharp staccato sound. "Right, we get it. No need to twist your knickers in a knot." Then he smacked his hands down on his knees and said, "Now, our news! The Christie's auction was a smash success. Wouldn't you agree, Anya?" This man changed the topic as easily as I changed TV channels.

She returned to her desk, picked up her laptop and set it on the coffee table in front of me. "Look at this. We just heard." Her lips softened into a wide smile as she scrolled through her emails.

A letter appeared on the screen; the famous Christie's C prominent in the letterhead. It itemized the details of the auction. An anonymous bidder had purchased both pol-ished ammolite fossils for 356,500 pounds—after deducting various fees, Peter and Anya would net close to five hundred thousand dollars Canadian.

Barely able to contain their excitement, they both started talking at once. The price was well above what they'd expected, it would boost their international rep-utation, it would be fantastic for sales. Peter was setting up another auction with Sotheby's and Anya had already updated the website.

"And Juve," Anya reached out to touch Peter's hand, "he'll be so excited!"

It wasn't until I replayed our conversation in the car

on the way back to the office that I realized I'd accomplished nothing. I told Keith I'd terminate our relationship with DreamStone if they didn't come up with a plausible explanation for Laura's story. They offered no explanation and they took no responsibility for Juve's behavior. They blamed Laura then shifted my focus to their amazing success with Christies.

Dealing with those two was like moving through fog. You were never sure where you'd end up. But one thing was certain, I'd been played.

CHAPTER 38

BETTER DEAD?

Instead of going straight through the traffic light and returning to the office I turned left and headed for Patrice's place. By the time I crossed over the bridge I was seething. I tested a few opening sentences: *Hi Patrice, lovely funeral, by the way I think Juve is bribing a government official. Get out now before you lose everything.*

When I pulled up in her driveway, my mind seized and I decided to let the conversation drift until I figured out how to drop this on her.

Patrice embraced me on the stoop and led me into the kitchen. Serving dishes, glasses, and utensils from yesterday's reception were stacked on the dining room table waiting to be returned to the catering company. We sat in the kitchen which was hot and muggy. The windows were open, and a squad of robins were having a party in the apple tree outside.

When I asked Patrice how she'd chosen a career as a military historian she sat taller in her chair, leaning forward with shining eyes. Her interest was sparked by her grandfather. "He told the most remarkable stories, terrifying and touching, about his time in Europe during the Second World War."

His brother, an enlisted man, had been lost in battle in Italy and there was very little information available at that time on how he'd died. Her grandfather developed dementia and became increasingly agitated about his brother's fate and Patrice, then a teenager, was determined to unearth some answers to ease his torment.

"This predated the internet," she said, "so I did it the hard way, tracking through dusty archives and brittle microfiche files, and writing to the government archive offices." She delivered these snippets of information to her grandad like a magpie returning to its nest with a piece of string. He died before she learned the truth, which made her even more determined to help other families solve their own wartime mysteries before it was too late.

"I wanted to study military history at university, but my father wouldn't hear of it, it was not a suitable profession for a young lady." Her lips twitched into a smile. "So I majored in art history, with a focus on war art."

"You studied the history of all the great battles, that was clever, Patrice."

Now, she was working on a multi-year project collecting oral history from Canadian veterans. "We have to move fast to catch the World War Two vets before they're all gone."

"Is it hard getting them to open up about their experiences?" I'd read somewhere that some vets refused to talk about the war. It was too traumatic.

She agreed. "It's understandable given what they went through."

Her eyes drifted to Finn's study, the shades were down and the light was dim. "The hardest stories involved soldiers who were horribly maimed in battle, patched up and shipped back home. There was no follow up, no one knew what PTSD was back then. Many of them couldn't step back into their old lives. They ended up losing everything, their families, their jobs, everything. For them, death would have been preferable. Better to go out a hero than come back a burden to everyone they loved."

She glanced out the window at Finn's cold frames. The ones closest to the house were propped open, empty.

"Finn could relate to that," Patrice said softly. "He was so vital, always outdoors, hiking, skiing, or birding. He loved flying all over the world, giving lectures and presenting papers. Then, just like that," she snapped her fingers, "he was broken, shattered. He would have hated me if I'd forced him to stay."

I inhaled sharply. "Patrice, did Finn regain consciousness? Is that what you're saying? That he told you to let him go?" Louisa's comment came back to me: Finn exhibited decorticate posturing; it was bad, really bad. Even if he'd lived his prognosis wasn't good, but he was a remarkable man, perhaps he could have cobbled together a decent life.

A look of shock crossed her face. "No, no. Nothing like that. His head injuries were too severe. But I knew the instant I saw him lying there, struggling to breathe through tubes. Wires and monitors everywhere." She squeezed her eyes shut and opened them again. "It's what he would have wanted. Death was a release. I owed him that." She gave me a small, brave smile, and stood up and walked over to the Kleenex box on the counter.

The jagged peal of the doorbell echoed down the hall. Patrice went to the front door and returned with Juve. He was wearing scuffed jeans, a tight blue tee, and thick socks. He'd left his mud caked work boots on the mat in the entry.

"Morning, Evie," he said. "Patrice. You doing okay?"

She nodded and he said he was on his way to the mine. The heavy rains had compromised the west side of the pit. They may have to notify their insurers. "Higher premiums, that's the last thing we need."

Patrice offered him a coffee, he nodded and sat down in Patrice's chair. The idea of him here in Finn's house with Finn's widow was unsettling.

His face hardened when he turned to me. "I hear you're looking for me."

So much for my plan to break it to Patrice gently. While she tinkered with the coffee, I laid out what Laura had told me, that Juve bribed her with a crypto tip which blew up and she lost everything. Patrice stiffened, then reached up into the cupboard and pulled out three mugs. Slowly she filled them and placed them on the table before sitting down next to me.

"Bullshit." Juve said, stirring sugar into his mug.

"You're denying it?"

"Damn right I'm denying it." A web of lines appeared at the corners of his eyes and he squinted as if he were looking into the bright sun. "I'm a geologist. I dig stuff up. What I know about crypto would fit into this spoon." He tapped the teaspoon on the side of his mug. "That bitch is stringing you a line." He finished his coffee in two large gulps, pushed his chair back from the table and stalked down the hall.

Patrice trailed after him. I could hear him grunting as he pulled on his work boots. Then the front door slammed and he was gone.

When Patrice returned to the kitchen, I said I was sorry but too many not-quite-right things were happening with DreamStone and we needed to talk about them.

"No, we don't." She pressed her lips together then said, "DreamStone is Peter's business. If you want to talk to someone about the company, talk to him."

"Patrice, I've tried that. They're stonewalling me."

She touched my cheek with curled fingers and out of the blue, said, "You look tired, Evie. I've got just the thing." She darted into the dining room, returning with a bottle of brandy, two glasses, and an envelope from London Drugs.

"Patrice, it's not even noon."

"As Finn would say, it's noon somewhere." She laughed and poured out two shots. "I developed Finn's photos." As the brandy did its job, we relaxed.

Finn was an accomplished photographer who created stunning, beautifully composed shots. Mountains loomed like guardians in snowy capes, streets gleamed in the moonlight, and the wildlife, big horn sheep, foxes, owls, and jays, looked like they were posing for Finn's pleasure.

"Finn had a unique eye," I said as I passed the photos back to her. "It's good Peter will have these to remember his father by."

She slid them back into the envelope and said, "I haven't shown them to Peter yet. It's too soon. You'd never know it to look at him, but he's taking the loss of his father very hard. I'll show him later when he's ready."

We drained our brandy glasses and when she hugged me on the stoop I thought she'd never let me go. As I put the SUV in reverse my cell pinged with a text from Juve:

You got it wrong.

CHAPTER 39

IT'S HAPPENING

Why do people do that? Leave cryptic messages when all they have to do is pick up the friggin' phone and talk to you? It was so aggravating I decided to ignore Juve's text until I got back to the office.

It was almost noon by the time I rolled into the parking lot. The sun was a pale flat disc barely visible in a grey sky. A cold wind packed the clouds so tight not a sliver of light could shine through.

Keith and I bought this building, a low slung one-storey structure, in the last real estate market crash. It was beautifully designed and nicely situated between a small, wooded hill and the river. Normally the river is a magical thing, transforming from an icy ribbon in the winter to a shimmering cascade of rapids in the summer, but today it was awful, a turgid brown mess heaving in the riverbed.

Yesterday, late in the day, the sandbaggers showed up, leaning on the horn and revving the motor of their rattly pick-up truck to announce their arrival. Madeline dragged a pair of gumboots out of the closet; they made a hollow rubbery sound as she marched outside to supervise 'her' crew.

AJ, Bridget, and I followed her and watched two sinewy young guys and a sturdy middle-aged man with a hard, round belly pile out of the truck. They hauled back the tarp covering the flatbed and flipped down the tailgate. Madeline disappeared around the side of the building with the older man. We joined the younger guys who joked with AJ while they waited for their boss to return. When he finally reappeared with Madeline in tow, he said the ground at the perimeter was relatively flat and he didn't anticipate any problems. In no time they were slinging floppy forty-pound sandbags into place, lapping and tamping them to create a tight seal. By the time we went home that night our office was a sandbagged fortress.

That was yesterday, today we had to secure its contents. A daunting task but we still had time, the river wasn't expected to crest for another day. The reception area was empty when I arrived. Down the hall someone grunted and someone else laughed.

"Now you're just showing off." That was Madeline. I found them in the photocopier room. AJ was standing on the second to last rung at the top of a rickety step ladder; it wobbled as he strained to heave a cardboard box up onto the top shelf of the stationery rack.

Bridget stood behind him, arms outstretched, ready to catch him if he fell, oblivious to the fact that if he did, she'd be flattened. "Don't twist like that," she said, "you'll hurt your back!" She turned and saw me in the doorway, her eyes full of concern. "He's going to kill himself if he doesn't get off that ladder."

AJ shoved the cardboard box into position then rested

his forehead against the metal rack and groaned. "I think I've wrecked my back."

"What did I tell you," Madeline said.

"I don't need an I-told-you-so right now, thank you very much. Someone help me down." His foot drifted around until Madeline caught it and guided him down to the ground.

Bridget grabbed two boxes and followed me back to my office. We dropped to our knees and began packing up my files. Something glittery caught my eye. I reached out and grabbed her hand.

"Bridget," I said, "is this what I think it is?" I called out, "Madeline, come take a look at this."

Madeline dashed into my office and snatched Bridget's hand away from me. "It's vintage, isn't it?" she asked as she turned Bridget's hand this way and that. On Bridget's finger was a stunning ring, one large diamond encircled by tiny diamonds, like a crystal daisy. Yes, Theo the internet boyfriend had proposed. And yes, it was vintage, it belonged to Theo's grandmother.

"Bridget," Madeline scolded, "you can't wear a ring like that to the office on packing day!"

Bridget replied that had she known she'd be preparing for Armageddon she would have left the ring at home. Just then AJ popped his head in the door, his back pain forgotten. "We just got another alert. Finish up, we have to leave."

Madeline waved Bridget's hand at him. AJ grinned and said, "Yeah, I know. Nice, isn't it?"

"You told him before you told me?" Madeline turned back to Bridget, green eyes wide in disbelief.

"He got in before you did," Bridget replied in a matter-of-fact tone.

I expected a crack from AJ about robins and worms,

but he wasn't listening anymore. He was staring, eyes wide with horror, out my window. The thin poplars and wolf willows crowding the riverbank were shaking violently as if a giant was yanking at their roots, dragging them underwater.

"Shit! We have to get out of here!"

That's when our phones went off. AJ pulled his cell out of his pocket. "Let's move!" The alert banner had changed from amber to red.

Critical alert, imminent life threatening danger

The flood gates on the Glenmore Reservoir had failed. A massive surge of muddy water was coming right at us.

Bridget and I jumped to our feet. I threw the half-filled cardboard box onto my desk and grabbed my purse and cell. Bridget, Madeline, and AJ were already out the door racing to their cars.

"Take Twenty-fifth Avenue," AJ shouted. "West to Hillcrest." Twenty-fifth ran parallel to the river for several blocks then cut up a steep hill to the neighbourhood where Mom and Dad used to live.

I waved, signalling I'd heard him. He nodded and jumped into his car. AJ and I were the only two who lived in the downtown core, close to the river: his warning was for me, to ensure I didn't, through dazed force of habit, take my usual route home.

Home! When I left this morning Louisa was out with the dog. We'd argued about the wisdom of running beside the river. The path was pitted, the gravel unstable, but she preferred that route to Fourth Street because she could set the pace and Quincy wouldn't slow her down by dragging her into bakeries and coffee shops, slobbering for treats.

Why hasn't she called? Or texted? It was past noon, surely they were back from their run by now.

I hesitated as I exited the parking lot. Left to go home and check on Louisa, or right, up the hill to safety? Stick with the plan. Trust Louisa. If she heard the alert, she'd be heading to Madeline's place. If she heard the alert, she'd have plenty of time. *If she heard the alert.*

Reluctantly I turned right and followed the others up Twenty-fifth Avenue.

My phone pinged. Louisa? I snatched it off the passenger seat. It slipped from my fingers, bounced off my lap and hit the floor. Feeling around by the gear shift I found it and scooped it up.

It was Keith. He hadn't come into work this morning. Large swaths of the acreage were flooding. He sounded frantic.

"What's happening? Are you guys all right?"

"We're fine," I said, "the office—"

"Forget the office, are you all out?"

"We're out, driving…" I peered ahead. Why was the traffic slowing to a crawl? Then I saw it. "Shit! Keith, I've got to go."

Filthy water boiled across the street, flooding the school yard on the other side of the road. Road? There was no road, just a wide, fast-moving river filled with cars crawling through what used to be an intersection. *Please don't let us slide off the shoulder and get mired in the muck.*

It was happening. It was really happening. The flood.

I geared down into first and plowed ahead until I reached the base of Hillcrest and began to climb. Behind me the river grew wider, the currents tugged harder. Soon it would be so high the cars would be swept away.

By the time I reached Madeline's house I'd completely forgotten about Juve's text.

CHAPTER 40

THE CONSERVATORY

That evening brought a perverse sense of calm: the waiting was over, the worst had happened. After the last flood the experts raised the gates on Glenmore Reservoir. Then the rains came. The reservoir filled, the gates buckled and collapsed. A wave fifteen feet high tore through the city, engulfing twenty-five neighbourhoods. Three people were dead, four were missing. The experts said we were prepared. They were wrong.

But for the moment, here with Madeline, we were safe.

When I reached her house and saw Louisa and that goofy dog, I hugged her so hard she said her back would break. Quincy popped up as I was bending down and cracked me in the nose with his rock-hard head, then scampered away as Louisa described their harrowing escape. The garage was already flooding when the critical alert sounded. She grabbed our go bags, even Quincy had one, and raced out to the car which luckily, she'd parked on the street. "I swear the basement and garage were under two feet of water before we reached the end of the block."

A half an hour later she pulled up in front of Madeline's place and waited for Madeline and me to arrive.

Madeline, unlike her yappy dog, was a gracious evacuation host. She gave Louisa free rein in her state-of-the-art kitchen—it turned out Madeline's cooking skills were no better than mine, but you'd never know it from the size of her Wolf oven. While Louisa tinkered with pots and pans, Madeline and I sipped drinks in the conservatory, a lush room jammed with palm trees, orchids, and ivies that curled up the pillars and clung to the struts of the glass dome high above.

The white wine went straight to my head; adrenalin does not dampen the effects of alcohol after all. I lined up ten miniature marshmallows on the arm of the wicker chair and flicked them one by one at the dogs. This was Madeline's idea. "It will divert Evangeline"—in my mind the Slipper Dog— "from that brute you brought with you." The flying marshmallows frustrated Quincy who wasn't as quick as the Slipper Dog at rooting out the tiny treats in the flickering candlelight.

Outside, the chop of helicopters rattled the conservatory's glass panes in their black metal frames and the harsh wail of sirens echoed through the treetops.

Quincy snapped up the last marshmallow, he'd finally found one, and flopped down at my feet. He cast a suspicious eye at the Slipper Dog and decided it was safe to take a nap.

Marshmallows reminded me of Doctor Death. His community, like AJ's, had been evacuated. AJ was staying with a soccer buddy, but I fretted about Gideon Gold. He was such an ornery old man; what if he refused to leave? Louisa assured me that the media reported the evacuation had gone smoothly. Even those who stubbornly refused to leave their homes changed their minds when they were forced to crawl up onto their roof for safety. Nevertheless I decided to call.

The phone rang four times. Good, if he doesn't pick up it means he's somewhere safe. He picked up on the fifth ring with a gruff, "What do you want?"

"Gideon, damn it. It's Evie Valentine. Why are you still at home? You're under an evacuation order, you can't be there."

"It's as dry as the Gobi Desert up here. I'm on the third floor, you'd know that if you were more observant."

"Gideon, your entire neighbourhood is under four feet of water. People are paddling around the streets in canoes for God's sake."

"True," he admitted, "that's what I told Jacob."

"Jacob? The pizza delivery guy? You ordered a pizza?"

"He won't come," Gideon said with a plaintive wail.

"Well of course he won't come, they're not open for business. His boss is too busy trying to save his store to make you a stupid pizza. Jeez, Gideon!"

By this point both Madeline and Louisa were eavesdropping. I rolled my eyes and made a cuckoo motion with my hand. "Gideon, I'm going to get my partner AJ to look in on you. Make sure you let him in when he buzzes." Assuming the buzzer isn't under water.

"He'd better come by boat," Gideon cackled and hung up.

AJ was nonplussed when I texted him Gideon's address but agreed to check in on my 'nutball' friend. It turned out his soccer buddy had a rubber dingy.

Madeline warned me that if Gideon needed rescuing, he could damn well go to a shelter because he wasn't staying here. She dragged her chair closer; it was a wicker peacock chair with a large fan back and a small base which made it tippy, and asked, "How did Peter and Anya react when you told them Juve gave what's her name bad investment advice?"

Louisa passed us a couple of bowls of popcorn sprinkled with parmesan and rosemary and sank quietly into her chair. She probably shouldn't hear this, client confidentiality and all that, but it had been an exhausting day and I didn't have the heart to send her away.

I scooped up a fistful of popcorn and said, "It was weird. Basically, they take no responsibility. They can't control what Juve does and if Laura listened to him, then that's on her." I glanced outside at Madeline's lush backyard, thinking of Peter's garden which ran right down to the river's edge. "It's a shame they didn't put in the flood barriers. The bank is unstable. They could be under ten feet of water by now."

Madeline flipped her shawl, a pretty paisley thing, around her shoulders; it made her look regal. She scooped the Slipper Dog into her lap. "I wonder," she said thoughtfully, "if that's why Finn wanted to meet with you? Maybe he figured out that something was amiss with Juve and Laura."

"How could Finn possibly know what Juve was up to?"

Louisa glanced from Madeline to me and said, "From what I've seen of Juve, he's tough and bull-headed. Nothing gets in his way. He could have had an altercation with Finn on the balcony."

"Good Lord, Louisa, we don't even know if he was there. Let's not jump to conclusions."

"No, wait," Madeline said, "Louisa has a point. Juve's been tight with Peter since their university days. If Finn was hounding Peter over a problem with the company, Juve may have stepped in to warn Finn off."

"I don't buy it," I said. "Peter would never let Juve intervene on his behalf. Besides, that was Patrice's job, she played the role of peacekeeper in that family."

"Speaking of Patrice," Louisa piped up again. "She lost no time pulling the plug on Finn. Sure, his chances of survival were grim, and he'd have been a mess physically and mentally for a long, long time, but at least he'd be alive."

"No, Finn would never forgive her if she kept him going, given the state he was in."

"Well, that's what she says, but here's the thing," Louisa persisted. "We'll never know his prognosis. She didn't send him down to Calgary where the experts could have examined him. He may have died in the ambulance on the way, but he may have survived and gone on to be one of those miracle patients who comes through a devastating diagnosis with flying colours. We'll never know because she pulled the plug before he could be properly assessed."

"Are you saying Patrice *killed* him without justification?" Suddenly I felt lightheaded.

Madeline interrupted. "My money is on Hadiza."

"*What*?" I glared at Madeline. "You're not serious. I've known Hadiza for a decade. The very idea is outrageous."

Madeline eyed me carefully and said, "I'm not saying it was intentional. It could have been an accident. Maybe they were arguing on the balcony and he slipped. She's not a small woman, she could have knocked him over... accidentally."

Earlier I'd told them Hadiza and Finn quarreled outside the restaurant, now I regretted it. "So what if they argued? They'd had differences of opinion in the past. They always ironed them out."

Madeline interrupted. "Sure, differences of opinion on legal issues, never about Hadiza's ethics and integrity."

"Well, they would have patched things up." My temper was rising and I'm sure it showed in my face because Louisa interrupted to say we'd all had a tiring day and we should finish our wine and go to bed.

Madeline stroked the Slipper Dog. "What I can't figure out, is your friend the chef."

"James?"

She slid the Slipper Dog off her lap and said, "Supposedly he saw something, maybe someone, on the balcony, but the police haven't found this mysterious person, have they? James could have pushed Finn off the balcony, then run downstairs to 'discover' his broken body, thereby covering his tracks." Her eyes were luminous, almost witchy, in the candlelight.

Madeline's comment unnerved me; I too had my doubts about James. How likely was it that after fifteen years of loathing Finn, James suddenly realized he'd been partially at fault?

Madeline shrugged. "Just saying."

Louisa got out of her chair and headed into the kitchen, "Right, this isn't getting us anywhere. I'm going to bed."

An hour later I was tucked under a fluffy duvet in Madeline's dove-grey guest room. The bed was comfortable, but I couldn't settle. Silvery light bathed the room; the moon shivered across the carpet when the wind rustled through the trees. What was it that Scarlett O'Hara had said? Tomorrow is another day. Tomorrow, or maybe a couple of days from now, they'd let Louisa and me return to our house to survey the damage. In a couple of days we'd be allowed back into the office. The sandbags would hold. Everything would be all right.

THE BIG BOSS

The next morning I was standing in Madeline's foyer feeling disoriented. All night long the choppers whomped overhead and I'd barely slept. My phone buzzed in the pocket of my fleece, as soon as I picked it up I was in trouble.

"Cory Russo here, am I speaking to Evie Valentine?"

Who the heck was Cory Russo? A former client? Another lawyer?

"This is she." I winced. I never talk like that.

Russo's voice boomed through the phone. We'd met at a political fundraiser, he said, hosted by his good friends at Gates, Case and White. He'd been meaning to get in touch. My mind raced; the Gates fundraiser was four years ago. Ah yes, I could picture him now. A large, heavy set man, big meaty hands. Demoted in a cabinet shuffle from Economic Development to Culture, but still bursting with self-importance. *No artifacts leave this province without my say so.* God, this was Laura Bazin's boss' boss' boss. What did he want?

"Evie, you represent DreamStone. Am I right? Great little company." Russo sounded like a used car salesman, slick but with an edge. He prattled on about the caliber of DreamStone's management team: Peter, Anya, and Juve, brilliant, absolutely brilliant. Exactly the kind of entrepreneurs this province needs. Then he gave a little sigh. "Look, I've been talking to Laura Bazin, you've met Laura, bright girl. She says there's been a misunderstanding in connection with your last permit application." His pseudo-caring tone hardened. "We have such a great relationship with you guys. I'm sure you can fix this little mix-up."

Mix up? There was no mix up. Just Juve passing along stupid investment tips and Laura blowing her life savings and threatening to hold DreamStone's disposition certificates hostage unless someone made her whole.

Russo paused.

I pressed my lips together. *Not one word from me, Mr. Russo. Not one word.*

He cleared his throat and said, "I told Laura, don't worry, the company will do right by you." Another pause, then a breezy, "Nice talking to you, Evie Valentine. Stay safe." And he was gone.

I blinked at the phone, then clicked the 'recent calls' button. it showed a strange area code and was identified as 'likely spam'. My heart skipped a beat. It does that now and then when I'm stressed. I dialed AJ's number.

"Can you meet me at BLV-2?"

"Where?"

"Madeline's place." I'd heard Bridget use this codename so many times—she likes cloak and dagger stuff—that I was using it myself. We'd turned Madeline's Georgian library into our command centre. Here we'd stay until the City gave us the green light to return to the office.

I found Madeline in the kitchen whipping up an omelet and cooing at the Slipper Dog, "Mmmmmm, Evangeline, your favourite, cheese!" She was unmoved when I pointed out that cheese omelet was my favourite too.

Halfway through my toast, AJ rang the doorbell. When he stepped into the foyer, Madeline laughed and said we looked like we were going to a team building event. We were both wearing blue BLV sweatshirts, worn jeans, and runners.

He swallowed a yawn. "I'd kill for a coffee."

"Come through," Madeline directed us into the library which had been transformed into a make-shift office with two computers, four flat screen monitors, a photocopier, a scanner, and a landline. Somewhere at the back of the house Rupert the cockatiel was barking. It took him less than a day to perfect Quincy's yips so now even I couldn't tell them apart.

"Where's the rest of The Menagerie?" AJ asked.

"The cats are sunning themselves in the conservatory and Rupert is amusing the dogs," Madeline said before she disappeared down the hall into the kitchen.

AJ glanced out the tall windows into the back yard and said, "Wow, this is a fantastic lot." We talked about the state of his place; the condo board was whipping out contradictory texts every hour. "We can come back, we can't come back. They're driving me crazy." Then he narrowed his eyes and said, "Then there's your friend, Statler."

"Who's Statler?"

"The Muppet, a.k.a. Gideon Gold, a.k.a. Doctor Death. I checked on him as per your request. He refused to let me in. Just stood on his balcony yelling at me to get lost."

It was hard to keep a straight face but I promised to

make it up to AJ; the next time we were at the Garrison, drinks were on me.

Madeline returned carrying a red enamel tray laden with coffee things and AJ and I opened our laptops on the polished walnut table.

I told them about Russo's call. "He's the Culture minister and Laura Bazin's boss' boss' boss. Russo says there's been a misunderstanding—his exact words were 'mix-up'—with DreamStone's application for a disposition certificate. He made it crystal clear he expects DreamStone, me, to fix it."

AJ frowned. "What mix-up? I thought she already granted their certificate. Did they apply for another one?"

Madeline pressed down on the plunger on the French press; the silver pot slipped on the glossy tabletop and I gripped its base to steady it.

"I'll be damned if I know. But Russo didn't call me from his office." I pulled out my cell and showed them my recent calls. Madeline reached out and took my phone, then retrieved her laptop from the sideboard and went to work.

AJ leaned back in his chair, stretching his arms above his head. "Refresh my memory: what exactly did Laura say when you guys met in Edmonton?"

The image of the crowded food court, the smells of greasy burgers and burnt coffee, came to mind; we could hardly hear each other over the shrieks of giddy teenagers and whiny toddlers.

"Laura said she expedited DreamStone's application and Juve told her to invest in ammolite-backed crypto tokens. She cashed out her RRSPs and her savings and lost all of it when the tokens took a nosedive. When I confronted Peter and Anya about it, they said they weren't responsible for Juve, and Laura was an idiot for taking anything he said seriously." I gestured at Madeline, was she making any progress on Russo's phone number; she shook her head, not yet. "As far as Laura's concerned, she did her part, DreamStone got its certificate and she expects to be paid, crypto crash or no crypto crash."

"Got it!" Madeline glanced up over the top of her laptop. "That phone number, it's a burner." Then she tilted her head to one side, the dogs were going berserk even though Rupert had stopped taunting them. She disappeared through the French doors and down the hall.

"A burner phone," I said as I crossed to the window. The garden was shimmering in the morning sun. A magnificent silver willow moved gently in the breeze. I flicked the latch, but the window sash was swollen shut from the rain.

"Here, let me." AJ thumped the heel of his hand under the transom until the window squeaked open. I leaned out and took a deep breath, the air was sweet and fresh.

"Hey," Madeline was back, "you're not making a run for it, are you?" She was carrying Evangeline who blinked at us, then started yipping and squirming, sliding out of Madeline's arms and onto the floor.

"We have to tell Keith we now have confirmation, or as good as it's going to get, that DreamStone is bribing Russo to expedite their certificates." I took another deep, slow breath.

"You believe this because Russo used a burner phone?" AJ sounded skeptical.

"It's the only plausible explanation. Russo made it clear when we met him four years ago that no artifacts left the province without his blessing, and Laura knew Peter and Anya were up against tight export deadlines and needed their disposition certificates fast. You scratch my back, I'll scratch yours. Then Juve screwed everything up by giving Laura a hot tip—whether it was in lieu of a cash payment or in addition to, it doesn't matter—and Laura lost everything. Peter and Anya are ghosting her so she went to Russo who expects me to force them to fix it, so everything can go back to the way it was."

"Keith is going to have a heart attack," AJ said.

That's when I remembered Juve's text:

You got it wrong.

CHAPTER 42

SCHRÖDINGER'S CAT

The Menagerie was quiet by the time AJ and I finally connected with Keith. He was at the acreage and his Wi-Fi was spotty, and the reception was iffy, but his apprehension came through loud and clear. "Russo is in on this? Can it get any worse?"

"We need to talk about Juve's text," I said, scrolling through my phone.

"What text?" Keith asked.

I explained I'd confronted Juve at Patrice's place about Laura's allegations and he denied everything. "But here's the weird thing, right after he stormed out, he sent me a text saying I'd gotten it all wrong. Last night he sent another, suggesting we meet at a craft beer market so he can tell me what's really going on."

"When?" AJ asked.

"Tonight."

"Works for me."

"No, not you, AJ. Just me, alone."

AJ grimaced and Keith leaned into the laptop camera.

"Is that wise?" His face was huge. "I mean, what do we know about this guy other than he's a miner?"

And waves guns around when you burst into his warehouse without warning. I pushed the thought aside.

"How can I refuse? On the one hand, it looks like DreamStone is bribing a government minister; on the other, Juve says I've got it all wrong."

Keith scowled and said, "Okay, but be careful. Don't get into a car with him. Don't go anywhere with him. Stay out of dark alleys."

"Dark alleys?"

AJ interrupted. "Keith, you probably can't see it on your camera but her face is turning red. You should probably quit while you're ahead. Let's assume she knows what she's doing."

Let's assume she knows what she's doing? This was going from bad to worse. "Thank you both for your vote of confidence. I appreciate it, really I do, but I know how to handle myself."

The skepticism on their faces said it all.

* * *

"Juve," I said as we sat down at a small round table at the Craft Market, "I have to admit I've never understood the attraction of craft beer, but then again I don't really like beer."

"Oh, don't tell me that!" His eyes darted from me to the server. He ordered something blonde for me and something Belgian for himself along with two plates of shareables: fried pickles and spicy cauliflower.

"Fried pickles?" I raised my hands in protest. "Since when are fried pickles a thing?"

He gave a pained smile and switched out the pickles for poutine.

"So, how did I get it wrong?"

I was referring to his text, but Juve didn't hear me. He was too busy ogling the server's backside as she wove through the tightly packed tables. It was all I could do not to snap my fingers in his face and shout, "Yoo-hoo! Over here!"

Slowly he turned his gaze to me and said, "Isn't this place incredible?"

The energy in the room was electric. After days of being on high alert, then being engulfed in turbid water, these people were celebrating being alive. Conversations swirled around us; stories about volunteering on clean-up crews, clearing out some rich guy's wine cellar and nicking a bottle of something expensive, and rescuing a goddamn cat off a goddamn roof because its hysterical owner refused to get into the rubber dingy without it.

"Let me tell you a little story about Peter and me."

"Juve, I don't have time for little stories. How did I get it wrong?"

The server reappeared with our beers, the food would be right up. Juve flashed her a broad smile and shrugged off his jean jacket, revealing a taut torso and well-muscled arms under his tee shirt. "Hot in here."

"Juve, I—"

"Peter and I met in university."

I sighed and took a sip of my beer, it wasn't bad, slightly sweet and not too bitter.

They'd both started in business but Juve switched to geology after first year. "EBITA and capital structure? All that shit went in one ear and out the other. But geology? Now, that's science, rocks are real."

"*Rocks are real.* You could put that on a tee shirt."

His face lit up as he described the thrill of identifying promising sites, taking core samples, analysing the data. "And then there's the eureka moment. There's nothing like it. Not booze, not drugs, not sex. Absolutely nothing. That ammolite's been there a million years. Just waiting for me to find it."

Juve rubbed his hands together when the server reappeared with our food. The cauliflower was intense, smelling of cayenne and lime, and my fork veered over to the poutine. Cheese curds and bacon will never let you down.

An entertaining storyteller, Juve painted a picture of Peter that was strikingly different from the Peter I knew. Yes, Peter was an intelligent, attractive man, but what I'd failed to see, according to Juve, was that behind those smiling eyes was a man wracked with insecurity, a boy desperate for his father's approval.

"Too late for that now." He gulped his beer. "The trouble with Peter is he's a sucker for lame ducks. In university he hooked up with one nutbar after another. Each one more screwed up than the last. Then along came Anya." He gave his head an imperceptible shake. "That woman is a piece of work."

Juve waved at the server, ordering another round. "Anya?" I said, reaching for my beer. "She's as smart as Peter, probably smarter. Didn't she get an engineering degree before she went to Wharton?"

He nodded. "Software engineering, computer science, something like that. After Wharton she became a venture capitalist." His tone was sarcastic as if a Wharton MBA was something to sneer at. "That was around the time she hooked up with Peter."

"She's one of the most confident women I know... and beautiful, to boot."

His beer glass stopped halfway to his lips. "Evie, you crack me up!" He crooked a finger, beckoning me closer. As I leaned in the server's arm swooped past my face and another golden beer with a foamy head appeared in front of me. I was developing a taste for this stuff.

Juve pushed his empty cauliflower plate out of his way. I stacked my poutine plate on top of it and the scent of cayenne mixed with bacon wafted over us. He raised his voice, it was very loud in here, and said, "Anya held it together just long enough to trick Peter into marrying her"—I hate it when men say stupid things like that, it's not as if Anya put a gun to Peter's head— "though I shouldn't be too hard on Peter; she had me fooled too, in the beginning, when they put together DreamStone."

"Back in 2016?"

"Yeah, that was a banner year for them. First the flashy wedding on Martha's Vineyard, her folks are loaded by the way, and then setting up the company." He glanced down at the table, searching for his plate, found it under my poutine plate and shot me a pitiful look.

"There was nothing left, Juve. You practically licked the plate clean."

He grunted then continued. "Everything was great in the beginning. Her dad invested in the company. Business was booming. Peter and I wanted to expand, and Anya used her famous 'venture capitalist skills' to hit up the banks and private lenders for more capital. Then a couple of years later her dad pulled out. He thought we were expanding too fast. He and Anya had a big fight. Cash flow was tight and Anya couldn't pay him out right away. By the time she got the money together they were barely speaking to each other. And that's when dear sweet Anya fell apart."

It was so muggy in the beer hall we were sticking to the seats, but I shivered. "What do you mean 'fell apart'?"

"Some kind of nervous breakdown. Peter checked her into one of those ritzy rehab places, it was all very hush hush, they didn't want to spook the banks with the news that DreamStone's CFO was batshit crazy. Then she came back, good as new and raring to go."

"When did all this happen?"

"Four, five years ago."

Around the time Finn invested in DreamStone. Around the time he asked me to become DreamStone's lawyer.

"This is all very interesting, Juve, but what's it got to do with Laura saying you screwed her on a hot tip and someone has to make her whole?"

His face hardened and he took another swig of beer. "Keep your shirt on, I'm getting there. Anya's dad did have a point. In the early days Peter and I made a big mistake, we expanded too fast and flooded the North American market with ammolite. The business lost momentum. We were stagnating. You know what they say: go big or go home. That's when we started thinking about Asia. Anya went back to the banks and borrowed against DreamStone's 'possible' reserves."

I nodded. "Then the pandemic hit. Everything went into a tailspin and the banks changed their lending policy. 'Possible' reserves weren't good enough anymore. They wanted 'probable' or 'proven' reserves, failing which DreamStone had to put up more security."

Juve lifted his eyebrows. "You've done your homework, Evie. Anya needed to show more sales, more receivables and better cash flow or the banks would call their loans. We had to get into Asia fast."

As my British father would say, the penny dropped. "Anya was desperate. She signed the Asian distribution agreements knowing full well the delivery deadlines were too tight. Then she needed to find a way to speed up the disposition certificates. Enter Laura Bazin and her rubber stamp. In return for a bonus, is that what you called it, Laura would push the certificates through in record time."

"You got it in one, Evie Valentine."

"So how does your hot tip on ammolite-backed cryptocurrency fit in?"

"Shit, Laura's always whining about money." He shrugged his shoulders. "The crypto tip was a freebie, it didn't pan out, no one told her to sink every penny she had into it."

The noise and the heat in the room was rising, Juve was on a roll, he couldn't stop talking and I pushed him harder. "Just to be clear. Those little bonuses you've been paying to Laura are bribes. You've been paying them since the pandemic, starting in 2021—"

"2022," he corrected me.

"And everything was fine until you tacked on the crypto tip and Laura lost everything."

His eyes wandered over to a table packed with laughing women, and he nodded.

"Does Peter know about it?" I asked. "The bribes?"

"Peter? Get real." Juve looked at me as if I'd just fallen off a turnip truck. "Anya's the financial brains of the business. Peter doesn't have a clue."

* * *

That evening when Madeline and I were sitting in the conservatory watching the bougainvillea drop tiny pink blossoms onto the white tiles, she asked if I'd had a chance to run Juve's story past Keith and AJ.

"Not yet." I'd had plenty of time to talk to them, but something held me back. "I'm missing something. Peter has to be complicit, but Juve says he has no idea what Anya is doing with the books. Surely, he's not that stupid."

The Slipper Dog floated by on tiny paws. Madeline scooped it up and arranged it on her lap. Quincy trotted in and flopped down on my feet with a groan. He gave me a look that said racing around with The Menagerie was exhausting.

"Did you hear that, Evangeline?" Madeline said as she kissed the dog on the nose. "There's something Juve's not telling us."

I shifted my feet out from under Quincy's bony elbows and said, "The only argument that supports Peter being oblivious to Anya's perfidy is he let his mother mortgage her house to support DreamStone. If he knew Anya was bribing Laura he wouldn't let his mother take that risk."

Madeline lifted the Slipper Dog up by the armpits the way you would a small child and said, "Oh Evangeline, shall we tell Evie what people will do for love?"

"Meaning what?"

"Meaning Peter knows... and he doesn't know. Like Schrödinger's Cat. As long as Peter doesn't open the box, he won't have to betray one of the two women he loves, Patrice or Anya."

"Well, Peter may not want to betray Anya, but Finn would want me to protect Patrice."

And that's how I found out what people will do for love.

CHAPTER 43

SCHRÖDINGER'S BOX

The next day was our first full day back in the office after the flood. Someone had dragged a large broken branch halfway across the parking lot and left it in my parking space. Cursing, I got out of the car and hauled it over to the garbage bin. I wrenched open the metal lid and was about to heave the branch inside when I stopped. What if the branch belonged to a beaver rebuilding his home? It would be a shame if he waddled all the way up here from the river only to find it gone. I set the branch down next to the concrete flower planter beside the bin.

On the way into the office the weather guys on the radio warned listeners that the river was still dangerous, swollen and running fast and high, the public should steer clear. Sure, I thought, tell that to the dolts who posted selfies of themselves hanging off bridges with nothing but a foot of air protecting them from the rushing river below.

Bridget was chatting with AJ at her desk. "Did we make it through unscathed?" I asked. A mouse couldn't lift a paw in this building without Bridget knowing about it. "Any leaks? Backed up drains? Anything?"

She beamed and flicked imaginary dust off the top of her immaculately clean privacy screen. She couldn't have done it with more flair if she were wearing white gloves. "Everything is dry. Madeline's sandbag guy is a genius."

"I heard that," Madeline's voice rang down the hall. "I'm calling him now; I'll pass along your compliments." Her door closed with a soft click, but not before she purred, "Hello, darling," into her phone.

AJ and I were heading to Keith's office when Bridget picked up a call. She glanced up and whispered *sotto voce*, "Doctor Death on the line for you."

I groaned.

"No, not you Evie, he wants to speak to AJ."

"Oh great," AJ muttered as he veered into his office. "I'll catch up with you after I deal with *your* friend."

Keith's office was full of half-unpacked cardboard boxes; books and files were spread across his chairs and credenza. "What a shame," I said as I sat down.

"What?" Keith put down his pen and stared at me. "What's a shame?"

"This. You've been back less than a day and already it's a mess."

His smile deepened. He was sunburnt, probably from spending the day digging swales and drainage ditches to protect the house and horse barn. "Yeah, that's what Wendy"—that was his wife— "said about the garage."

AJ barged into Keith's office, making a noise like a horse blowing through its lips, and dropped into the chair beside me. "I should never have agreed to look in on that curmudgeon."

"Doctor Death?" I asked innocently. "Dare I ask why?"

"Damn right Doctor Death. He wants me to pick up a rotisserie chicken and some scotch on my way home. The delivery guys still can't get into his building, that makes me his personal errand boy."

I grinned at Keith and said, "It's karma. We were stuck with him in law school, now it's AJ's turn." AJ harrumpffed and said he'd forgive me... in the next millennium.

"So, about my meeting with Juve."

Immediately I had their full attention. "He and Anya have been bribing Laura since 2022. The way Juve tells it, he's just the delivery boy, Anya is the mastermind. Oh, and get this, Peter knows nothing about it."

"Do you believe him?" Keith asked.

I scratched the back of my neck. "Yes and no."

AJ interrupted before I could continue. "Did Juve confirm that Russo is in on it?"

"No. He only talked about Laura."

Keith raised a hand. "Hold on, why yes and no?"

"Well," I said, "I think he's telling the truth as far as Peter not knowing about the bribes, but he was too quick to fess up. Like he wanted to give me something to throw me off the track, to make me go away. There's more going on."

Keith furrowed his brow; it was his I'm-processing-this-bear-with-me look. AJ, who thinks like I do, said, "Patrice should call her loan."

"Yep," I said, rising to my feet. "I'm heading out there now. And Peter has to be told. It's time to rip the lid off Schrödinger's box."

CHAPTER 44

ANYA

Downtown was covered in sticky brown sludge. Abandoned cars jutted out of drowned ditches. Boarded up storefronts stared blindly into the street. It looked as if the place had been destroyed in an alien invasion. To make things worse, the heat was rising and everything smelled horrible.

My trepidation eased as I drove through Patrice's neighbourhood; here, high up in the north-west quadrant of the city the streets were clean, the shops and playgrounds free from filthy water.

Voices floated out from the back of Patrice's house. I followed the narrow pavement in the side yard, ducking under the lilac trees heavy with sweet purple flowers, and pushed open the creaky low gate.

All the cold frames were open. Patrice was kneeling on a sheet of newspaper; Peter was hovering over her. "Just give it a good yank, Mom," he pointed with a small spade at the ropey vine twisted around her gardening gloves.

She sat back on her heels, slipped off a glove and swept

her hand across her forehead. "I did give it a good yank, Peter. It won't come out. You try."

I hesitated for a moment. I'd hoped to talk to Patrice first, then Peter. But here he was. It was time to end this.

"You two look busy," I said. They turned to face me, Patrice's smile widened and Peter nodded hello. "Can I talk to you for a minute?"

Patrice rose, brushed the dirt from her knees and said, "Of course, Evie."

"Mom, don't we..." his voice faded as he glanced at his watch.

She swivelled her hips in circles and groaned. "Your old mom needs to take a break, Peter. Get the lawn chairs out of the garage, will you? Evie, anything to drink? Coffee? Tea?"

I shook my head. "I won't be staying long."

Peter disappeared into the garage and returned carrying three plastic lawn chairs, he flapped them open and we sat on the small wooden deck by the back door. The sun bouncing off the white siding warmed our backs while the breeze swishing through the evergreens cooled our faces.

Where does one start a conversation that ends with: you've been betrayed by someone you love? At the beginning, I suppose. I described my meeting with Laura in Edmonton and my phone call with Russo, the government minister. Patrice nodded politely, not sure where all this was leading. Peter became very still, like a block of marble too heavy for his flimsy plastic chair.

I took a deep breath and said, "Juve admits he's been delivering bribes to Laura—"

Peter cut me off. "No, we've already gone through this. Juve gave Laura a hot tip, it's not his fault she went overboard."

"There's more," I said, raising a hand to silence him.

"Juve says the bribes started in 2022 and they were Anya's idea." Juve said a whole lot more about Anya, nasty, vicious things, but nothing good would come from repeating them here.

The air grew still. I waited. Then Peter exploded, flying out of his chair. It shot backward, hit the wall, and clattered over onto its side. "That's insane! You can't waltz in here and accuse my wife of bribery!" The words caught in his throat. "Who the hell do you think you are?"

I stood up. Our faces were much too close for a civilized conversation. "As your lawyer it's my duty to tell you when your company is breaking the law." I tried to depersonalize the accusation but in this case the company and Anya were one and the same.

"You're calling my wife a crook." His breath was hot in my face.

I stepped back. "That's exactly why we have to get to the bottom of this," I said. "Laura accused Juve, and Juve accused Anya." *What's that old saying: where there's smoke there's fire.*

Patrice tried to push herself up out of the rickety lawn chair, she was trembling and her hand slipped off the thin metal arm, she listed to one side. I caught her arm to keep her from falling.

"Let's go inside, Patrice," I said as I steadied her. "We'll sort this out." I wanted to get both of us away from Peter.

She nodded and in a quiet voice said, "I'm sure it's all a big misunderstanding."

"Jesus, Mom, you're not buying this shit?" Peter glared at Patrice, imploring her to side with him. She pressed her lips together but didn't speak.

He kicked his lawn chair and sent it flying across the grass, then stormed around the side of the house and started his car. We heard the gears grind as he reversed down the driveway and sped into the street.

When he was gone Patrice turned to me, her eyes were red, and said, "Evie, this can't be true."

"I'm afraid it is. As far as I can tell, Anya, that is, Dream-Stone, is desperate for cash."

"No, she's not," Patrice said with a determined shake of her head. "Come inside, I want to show you something."

She led the way into the house and sat me down at the kitchen table while she went into Finn's study. I could hear her rummaging around in his desk. "Here it is," she said, returning with a piece of paper that she put into my hand. It was a letter from DreamStone saying the company was repaying $250,000 of the $500,000 loan. "You see," she said triumphantly, "they don't need the money."

I handed the letter back to her. "Patrice, all I know is what Juve told me."

She put the letter on the table, then crossed to the kitchen sink and poured herself a glass of water. Turning to me she said, "I've known Anya since 2016. From the minute I saw her I knew she was different from Peter's other girlfriends. This girl had a head on her shoulders. She took business at Wharton, she was bright, confident, beautiful. Look at her." Patrice pointed to a wedding photo sitting on the small work desk in the corner of the kitchen. Anya was nestled into Peter's side. Her thick black hair was piled high on her head, her strapless wedding gown showed off her delicate shoulders and lovely long body. Her face was upturned and she was looking into Peter's eyes. Even in profile you could see Peter was besotted.

"Evie, she's a lovely girl. And her parents are charming. They were delighted Anya had finally found someone."

"Finally? Peter and Anya were in their mid-twenties

when they married. They had all the time in the world to find a mate and settle down."

Patrice dismissed my comment with a smile. According to her folks, Anya had a habit of falling in love with promising young men but it never worked out. "They'd flutter around her like moths to a flame, then fade away. But not Peter, he worshipped the ground she walked on. He still does." She crossed the room, picked up the wedding photograph and set it in front of me. "Beautiful and rich. She helped Peter achieve his dreams."

"Were you and Finn close to her parents?" The other photo on the small desk was a family shot, the bride and groom and the proud in-laws clustered together under an arbour heavy with climbing roses.

"No, not really," she said, her eyes fixed on the photo. "Certainly not since her father pulled his money out of DreamStone." She gave a quick smile and shrugged. "You know how it is with families, sometimes they're close like Peter, Finn, and me, sometimes they're not."

As Patrice reminisced about the wedding my mind drifted. Peter's outrage at the idea that Anya was bribing a government official seemed sincere, but they lived and worked together day after day for years. How could he not know what she and Juve were up to?

CHAPTER 45

EMERGENCY

Bridget was in a flap when I returned to the office. "Where the heck have you been?" she demanded as she sprang up from her desk. "Why didn't you answer your cell?"

"The roads are a mess." But that wasn't the real reason I was late. I'd pushed Patrice as hard as I could but she refused to call her loan to DreamStone. They'd repaid half the debt and she was confident they'd repay the rest soon. I was embarrassed to admit it but I'd snapped at her. It was terribly unprofessional. "Patrice, for the love of God, your son and his wife are multi-millionaires"—although who knew for how long— "you need that money more than they do." The minute I said the words I regretted them. Patrice accepted my apology but it wasn't long before she'd shown me to the door.

Distracted, I'd missed the turnoff and shot down a side street only to get mired on a mucky road next to a playground. My tires spun and mud flew all over the place. It took twenty minutes and a passing stranger to extricate the Mini from the quagmire. I was furious by the time I returned to the office. Two hours gone and all I'd managed to do was alienate Finn's widow.

Bridget thrust a wad of pink telephone slips into my hand. "Call Peter Tanberg. Something's happened to Anya."

"Peter called?" Many times, from the looks of the messages in my hand. "I just saw him a couple of hours ago."

"Be that as it may, he wants you to call him ASAP, he says it's urgent."

Dropping my briefcase onto my desk, I punched in Peter's number. It rang six times and went to voicemail. I left a message and did it all over again ten minutes later and fifteen minutes after that. Too agitated to work I killed time lobbing balled up telephone slips into the waste basket on the other side of the room.

Madeline spotted me on her way down to the coffee room. "What's up?" she asked as she picked up the crumpled paper balls, only three of the five made it into the bin.

"Something's happened to Anya."

My phone buzzed. I snatched it off my desk and held up one finger, indicating Madeline should wait. "Peter, what's going on?"

He and Anya were in the ER. Patrice was on her way. Right after Peter had left us, he picked up Anya and took her out to brunch at Red's Diner. She was spreading cream cheese on a bagel when something weird happened. "It was as if her brain glitched. The butter knife slipped out of her hand and she kind of threw her bagel to the floor." When he asked her what was wrong, she opened and closed her mouth like a goldfish, but no sound came out. "No words, not even a murmur." He thought she might be having a stroke and rushed her to hospital.

A keening cry sounded in the background. Peter's voice

faded as he turned away from the phone, "I'm here, Anya, darling, I'm here." The wail dropped to a moan. His voice became louder. "They've got her on an IV, they're pumping fluids into her and running tests. Hopefully we'll know something soon."

"Peter, I—"

"Evie, that's not why I'm calling." In the background people were talking loudly. Someone asked Peter to please step outside, the phone made a rustling sound as he went out into the corridor.

He spoke quickly. "Listen, Juve needs a copy of the latest disposition certificate, it's on Anya's laptop back home. The City won't let us back in, supposedly it's not safe." Like Peter, Louisa and I were still locked out of our place; three people had died in the flood, one in their own basement, the City was right to be cautious.

"No problem, Peter. We've got the certificate here." I raised my eyebrows at Madeline who nodded in agreement. "Where do I send it?" He gave me Juve's email address. Anya started screaming. A firm voice told her to calm down. And Peter hung up without saying goodbye.

Madeline's eyes were wide. "Wow. That sounded brutal."

We crossed the hall to her office and she scrolled through the DreamStone files until we found the most recent disposition certificate and sent it to Juve.

"Madeline, while we're here can you pull up the Asian distribution contract?"

She scrolled and clicked until it appeared. The shipment had two days to make it from the Bear's Paw mine to Vancouver where it would be loaded onto a freighter. If DreamStone missed the shipping window the ammolite would sit on the dock for a week until the next freighter was ready to depart. They'd be in breach of their agreement and liable for thousands of dollars in fines, to say nothing of lost sales. The house of cards was beginning to teeter.

"What if they ship by air?" I asked.

Madeline did a Google search and clicked a new link, bringing up an air freight site. The quickest route would be Vancouver International Airport to Beijing. "That's no better. China Eastern only flies once a week."

"It probably costs a lot more, too."

Madeline closed the DreamStone file and sighed. "We've done everything we can."

We had, and once this shipment was gone, we'd wash our hands of them forever. I gazed past Madeline into the parking lot and the small wood that slopes up the hill. "Madeline, I meant to thank you for connecting us with your sandbag guy."

She smiled and was repeating Keith's comment about the sandbags falling off the back of a truck when my phone rang again. It was Peter. He started yelling before I could say hello.

"Jesus Christ, Evie. That's the wrong one!" A tiny line appeared between Madeline's brows.

I put the phone on speaker and set it on the desk. "Juve," Peter shouted, "you still there?" Juve grunted yes. "Tell her which certificate you want."

I glanced at Madeline who clicked open the file, pulled the certificate up on screen, and waited. Unlike Peter, Juve was calm and unhurried. "I've got the packing invoice here. I need the certificate. Here's its identification number." Carefully he recited a string of numbers. Madeline stared at the image in front of her, tracking the numbers with her fingertip.

Finally she said, "Juve, the numbers don't match." Juve told her to check the weight/count column. Our eyes scanned the page. She found it and read out the information. We waited. Other than the sounds of nurses talking in the background, no one said a word.

Juve rustled some papers at his end, then said, "Peter, they've got the wrong one."

Madeline sat back in her chair and said, "That's the most recent one we've got, unless you guys applied for another certificate and didn't send us a copy."

"Peter," Juve repeated, "they don't have it."

"Shit," Peter said. "It's got to be on Anya's computer at home. Evie, if I get you access, can you send the certificate remotely from her computer?"

I glanced at Madeline. She said yes.

We heard the sound of the phone rubbing across Peter's cheek. "Anya, darling, listen to me. I need your password."

Her breathing was ragged, she sounded as if she were thrashing around.

"Anya, please, look at me." He coaxed her. "I need your password. Anya?"

"Carol... Channing... ninety... seven." The words came in staccato bursts. "All... one... word."

"Did you catch that?" Peter asked.

Madeline repeated the password. We had it. Someone called Peter's name. They wanted a word. He dropped off and the harrowing sounds of the ER disappeared.

Juve stayed on the line, waiting. Madeline tapped her keyboard; screens came and went until Anya's home screen appeared. Madeline clicked through a couple of files until she found the right one and with a few more keystrokes the disposition certificate was on its way to Juve. "Thanks," he said, "Got it." He hung up.

Bridget rapped on Madeline's open door, wide-eyed

with worry. "Is Anya going to be all right? What happened? It sounded like she was dying."

We had nothing to tell her, we didn't know.

I returned to my office and set the DreamStone file aside, looking for something boring and mundane; a little less histrionic.

And for a couple of hours life at the firm returned to normal. Bridget greeted clients and escorted them to Keith's office. AJ's phone rang in the next office, his rich laugh echoed in the hallway. Six o'clock rolled around and the office grew quiet as computers were shut down, lights were turned off and everyone left for home. I was rummaging for my car keys when Madeline's door swung open and she said, "Evie, you need to see this."

I hung over her shoulder as she walked me through the rows and columns in the documents displayed on her computer screen. By the time she was finished I was so pale she made me sit down, I didn't feel faint but apparently I looked like I was going to keel over and die. She walked me through it one more time just to be sure, then I sent Keith and AJ a text:

New development on DreamStone.

Meeting 8 AM tomorrow.

Urgent.

CHAPTER 46

NEGLIGIBLE VALUE

The next morning was a radiant Friday: humidity hung heavy in the air, and the sun was high in a clear blue sky. I heard them before I saw them, their voices floating up from the river behind the building as I crossed the parking lot. Bridget and Madeline were picking their way through the woody scrub like a pair of pixies in gumboots. Bridget crouched down, her stick poked tentatively at a sodden mass of leaves and twigs, Madeline bent gracefully over her shoulder. "It's nothing, Bridget," she said gently, "the burrow is empty."

"Did they survive?" Bridget asked.

Madeline patted Bridget's shoulder. "I'm sure they did."

Bridget dropped the stick when I called their names and they made their way unsteadily back to me, their rubber boots squelching in the muck.

Madeline's expression signalled I was not to contradict what she'd told Bridget. I nodded. Got it. Even I knew that small animals were the least likely to survive a flood. The surge hits them so fast they can't escape which was why Bridget's search for survivors was futile.

"Keith and AJ aren't here yet," Madeline said. I already knew that. Their cars weren't in the parking lot. Keith usually gets in by six and AJ rolls in at seven-thirty, the same time as I do, but the flood-ravaged roadways made everyone's commute treacherous and unpredictable.

Madeline deposited her wellies in the trunk of her car, replacing them with a pair of red Jimmy Choos. In her white sleeveless sheath she could be auditioning for a role in *Mad Men*.

Bridget unlocked the doors and clicked on the lights, whistling softly under her breath as she went off to start the coffee.

"Ready?" I asked Madeline as we entered the conference room. I felt like we were in the eye of the storm, that quiet period before all hell breaks loose.

"As ready as I'll ever be," she replied, turning on her laptop and loading up Anya's files. They were huge and the laptop's fan started to whir. We'd spent a good half hour last night debating how to tell Keith. Do we rip the band-aid off slowly or do it all at once? AJ would roll with it either way we played it. Keith, on the other hand, might not.

AJ's MGB roared into the parking lot sending the crows and magpies screeching high into the sky. Keith's SUV pulled in right behind him. We heard Bridget tell them we were waiting for them in the conference room.

I called out. "Grab yourselves a coffee or a whiskey"—I was kidding, we didn't keep alcohol in the office— "you're going to need it." This was me telegraphing Keith that there was trouble ahead.

A minute later they strolled in and sat in their usual chairs.

"What's up?" Keith asked.

"We've got a big problem with DreamStone," I said.

"We always have a big problem with DreamStone," he replied. "The sooner we're rid of them the better."

"Yeah, well, little things like Finn's funeral and a mass evacuation and Anya screaming her lungs out in ER got in the way."

"Anya's in the hospital?" Keith was genuinely concerned. "What happened?"

"Her health is the least of my worries." I explained the hysteria of yesterday and how Peter had given us Anya's password so we could access her laptop and send Juve the most recent disposition certificate. "In the process, Madeline discovered something." *Here it comes, rip off the band-aid in one fell swoop.* "Anya is running two sets of books: one for the tax man and one for herself."

AJ choked on his coffee, coughed, and wiped his chin with the back of his hand.

The colour drained from Keith's face. "Two sets of books? DreamStone is engaged in tax fraud on top of bribing a government official? Isn't that just ducky."

"It gets worse," I said brightly.

"Sure," he replied, sarcastically, "why not."

Madeline put the key documents up on the big screen but the numbers were hard to read with the glare coming in from the windows.

"I think they're smuggling ammolite into China," I said.

"Jesus Christ!" Keith went from ash grey to blotchy red. It's times like this that I worry about his blood pressure.

"Shit," AJ muttered under his breath.

I explained that when Anya gave us her password, we had a chance to compare the numbers set out in the government-issued disposition certificate with Dream-Stone's internal documents.

"The numbers don't line up. The last shipment is a good example." I glanced up at the documents on the big screen, Keith and AJ did not. Their attention was riveted on me. "The disposition certificate shows DreamStone is shipping six containers. Five contain ammolite jewelry valued at ten million. The sixth contains something called 'promotional materials' valued at 'negligible'.

"However, DreamStone's internal ledger for the same shipment shows five containers valued at ten million, and the sixth container—the so-called promotional materials—is valued at two million dollars."

Keith chewed his lip, still processing this information, but AJ leapt ahead. "Okay, so this could be evidence of tax evasion, but how did you get to smuggling?"

How indeed? Intuition? The uneasy feeling that Juve was willing to tell me about Anya's bribery scheme because he was steering me away from an even bigger secret: they were smuggling ammolite to Asia.

"AJ, they're hiding it in plain sight."

"How?" he asked.

"By disguising it as something else. Just like ivory smugglers who paint ivory black and pass it off as ebony wood, DreamStone is disguising real ammolite as fake ammolite—promotional material of negligible value—and shipping it out of the country under an expedited disposition certificate. Once it reaches its destination it's sold to private collectors."

I told them about the day Louisa and I drove out to the mine and Quincy got loose and chased a jackrabbit up the hill to the warehouse. Just thinking about it sent a shiver down my spine: Quincy smashing through the door, dragging poor Louisa over the threshold. Juve grabbing a rifle and pointing it at her head. And his feeble explanation, a problem with coyotes—coyotes don't break down doors to attack the people inside. But criminals do.

Criminals steal perfect ammolite fossils worth millions of dollars. It's not as if DreamStone could report the theft, there being no records to prove the ammolite existed in the first place; it hadn't been logged by the government or assessed by the Tyrrell Museum, so when Louisa burst through the door the first thing Juve did was reach for a gun.

I'll say this for him, Juve has good instincts. He wanted to keep us away from the giant ammolite shell resting on the workbench behind him. What's the harm, Peter said, it's a fake. A perfect replica made of resin, mica, and ammolite chips. Marvelous, isn't it. Yes, it was. And it belonged in a museum, not in the private collection of an overseas buyer.

I waited, expecting Keith to explode. To rail on about the untenable position I'd landed him and the firm in. But he didn't. Instead, he came over to my side of the table and sat down. He took my hand in his and looked me in the eye. Gently he said, "Evie, I want you to repeat after me: DreamStone is smuggling priceless artifacts out of the country and there's nothing I can do about it."

"We have to report them," I said.

"We can't. Client confidentiality."

"Oh Keith, not the bloody Code again."

"I'll look into it, but off the top of my head I can't think of an exception to the client confidentiality rule. You have to stand down." This time his voice carried an edge.

"After I drag them in here and read them the riot act." I slipped my hands out of his. "Then we fire them."

My head said it was a good plan, but in my heart I knew
it wasn't enough.

CHAPTER 47

THE ZOO

Louisa was dancing around in the upstairs window when I pulled up in front of Madeline's place. God knows what she was listening to but she was flailing around like a woman possessed. By the time I reached the front door I could hear her thundering down the stairs. Maybe she'll greet me at the door with a martini, I thought. No, she'd better not. Ever since we'd arrived on Madeline's doorstep we'd been tippling way more booze than we did at home. I blamed it on too many crappy days like today.

It had taken me hours to track down Peter and when I finally did, I had to pretend I was worried about Anya. "How is she? What's the diagnosis?"

"Disorientation caused by extreme dehydration. They kept her overnight, filled her with IV fluids, that kind of thing. I just settled her at home."

"Patrice's place?"

"No, we've got a suite at the Palliser Hotel. Anya needs her rest."

I said I wanted to meet with them on Monday. He

resisted, not surprising given that I'd alleged his wife was up to her neck in a bribery scheme, but I prattled on about Patrice's loan, bank security, things BLV could do to lighten their debt burden—all legal bafflegab to force them to see me—and eventually he acquiesced. Anya might have the strength for a short visit on Monday if she did nothing but sleep all weekend but I would have to come to their hotel. She was much too weak to come to me. I rolled my eyes so hard they almost fell out of my head.

Louisa flung open the front door before I touched the doorknob and did a little dance on the checkerboard-tiled floor. Her eyes sparkled and she grabbed my hands and started singing that silly little song we used to sing when we were kids: "We're going to the zoo, zoo, zoo, that's what we're going to do, do, do."

"No, that's not what we're going to do, do, do," I sang back, shouting a little to be heard over Rupert, the cockatiel, who'd chimed in. "I'm exhausted." But Louisa was insistent. It's the weekend. A trip to the zoo was just the thing I needed to put DreamStone out of my mind for a couple of days.

At that exact moment Madeline sailed around the corner and declared Louisa was right. "I'll take you as my guests. They'll give us the red carpet treatment. I'm a VIP, you know." She arched her eyebrows and sucked in her cheeks. The zoo was on her charitable contribution list. Knowing Madeline, her contribution would be a sizeable one.

"Well," Louisa said, "if this is going to be a girls' outing, we'd better invite Bridget."

So we did.

Bright and early on Saturday morning Madeline, Louisa, and I were in the car rocketing past the concrete dinosaurs in Dinosaur Park, searching for the zoo's north entrance where we'd arranged to meet Bridget. The minute we pulled into the parking lot she leapt out of her car and rushed over for hugs, you'd think we hadn't seen each other for months, then insisted we head straight to the penguin enclosure. "It's such a beautiful day, the exhibit will be packed and we won't be able to get close enough. Come on!"

It turned out Bridget was an expert on penguins: she pointed out the Kings, the Humboldts, the Rockhoppers and Gentoos, and provided a running commentary in a squeaky little voice of what they were thinking as they bumped each other off the rocks and flopped into the sparkling blue pool.

Their keeper, a young woman wearing blue latex gloves and carrying a tin bucket, was tossing silvery fish into the water. Bridget pulled out her phone and crouched behind the plexiglass barrier to make a video— "hashtag penguins"—of the penguins pitching themselves off the rock ledge into the frothy pool and popping back up with a fish clamped in their orange beaks.

I was watching the crowd, a small child demanded to be picked up so she could see better, when I heard a loud thump. A large King penguin had shot out of the water, slamming its hard sleek body against the plexiglass, startling Bridget who flung herself backwards. Her phone flew out of her outstretched hand and bounced across the path into a flowerbed.

"Oh my goodness!" She tried to haul herself to her feet, then yelped with pain and sank back down to her knees. She tried again, reaching for the plexiglass railing while we grabbed her arms and hoisted her up. "My phone," she said anxiously, "where's my phone?"

"Forget the phone. Are you all right? Are you hurt?" We buzzed around her.

She gave a weak smile. "Twisted my ankle, I'm okay."

Louisa fussed, saying we should take Bridget to the First Aid station to make sure nothing was torn or broken, while Madeline scoured the path and the flowerbeds until she spotted Bridget's phone. She dusted it off, saying, "You'll need to get a new screen, it's scratched." And handed it back to Bridget.

Bridget tested her weight on her ankle but refused to leave the penguin enclosure until she checked her video. After a moment she smiled and turned the phone so we could see the screen. The short clip started with frolicking penguins, then bam! something that looked like an Orca blasted across the screen; blue sky and the green grass whirled by, then a small bounce. The sky and a few trembling leaves waited until Madeline's hand appeared.

"It's perfect," Bridget declared. "All it needs is the right music, something ominous like the theme from *Jaws*."

"You can do whatever you like as long as I'm not in it," Madeline said. She has a thing about voluntarily giving up her privacy on social media. I used to tease her about being in witness protection, but she didn't think it was funny.

We set off down the path to the Kitamba Café. As we ambled past enclosures and street signs pointing the way to Destination Africa and Exploration Asia, I said to Madeline, "It looks like all the exhibits are open, the flood's had no impact on the zoo whatsoever."

She gave me a small self-congratulatory smile. And I knew she'd donated a substantial sum to ensure the zoo and all its inhabitants, right down to the tiniest deadly spider, would be safe.

"Evie!" Louisa shrieked and clutched my arm. A peacock

strutted down the path toward us. "Do something. Shoo it away!" The zoo was packed with ferocious predators and the only creature that terrifies Louisa is this ridiculous bird. It fanned its magnificent tail, the feathers swished and shivered in the sunlight, and dismissed us with a flick of the crest on top of its head before it marched away. Louisa exhaled slowly and I said I was relieved not to be pressed into service; the last time we'd encountered a peacock I'd had to stand between them waving my arms like a crazy person.

Kitamba Café wasn't crowded and the line in front of the food counter moved quickly. We placed our orders and were soon back outside sitting on the patio. Corn dogs, cheeseburgers, coffee, and a bright blue cold drink for Bridget. Not healthy choices but all a part of the zoo experience. Across the way on the far side of the lawn beyond the brilliant yellow flower beds, small children clambered onto a giant red Adirondack chair and sat pretty and smiled nice for their parents who were madly snapping photos on their cell phones.

As we headed back to the car, past the flamingos strolling on unhinged legs and large spikey porcupines, I realized I hadn't thought about DreamStone all morning. At first, I was relieved, but then something flickered in the back of my mind, a memory tugging, waiting for me to recognize it.

CHAPTER 48

THE DARK WEB

The beauty of having AJ's cell number is I can call him any time of the day or night and he always picks up. Always.

It was Monday morning, just before sunrise and Quincy and I were jogging through Madeline's neighbourhood. The air was luminous, unlike my community where the stink of standing water rose up from the flooded basements and settled over the neighbourhood like a rotting blanket. The cleaning crew was halfway through ripping our basement apart, they'd be finished in another week, they said. I had my doubts, but we couldn't complain, we were lucky to get them. Our job was tiny compared to the mansions like Anya's place, but luckily, Madeline knew a guy.

Quincy wound his leash around my legs and snuffled the grass while I punched in AJ's number. The phone rang three times before a sleepy voice said, "Do you have any idea what time it is?"

"I believe it's five or thereabouts."

"Four-fifty in the morning. In. The. Morning."

"Well, you're awake now, so stop whining and listen to me." I could hear the rustle of bedding as he moved around trying to get more comfortable, moaning and grunting for effect. Then he yawned loudly and said, "Okay, I'm up. What do you want at this ungodly hour?"

We talked for a few minutes and he agreed to meet me at the office as soon as he'd had a shower.

The Mini rattled across the office parking lot; if it wasn't regravelled soon, I'd wreck its suspension. In the distance I could hear the sound of AJ's MGB roaring through the streets. He wheeled into the lot and fishtailed to a stop a metre from my car.

"It's always drama with you, isn't it AJ?" I said with a small smile.

He grinned and followed me into my office. "Here, this will improve your mood... or mine at any rate." He placed two Seb's coffees and two small paper bags on my desk.

"Breakfast bagel." He nodded as he tore his bag apart and I handed him a wad of Kleenex to catch the grease and crumbs.

"Thanks for coming in, AJ. I really appreciate it." My bagel was hot and the first bite was delicious, the bacon crispy just the way it should be.

"Anything to oblige." He grinned like the farm boy he pretends to be. "So, what's up?"

I'd booked the 'you are crooks and you're fired' meeting with Peter and Anya for ten this morning. It was going to be messy but, for Patrice's sake, I had to make them stop.

"AJ, I'm only going to get one shot at this. I have to get it right."

I've worked with many lawyers over the years, but no one, not even Keith, is as good at helping me frame a killer argument as AJ. I lob ideas at him, he lobs them back and when we were done, I'm bullet proof, or as close to it as I'll ever get.

AJ chewed thoughtfully as he listened to my arguments, then pointed his bagel at me and said, "If I'm Anya, the first thing I'm going to do is throw a hissy fit. The second thing I'm going to do is say you've got no proof." He picked up his coffee and blew on it.

I pulled out a yellow note pad and uncapped a new Bic. "Juve admitted to bribing Laura. Even if Anya denies it or says Juve was on a frolic of his own—don't you love legal jargon—I've still got Juve's admission and Russo's phone call. Admittedly Russo was pretty vague, but why else would he be calling me if not to keep the bribe money flowing? Can you believe Laura assumed we're in on it?"

"She's not the sharpest pencil in the box," he said, sipping his coffee and grimacing as it went down. It was blisteringly hot.

"Or maybe she's desperate. She did have a 'fire sale' look about her when we met in Edmonton."

My Bic stuttered across the page, the ink refused to flow. I scribbled little circles on the corner of the pad trying to get it started. "We have Anya's duplicate set of books, that's hard evidence of tax fraud and smuggling."

"Unless she has an explanation. Unlike Laura, Anya is as sharp as they come. Remember, she was an early investor in crypto; she made a bundle and was smart enough to get out before it crashed."

Something clicked in my brain. The Bic flew off the edge of the yellow pad and my hand grazed AJ's coffee cup, slopping hot coffee over his fingers. "Jesus!" he yelped.

"AJ! That's it. What if she didn't get out? How much do you want to bet that she's still using her crypto account—"

"On the dark web?" He understood me immediately. "To launder her illicit profits from smuggling."

"Bribery, tax evasion, smuggling, money laundering. God, AJ, I've got to get Patrice out!"

There was a commotion in the reception area. Madeline was complaining to Bridget that she'd almost broken an ankle in a pothole in the parking lot. Bridget chided her, "What do you expect in those skyscraper heels?"

As Madeline passed my office, she broke her stride and said, "This is it, isn't it? You're thrashing it out with them."

"Damn right," I glanced at my watch. "I'm meeting them at their suite in an hour."

"Do you need me to ride shotgun?" AJ asked.

"Nah," I said, sweeping a wad of greasy Kleenex off my desk and into the trash can. "We're all civilized people. I can handle it."

CHAPTER 49

THE PALLISER HOTEL

The Palliser Hotel, unlike the Banff Springs, is not nestled in the rugged mountainside but sandwiched between the downtown office towers and the CP rail line. Day and night the trains rumble by, screeching and rattling from one side of the country to the other. I've often wondered what would happen if a train carrying oil or noxious chemicals derailed on the Palliser's doorstep.

Still, the historic sandstone building is beautiful. Peter and Anya were staying in a luxurious suite on the eighth floor. The thickly carpeted hallway muffled the sound of my footsteps, they wouldn't know I was coming until I was practically on top of them. I tapped on the door to Peter's suite, he eased it open, a finger to his lips, "Anya's sleeping," and ushered me in.

He padded around barefoot and looked a little silly in his pressed slacks and cashmere sweater as if he couldn't make up his mind whether to go to work or go back to bed.

"Peter," I said, glancing toward the bedroom door which

was firmly closed, "I really need to speak with Anya. This is urgent."

He gave an apologetic smile and said, "She's been through a lot, she needs to rest." Then sat down on the sofa. I sat down next to him. *Fine, we'll play it your way.*

Quickly I outlined the points I'd refined with AJ earlier: In 2021, DreamStone ran into financial trouble. The banks refused to lend Anya any more money unless she put up more security. She mortgaged everything she had, but the banks kept pressing, it still wasn't enough. Desperate for cash flow she and Juve started bribing Laura to expedite the disposition certificates so they could move the ammolite inventory even faster.

"Hold on," Peter raised a hand to interrupt me. "So what if we gave Laura a few tokens of our appreciation. Is that a crime?"

"Yes, it is. It's called bribery." I pulled my laptop out of my bag and set it down on the coffee table in front of us. "I have to show you something." He glanced at the bedroom door, then back at my computer, looking confused, like an aging boxer who's been in the ring too long.

Two documents appeared on the screen. "Peter, this is your last transaction. Promotional materials. Here its value is nominal, and there the value is two million dollars. That's impossible. It can't be both at the same time. Anya is committing tax fraud." His mouth dropped. I took a deep breath. "She's hiding the two million because she and Juve are smuggling ammolite into Asia. Two million is its true value."

He reared back, his face was so pale I thought he was going to be sick. Before I could speak the bedroom opened and Anya crept into the room. She looked frail, like a Victorian damsel in search of a fainting couch.

"Peter, what's going on?" She clutched her hotel bathrobe tightly at her neck, her eyes widening when she saw me.

"Anya, I think you know exactly what's going on." I turned the laptop to face her. Her eyes flicked down to the documents on the screen. She inhaled sharply then turned to Peter.

"I can explain. That was just an exercise to illustrate what we would have made if those ridiculous export restrictions had not existed. In fact," her voice was stronger now, "I'm lobbying Cory Russo to get rid of them."

I shook my head. "Not true, Anya. Let me spell it out for you. You bribed Laura, you smuggled ammolite into Asia, hence the fake documentation, and you're laundering your illicit profits on the dark web."

Anya turned to Peter. In a firm voice she said, "Make her leave." As he came toward me, she crossed her arms. "You're fired, Evie. Send our files, hardcopy and electronic, all of it, to me immediately."

Peter swung the door open. Just before I stepped out into the hushed hallway, I said, "Peter, you dragged your mother into this mess. You, Anya, and Juve will go to jail if you're caught. Stop it now before you destroy Patrice and she loses everything."

"You'd better leave," was his curt reply.

The door closed softly behind me but not before I heard him say, "What the fuck, Anya?"

CHAPTER 50

THE PHOTO ALBUM

We're getting pretty good at this," I said to Louisa. We were standing at the granite counter in Madeline's huge kitchen, studiously ignoring the cats and dogs at our feet who seemed to think we were preparing dinner. A large, wet cardboard box was slumped in the kitchen sink. It was packed with broken Christmas ornaments and a fat, soggy photo album.

Earlier in the day Louisa went to the house to meet with the cleaning crew. They'd made good progress in the basement and wanted to know what to do with two foul smelling carpets and a stack of mildewed bedding. Everything was going well until Louisa spotted the mashed Christmas box sitting on the workbench in the garage. "Ah, that," the workman said, "it crossed paths with a high-pressure water hose."

"What?" Louisa was aghast. "The box sprouted legs and wandered into a blast of water just for the hell of it?" Hours later she was still seething.

With good reason. The Christmas album was Mom's

life's work. Every Christmas from the day Mom and Dad got married to the day they died was preserved in that album. Opening the album's green and gold embossed cover was like stepping into a time machine. Mom's hair went from jet black, to brown, to her short-lived redhead phase, to glossy white; Dad got smaller and frailer and balder but never lost his ramrod straight posture. Various cats and dogs came and went. Louisa and I were transformed from tiny babies to toddlers slung up on their hips. From little girls sitting under the tinsel tree, our arms wrapped around matching Puffalumps, to adults wearing silly grins as we stared at the camera waiting for its timer to go off.

Louisa set the photo album on a thick towel. We worked diligently, peeling the photos off the cardboard pages and rinsing them in clean water before patting them dry and spreading them out on multiple layers of paper towels to dry.

"You're awfully quiet," Louisa said as I blotted a curling photo. "We won't be able to salvage all of them, Evie. Mom always said it's the memory, not the picture, that counts."

"I was thinking about photographs. How everyone collects images of the things they love and saves them in different ways. Mom developed her photos at London Drugs and put her favourites in photo albums. Finn kept digital images in his camera, some of which find their way to his fridge, and Bridget takes thousands of photos with her cell phone and posts them to her Instagram account."

The cardboard pages made a wet, sticky sound as I peeled them apart. Mom used tiny silver corners to glue the photos down. Where on earth did she find them? I slipped my fingernail under a snapshot and gently pried it off the page.

My mind wandered to something Gideon had said at

Finn's funeral. Someone made the banal comment that Finn died doing what he loved; later in the car Gideon said that was the stupidest thing he'd ever heard. "Name one person, just one, who loves falling off a balcony to their death." I'd dismissed it as Gideon being his snarky old self, but—

"Oh my God!" I dropped the photo onto the sheet of soggy black paper.

Louisa straightened up; she'd been hunched over the countertop waving a red folding fan, Madeline's naturally, over the photographs. "What?" The fan hung motionless in the air.

"I know who did it! Finn was pushed off the balcony and I know who did it!" My hands shook so hard I could barely peel a tiny silver corner piece off the tip of my finger and drop it onto the paper towel.

"Where's Madeline?" I spun around so fast I stepped on Evangeline's paw. She yelped and we both raced into the living room looking for Madeline.

"She's out," Louisa called after me, "with that guy from the construction company," and went back to waving her fan.

"When will she be back?"

Louisa arched an eyebrow. "It's Madeline. She said not to wait up."

*　*　*

The house was quiet but for the antique clock ticking loudly on the mantle. I was half asleep in a wingback chair when I heard Madeline unlock the front door.

"It's after two!" I said. "Where have you been?"

She blinked a couple of times, then slipped her silky

grey evening coat off her shoulders, and said, "I beg your pardon, are you my mother?"

"Sorry, sorry. I need your help."

"Now?"

"Yes, now."

"Fine," she said, "let me get out of this dress." She kicked off her pointy black stilettos and padded off to her bedroom. The Slipper Dog yipped a greeting, Madeline cooed softly and told Evangeline to go back to sleep, a few minutes later she reappeared in a flimsy white satin robe.

We went into the study and she poured herself a drink. "Scotch?" she asked. I shook my head; I was too keyed up to join her. We talked about Finn's funeral and the reception Patrice hosted at her house. I grilled her mercilessly, testing her recall until I was convinced her memory was sound.

"Jesus, Madeline, the answer was right there, staring us in the face the whole time!"

She eyed me over her whiskey glass and said, "Yes, but it's all speculation. You can't go to the police with this; you've got no proof."

"True, but if I confront them, they'll crack, I know they will."

She made a dismissive sound. "Good luck with that. They fired you, remember. None of them will ever speak to you again."

CHAPTER 51

BREAK-IN

At four in the morning The Menagerie went nuts. Quincy and Louisa were in the bedroom next to mine, and Quincy's barking woke me from a dead sleep. The Slipper Dog and Madeline were down the hall where Evangeline was making the strangest yelping sounds. Rupert the cockatiel echoed the shrill pitch of the security alarm, then shrieked "Stop it!" in Madeline's voice.

I leapt out of bed and raced into the hall. Louisa was just ahead of me, clinging to Quincy's collar as he dragged her toward the library. "Someone's in the house!" she shouted over her shoulder.

Madeline sprinted around the other way, running through the kitchen and the dining room, her white robe fluttering around her like angel wings.

Something crashed to the floor in the library, the French door banged open on its hinges.

"I'll let the dog go!" Louisa screamed down the dark corridor. "He'll tear you to shreds so help me God!" Quincy snarled viciously. I had to get in there before she released him because he just might do it.

I charged past them into the library. "Get the lights!" My thigh throbbed with pain when I ricocheted off the mahogany table and knocked over a chair. A flash, the chandeliers exploded in bright white light. Then Madeline was next to me, reaching for the door latch on the French door and yanking it up, then down again until we heard the double lock click.

"Did you see him?" Louisa released Quincy who tore across the library and thumped broadside into the French doors. He was vibrating with adrenaline. We all were.

In the garden; a shadow of a man moving across the lawn in the moonlight. He dove into the cotoneaster hedge and disappeared into the night.

"Did you recognize him?" Louisa asked again.

"No," I said, "Someone in a hoodie. I didn't see his face. Madeline?"

She shook her head and picked up the Slipper Dog, which was shaking so hard it looked like a broken toy, and went out to the kitchen to turn off the alarm. We could hear her on the phone with the security company saying we'd had a break-in but we didn't know whether anything had been stolen. "We'll take inventory tomorrow and get back to you."

On her way back to the library she beelined to the drinks cabinet. "Nightcap, anyone?" Halfway through setting some glasses and a bottle of port on the table she stopped. "Where's my laptop?" It wasn't on the table where it belonged.

"There, by the planter." I pointed at the laptop tossed behind the Ficus tree in the corner of the dining room. "He must have panicked and tossed it when the dogs started up. No, that makes no sense. Of all the precious things he could have taken," I gestured at the art, the antiques, and the silver, "why would he waste his time with a laptop?"

Madeline retrieved her laptop, set it on the dining room table and turned it on. "Oh good, it works. Why would he take it? Because I have all sorts of important stuff on here, that's why." She stopped and stared at Louisa, just noticing her oversized tee shirt. "*Hello Kitty*? That's what you wear to bed?"

I laughed. "It's mine."

"Let her keep it," Madeline said as she finished pouring out three glasses of port. "Although technically you're not much better."

I glanced down at my cotton tee and plaid pyjama pants, then accepted a glass of port and passed the other to Louisa.

Louisa took a sip, made a face, and said, "We're going to regret this in the morning."

"We'll worry about that tomorrow," Madeline said, as she took a long swig and topped up her glass.

CHAPTER 52

SHE'S GONE

It's amazing how fast six-thirty in the morning rolls around when you start drinking at four A.M. I yawned and shuffled into the kitchen.

"Snap out of it," I said to myself in my best Cher voice. Quincy tilted his head. "No, not you, you silly dog." I rubbed his ear and wondered where Madeline keeps her cereal. The cupboard door banged shut, making my temples throb.

Madeline drifted into the kitchen in a white terry robe, her thick red hair was wrapped in a white terry towel. She looked fresh, as if she'd just returned from the spa. "Snap out of it?" she asked. "What? You can't cut it anymore?"

I looked down at Quincy and whispered, "Tell her I can't cut it anymore. And tell her my head hurts and she's talking too loud." I glanced at her. "I have to get them to admit how Finn died. And I can barely function thanks to you and your well-stocked liquor cabinet."

Madeline stifled a yawn and said, "Oh yeah, that's right." She wandered over to the coffee machine and turned it on. "A meeting with the DreamStone team? Good luck with that."

Rummaging through the cupboard I found a cutting board and a loaf of sourdough bread to settle my stomach. My phone vibrated on the counter. Madeline picked it up and handed it to me.

"It's Patrice. Here's your chance."

I nodded. "Good morning, Patrice. How—"

"Is she with you?" Patrice was short of breath. "Anya?" she said, speaking more clearly now. "Is she with you?"

"Me? Are you kidding? Why on earth would she be with me?"

Patrice gave a slow shuddering sigh and explained. "Peter called me this morning looking for Anya. He said you came by yesterday and accused her of doing illegal things—oh Evie, I wish you hadn't done that—Anya, well she's— you don't know her. He demanded an explanation and they had an argument. Anya, she's such a sweet girl but she has a terrible temper. She locked herself in the bedroom and he hasn't seen her since."

"Since when? How long has she been gone?"

Madeline edged closer and put her head next to mine so she could hear Patrice's side of the conversation. The delicate scent of herbal shampoo wafted over me.

"I don't know." Her voice thickened and she started to sob.

"Didn't he check on her last night?"

"The bedroom door was locked; he spent the night on the sofa in the study." I remembered their hotel suite, all white and grey and cream. It was huge with a bedroom on one side of the seating area and a study on the other. Anya could have crept out in the dead of the night and Peter would be none the wiser.

"Poor Peter," she said. "He left her alone to cool off. And now she's gone. If something's happened to her, he'll never forgive himself."

I shook my head at Madeline. She pulled a pen and a note pad out of the junk drawer and scribbled: *Usual haunts?*

"Patrice, listen to me. Where would Anya go? Other than your place. Does she have close friends? Would she fly home to her parents in New England? Did she take her passport?"

"I don't know, I just don't—wait, it's Peter, hang on." She put me on hold. Madeline and I stared at each other, waiting for her to return.

Thirty seconds later she was back. "Peter just talked to Juve; she's not at the mine."

Well, of course not, I thought, what solace would she find in a dirty, noisy pit of a mine. No, she'd go somewhere she felt safe. "Patrice, what about the house? It's her home and her office. People are like cats. When they're distressed, they return to their familiar places. Has anyone checked the house?"

Madeline wrinkled her brow and whispered, "Mandatory evacuation order." I shrugged, it might not be safe to return, but that wouldn't stop her.

Patrice agreed it was worth a try. She'd call Peter.

I threw on a pair of jeans and a hoodie raced out the door.

* * *

The thick brick wall protecting Anya's mansion from the street was caked with mud. Three cars were parked haphazardly in the street, the driver's side door on the Porsche was wide open. I abandoned my car in the middle of the road and ran up to the wrought iron gate. It was wedged open in a sticky mound of muck and debris. Angling my body, I squeezed through the narrow gap. My runners squished in the mud as I crossed under the Japanese maple by the front door.

The front door was secured with a smart lock keypad, but it didn't matter, the door was wide open, and I slipped inside. The stench was overwhelming. Muck and rotting vegetation. Sisal carpets crumpled up against the living room walls. Italian chairs and glass-topped end tables smashed into pieces and strewn across the warped hardwood floors. The office facing the back garden was completely destroyed, the furniture cracked and splintered. Behind Anya's desk lay the plexiglass box containing the architectural model of her new office building, it was nothing more than a sodden mush of foamboard.

Footprints tracked across the muddy floor to the folding glass doors and out across the heaving flagstone patio to the back garden. The greenhouse down by the river was destroyed, broken sheets of glass littered the grass, torn from their metal frames when the river burst its banks. Angry voices rose from the secret garden behind the tall cotoneaster hedge.

Peter was pleading with Anya to come back with him to the Palliser. "I'll send someone around to get your car. Please darling, you need to rest."

Patrice fluttered around them, urging Anya to listen to her husband. For some reason this infuriated Peter who rounded on his mother, barking, "Mom, stay out of this! Go home, you don't belong here."

"Actually, she does," I said as I approached them. Their faces turned to me, registering shock and surprise. That's when I noticed Juve was missing. "Patrice," I said, "please stay."

"Jesus Christ, this is all we need." Peter stepped forward as if to shield Anya from me. "Evie, you are not welcome here. Get out."

"No," I said, stepping closer. "This concerns Finn, so it concerns Patrice. You can hear it from me now or you can hear it from the police later, your choice, Peter."

Anya blinked as if the sight of me had awakened her from a trance. Behind us came the roar of a loud car engine rumbling in the street. A moment later the patio doors screeched open and there he was, loping across the lifting flagstones into the garden. Juve.

"Perfect timing, Juve," I said. "I was about to explain why Finn sent me an email after his death." I winced as I said it, my tone too casual for the gravity of this conversation.

"Just before he died, Finn sent me a scheduled email. He wanted to meet to discuss his concerns about Dream-Stone's finances. He said it was urgent. At the time I didn't know precisely what he wanted to discuss... but I do now."

They stood very still. A breeze coming off the river was cool and ruffled Anya's hair, blowing it into her eyes. Peter swept a strand of hair off her face, she didn't appear to notice.

"He couldn't figure out how DreamStone stayed afloat."

Patrice glanced from Peter to me. "He never said anything to me."

"I think he wanted to talk to me first, Patrice. But he didn't get the chance. However, he did raise it with someone else and they pushed him off the balcony at the Banff Springs Hotel."

Please confess, please don't make me drag Patrice through this.

CHAPTER 53

OPENING SCHRÖDINGER'S BOX

One minute he was standing next to Patrice, the next he was shaking me like a ragdoll, his red face close to mine, screaming, "That's enough!"

I slipped in the mud and almost fell to the ground but he wrenched me back upright.

"Peter, stop it!" Patrice grabbed his hand, trying to pry it off my arm. "What are you doing? Let her go. Let her finish what she's saying." He shot a disgusted glance at his mother then released me.

A zing of pain shot across my shoulder blades. I flexed my arm and said, "Peter, the day Finn died, you and your father had a nasty argument. Here it was, Finn's big day and you two had been fighting all weekend." Peter set his jaw but didn't deny it. "When I walked in on you, Finn was complaining about how much money you were spending on the room, on the banquet, on everything. He taunted you, saying even with all your money you couldn't bring Patrice back from Europe in time for the celebration. To your credit you kept your temper and left to have breakfast with Anya."

I caught Patrice's eye. "The last time I saw Finn, the very last time, was later that afternoon. He was racing down the corridor heading back to his room to get his camera. He was so excited. He wanted me to come with him, but I said Hadiza and I had to take care of some last-minute details." I felt a stab of regret. If I'd gone with him, none of this would have happened.

"What does this have to do with anything?" Juve's voice cut like flint. It was the first thing he'd said since he arrived.

I continued. "At Finn's funeral, everyone gave such moving eulogies. Anya's eulogy was especially touching with her story about Finn making her feel welcome at Sunday dinner and letting her make off with the last falafel. The bit that caught me by surprise"—the bit that infuriated Gideon Gold— "was when Anya said Finn died doing what he loved."

Gideon's derisive tone came back to me. *Finn didn't fall off a mountain, for Christ's sake, he fell off a balcony and landed behind a dumpster.* The words echoed in my mind for days until I finally figured out what was wrong. Anya, so cool, so analytical, not one for mushy platitudes, when she said Finn died doing what he loved, she meant it.

"So here's the thing, Anya, you were right. Finn did die doing what he loved. He was on that balcony. Taking photos of a Steller's Jay—you called it a blue jay in your eulogy—which had eluded him for years. Then something happened. He went over. And you were there."

Peter interrupted. "A blue jay? That's ridiculous. Anya didn't have to be on the balcony to see it, she'd have seen the photo on the fridge." He glanced at his mother. "That's where all of Dad's photos end up, isn't that right, Mom?"

This was where Madeline and her remarkable memory came in. Last night she described every photo stuck to the fridge, pictures of all the places Finn and Patrice had visited which, by strange coincidence she and her lawyer friend had visited as well. The only photo Madeline didn't recall seeing was Finn's photo of the Steller's Jay. She didn't recall it because it wasn't there.

Patrice's eyes flew from Peter's face to mine. It was an eerie moment, just before Schrödinger opens the box, that split second in time where the cat is both dead and alive. At that exact moment Anya was both innocent and guilty; her fate depended on how Patrice answered my next question.

"Patrice, is there a photo of the Steller's Jay on the fridge?" Would she tell the truth, or would she lie to protect her son's wife?

"Oh, Peter," Patrice looked at her son and said quietly, "there's no photo of the Steller's Jay on the fridge. It's still in Finn's camera."

"Then Anya saw it in Dad's camera."

"No," Patrice stared steadily at her son. "The camera was damaged when your dad fell." She turned to face Anya. "I didn't show the photo to Peter, and I certainly didn't show it to you." In a voice riddled with grief, she said, "Anya, what in God's name have you done?"

Anya recoiled as she'd been slapped. "Make her stop. Peter, please!"

He hesitated. Who should he believe? His mother or his wife? That split second of indecision was not lost on Anya. She recovered quickly and took control of the conversation.

"Darling, there's no need for all this fuss. Of course I saw the photograph. Finn showed it to me when I bumped into him on the balcony. He was still taking photos, happy as a lark when I left him."

"That's not true." Everyone tore their eyes away from Anya and back to me. "Finn took four shots of the jay, the first two were blurry, the third shot was perfect, and in the last one it flew out of the frame. After that there is nothing. No more photos in the camera. And there's no record in Finn's Merlin app of the sighting. He's been tracking that bird for years, there's no way he wouldn't record when and where he found it." This was one of those rare cases where the lack of evidence was evidence of the crime.

Peter reached tentatively for Anya as if he were trying to pull her closer. "Darling," he said softly, "what happened? Just tell me what happened."

She lifted her face to him, her voice was firm. "Nothing happened, Peter. Absolutely nothing."

"Anya," he pleaded, "we're family, please."

Her hand shot up. She slapped his arm away and stepped back, out of his reach. "Family? Don't you talk to me about family. Your precious father didn't care about his family. All he cared about was money. He wanted to see DreamStone's financials. If I didn't give them to him, he was going to turn us in. Turn you, Peter, his own son, over to the police."

"For God's sakes Anya, that's ridiculous." I couldn't keep the anger out of my voice. "He wanted to see the financials, you refused to show them to him because you were engaged in tax fraud, smuggling, and money laundering, and the financials made no sense. That's why he emailed me requesting a meeting. He wanted to understand his legal options before he raised his concerns with Peter. Do you honestly expect us to believe he'd turn Peter over to the police without discussing it with Patrice first? Come on!"

Anya did not appear to be listening to me anymore. Her gaze was fixed on the greenhouse glittering in the sun. A tiny blue vein pulsed in her temple.

She dismissed me with a wave of her hand, locked her eyes on Patrice, and said, "He mocked me, he mocked my intelligence and my education. I went to Wharton, for fuck's sake. I was the one who made us rich playing the crypto market. Me, not Peter. I was the one who created a successful global business, me, not Peter." She spun around to glare at him. "You went bankrupt twice. You achieved nothing until you met me. But did that count for anything? Not with Finn. He sneered at me—*you fancy yourself a financial wizard? You're a joke!*"

I grabbed her arm. "That's when you pushed him off the balcony."

She shook me off and moved closer to Peter, speaking in a whisper. "No, I wasn't there when he died."

"You're lying," I said. "Someone saw you."

CHAPTER 54

A TANGLE OF CANES

The air was so still I could hear the river splash against its banks and the cries of the gulls wheeling overhead. Anya pulled back her shoulders and tightened the belt on her nylon jacket. For a moment I thought she was going to leave, but she stood her ground, waiting. Daring me to continue.

"Someone saw you, Anya, up on the balcony right after Finn fell."

"That's a lie." She fixed her clear blue eyes on Peter. "Darling, she's lying, you know she's lying."

"Cedar James McQuinn," I pressed on.

"Who?" Peter glanced from Anya to me.

"James, the head chef at the Banff Springs Hotel. He found Finn slumped behind a dumpster under the third-floor balcony. A flash of light on the balcony caught his eye. Anya's pendant."

Her hand flew to her throat. The pillar bar pendant, ammolite edged with glittering diamonds. She never took it off.

"James yelled up, telling you to call 9-1-1. When you didn't respond, he called the EMTs himself. He saw you, Anya, and he told me all about it." In truth James didn't recognize the shadowy person on the balcony, but Anya didn't know that.

Something shifted in her eyes, her bravado melted. In a small, sad voice she said, "Peter, I'm so tired. Let's go home."

Peter grabbed her roughly by the shoulders, forcing her to look at him. "Is it true? Were you there when Dad died?"

"It was an accident." Tears streamed down her face. "Peter, he was so vile to me. Screaming he was going to destroy us. He was angry and abusive." She crept closer to Peter, trying to nestle in his side. "You must understand. He grabbed my hair and yanked me to the balustrade; I thought he was going to throw me off the balcony. I pushed him. Away from me. I had to. And... he slipped. He just slipped. It was an accident, my darling, I swear."

My head were buzzing, I was losing control. I clenched my fists, digging my nails into my palms. In all the years I'd known him, never once had Finn been physically aggressive. The idea he'd threaten Anya with violence was a vicious lie.

"Anya? If it was an accident, why didn't you get help?"

She wouldn't look at me. She continued to stare at Peter with those sad, blue eyes and said, "The cook, that James person, had it under control. There was nothing more for me to do."

She just confirmed she was there when Finn went over. I continued. "So you left. And what did you do next, Anya? You got ready for dinner. You put on your pretty gown, you did your hair, you applied your makeup, then you joined Peter and me at Finn's celebration dinner. He was late, very late. And yet you said nothing, Anya, absolutely nothing. Knowing full well Finn would never show up. For three solid hours, from the time you pushed him off the balcony to when Patrice called Peter to tell him Finn was in the hospital. You sat there and said nothing."

My heart was thumping wildly in my chest. "You know what I think? I think you wanted Finn to die before the family got to the hospital so he couldn't tell them what you'd done. To protect yourself you stole the last few hours Peter could have had with his father. And when Finn died without regaining consciousness, you thought you were home free."

She turned on me, eyes blazing. "How dare you judge me. You're nothing. A two-bit lawyer throwing malicious accusations around. How dare you!"

That's when her hand shot up and she slapped me. Stunned, I staggered backward. She lunged, ready to strike again, but Peter caught her wrist and hauled her back.

"Anya, stop. Now." His voice was strong and carried authority. "Stop. Breathe. Just breathe."

She exhaled loudly and curled forward. I thought she was going to fall into Peter's arms, but she broke free and sprinted toward the river glittering at the end of the garden. As she ran, she darted around soggy heaps of uprooted shrubs and shattered fragments of the gazebo, her breath coming in short, harsh gasps.

Peter charged after her down the muddy slope. I went to follow but Patrice held me back. "Give them space," she said. "Peter will calm her down, he always does." At first it appeared Patrice was right. He'd caught Anya and she went limp in his arms, wailing and sobbing pitifully. But she pivoted and darted even closer to the edge of the crumbling riverbank.

Then she tripped. Her arms flew up into the air. She

pitched forward. Screaming as she fell into a tangle of raspberry canes. Glass shattered. Then silence. We raced across the mucky ground. Peter reached her first. She was lying face down on a large sheet of glass, ripped from the greenhouse by the raging river and hidden in the brambles under a crust of mud.

"Peter?" She sounded bewildered. He dragged her out of the brambles. Her white shirt was streaked with dirt and blood. He tried to lift her to her feet, but her knees buckled and she slumped against him.

"Mom!" he screamed. "Help!"

I whipped out my phone and dialed 9-1-1.

Anya's hands were shredded. Covered with blood. Shards of glass. Blood everywhere. Soaking her blue nylon jacket and her white slacks. Coating Peter's shirt. He lowered her slowly down to the grass.

"Peter," I screamed, "What's the address? Where are we?" He told me and I repeated it to the 9-1-1 operator. Switching the phone from ear to ear as I followed the operator's instructions, ripping off my hoodie, throwing it to Patrice. "Try to stop the bleeding!" I was shaking violently now, pleading with the operator to hurry.

Peter rocked Anya gently, whispering and stroking her cheek. The wail of the sirens eclipsed the cries of the gulls overhead.

I looked around. Juve was gone.

CHAPTER 55

NO GOOD DEED

Two days after the horror of seeing Anya sliced to ribbons on the soggy riverbank behind her ruined mansion, Louisa sensed my mood lifting. My guilt-filled stupor had eased. I was ready to talk about it... as long as she didn't push me too hard.

"What would you say to a hot tea?" she asked, as she followed me into Madeline's conservatory. Dad was British, we learned at a very young age that a 'cuppa' cures everything.

"'Hello. Where's your friend Mr. G and T?'" Mom had her own way of easing a sad mood. In her case it was a bracing shot of brandy served in a *stampedli.*

Louisa picked up the Slipper Dog and stared into its eyes. "What say you, Evangeline, should we get Evie a drink, maybe a little one?" Apparently the dog said yes because Louisa and Evangeline disappeared into the kitchen to fetch some glasses. "But just a little one. Ever since we got here, we've done nothing but drink." It was unclear who that last bit was directed at, me or the Slipper Dog, but

Louisa was right. Madeline's liquor supply rivalled that of a trendy cocktail lounge.

Quincy charged into the kitchen when Louisa set Evangeline down on the floor, the sound of their scrabbling paws on the black and white tiles attracted the attention of Rupert the cockatiel who barked at them for a few minutes.

Madeline and a fluffy white cat joined me in the conservatory. Some of the higher windows were open and a soft breeze rippled through the greenery. A strand of ivy drifted down from the ceiling, grazing her hair. She shuddered and flapped it away. "I hate it when that happens!"

"It's not a spider," I said. "But it could have been. A big, black, hairy one."

"Ugh, don't say that." She shuddered again and threaded the vine around a filigree metal strut before settling into the fan-backed wicker chair. We're all afraid of something. Louisa is terrified of peacocks, Madeline hates spiders and me, I'm afraid of bears; thankfully I'll never see one; I never go hiking or camping. What was Anya was afraid of? Not that it mattered anymore.

Madeline was in an Audrey Hepburn mood tonight, casually elegant in black capris and a loose-fitting white shirt. She crossed her legs and eyed me carefully before asking, "How are you doing?"

I was doing fine until she asked me that question and the memories flooded back. Anya, her face so pale and her hair so black, lying on the grass drenched with blood. Peter on his knees rocking her gently and Patrice desperately trying to staunch the bleeding while I was on the verge of hysteria with the 9-1-1 operator.

The ambulance arrived within minutes. The EMTs assessed Anya's injuries and grimly loaded her into the ambulance. When one suggested Peter should ride along, he and his mother scrambled into the back.

Later that evening, Patrice called. Between tight sobs she described their harrowing ride to the hospital. Lurching from side to side through traffic, wailing through red lights with Anya strapped to the gurney, eyes wide, terrified and whimpering. Patrice said she kept repeating she was sorry. She hadn't meant to hurt anyone, "Not Dad, not Finn."

Peter bent close and whispered, "Darling, don't talk. Your father is fine, he's in New England, he's fine." For some reason this agitated her even more. Patrice wondered whether Anya was blurring Finn with her own father.

Finally, Patrice took a deep breath and said the words I'd been dreading. "Evie, Anya didn't make it. She was gone before they could get her into the OR."

"When's the funeral?" Madeline asked, breaking into my thoughts.

"Sometime next week. Patrice is planning a private service. Just the two of them, Peter and Patrice."

"Not Juve?"

I scoffed. No one had seen Juve since that morning at the house. Peter drove out to the mine in a daze the next day. He was dismayed to discover the warehouse had been stripped bare. Every scrap of ammolite and most of the finishing tools had been packed up and carted away. Even the rattly company truck was gone. Peter said the only reason the excavators were still in the pit was Juve couldn't drive them down the highway without being pulled over by the cops.

"Juve could be anywhere from Montana to Madagascar by now," I said.

"So Patrice lost her investment?" Louisa was following our conversation from the kitchen.

"Well, that's up to Peter. Anya's dead and Juve is gone, but DreamStone the company still exists. This is Peter's chance to do right by his mother, to do whatever it takes to pay her back."

Rupert the cockatiel was strutting around on the kitchen table still screeching at the dogs. Louisa flung a piece of broccoli at him and told him to pipe down, then returned to the conservatory carrying two tall frosty glasses. With an impish twinkle in her eye she said, "A G and T for Evie... and a Perrier for Madeline."

Madeline accepted the glass with a look of disdain, set it on the low table next to Louisa's chair, and went off to rummage in the liquor cabinet. The fluffy white cat followed her, peering into the cabinet when she opened the doors.

Louisa picked up Madeline's Perrier and took a long sip before settling in her chair. "So, Finn was right to be worried about DreamStone. What tipped him off?"

"I think he suspected something was wrong way before I did. Back in January when the Justice Department lawyer grilled him about ammolite-backed cryptocurrency. Her questions were so out of context he would have started researching crypto to try to understand its connection to ammolite. I'm sure he pestered Peter for information, Peter would have pointed him in Anya's direction. Peter wasn't the money guy"—*Juve finds it, Anya values it, and I sell it,* how many times did Peter say that— "and the harder Finn pushed, the more evasive Anya became."

"And paranoid," Madeline said as she carried a small dusty bottle into the kitchen. She returned a minute later with a glass of cloudy liquor, diluted with water and sweetened with a sugar cube. Absinthe. She lowered herself gingerly into her tippy Peacock chair and said, "It's a shame he didn't come to us earlier."

Her comment struck a nerve. Because he did. Last month Finn called, wanting to meet about DreamStone, but I was in the middle of a trial: a coal mining company was being prosecuted for dumping toxic chemicals into a pristine waterway and I was advising the prosecution. I had absolutely no time to spare. We agreed to meet after Finn's celebration in Banff. If I'd managed to give him even ten minutes...

Louisa said, "It's funny how you started in different places, Finn with the Justice Department lawyer and you with Laura Bazin, and came to the same conclusion: that Anya was corrupt. What about Peter? He must have known something was wrong."

"If he knew, he was in denial." I said, rolling the G and T around in my glass. "Peter's biggest mistake was hooking Anya up with Juve. She knew the crypto market, Juve saw ammolite as the next gold rush and was hell bent on cashing in. Ambition and greed. Put them together and boom, you've got a slick smuggling and money laundering operation."

My drink went down smoothly. "You know, it's strange but I think Juve was sincere when he said he was just trying to help Laura with that hot tip on crypto. That it wasn't part of the bribery scheme."

"Oh, give me a break!" Madeline's next words were cut off by the sound of the doorbell. Quincy and the Slipper Dog raced Madeline to the front door and the fluffy white cat claimed her unoccupied chair. It hopped off again when Madeline returned to the conservatory with Hadiza in tow.

Hadiza set a bulky paper bag down on the brass coffee

table. Madeline offered her a drink but she declined, asking for tea. Louisa jumped up to make it.

Turning to me Hadiza said, "Evie, how awful for you. Are you okay?"

Dear God, not again. Tears pricked my eyes when Hadiza embraced me. They weren't tears of sorrow but of guilt. If I'd joined Finn on the balcony when he wanted to show me that stupid little bird...

"What's in the bag?" I asked, coughing a little to clear a husky throat.

Hadiza opened the bag and lifted out a pink, cellophane-wrapped bucket. It looked like a floral display. She gestured, tentatively. "Strawberries and unicorn fruit dipped in chocolate. I hope you like chocolate."

The unicorn fruit turned out to be little unicorn-shaped pineapple slices dredged in white chocolate. I bit off a rainbow unicorn horn. It was sweet and tart on my tongue.

By the time Louisa returned from the kitchen with the tea tray Hadiza was deep into a story about her admin law class. "Gideon Gold is auditing the course for real now. He's got to be the oldest auditing student on the planet. The kids call him Doctor Death... to his face! Can you imagine?

"I don't know where they picked it up, I certainly didn't tell them. He probably leaked it himself to put the fear of God into them. In any event, I think he likes it." Hadiza's tone conveyed a mix of surprise and grudging admiration. Perhaps they'd finally put their differences behind them— no, given Doctor Death's penchant for stirring up trouble, the feud between the Jets and the Sharks would last until the end of time or until he died, whichever came first.

Louisa nibbled thoughtfully on a chocolate covered strawberry and pulled the green stem through her teeth, depositing it on her plate on the coffee table. "I still can't figure out who broke into our room."

Madeline raised her head in surprise. "Someone broke into your room? When?"

"When Louisa and I were staying at the Banff Spring Hotel. After what's his name dumped her," I said.

"For the record, I dumped him." Louisa wrinkled her nose.

I reached for another unicorn and said, "My money's on Juve."

"Why on earth would Juve break into our hotel room?" Louisa asked. Her head was down, she was prying the white cat's paws off the edge of the end table, it was determined to sneak off with a strawberry.

"For the same reason he broke into Madeline's study, to steal my laptop. He didn't succeed in Banff because Louisa, the die-hard Dwayne Johnson fan, took my laptop into the bathroom to watch a movie—"

"I was having a leisurely bath," Louisa said sheepishly.

"And he didn't succeed here because the dogs and Rupert went nuts and scared him off."

"Back up," Hadiza said, "why did Juve want to steal your laptop in the first place?"

I'd been brooding about this ever since Patrice told me Anya was dead. She described Anya raving in the back of the ambulance, frantic that Finn had sent me a dangerous email, insisting Peter get it back.

I rubbed the corner of my eye with the heel of my hand and told Hadiza that Finn had sent me an email that arrived after he'd died. I'd asked Patrice whether she'd received one too. When she said she hadn't I'd asked her not to mention it to Peter. "But she did. Then Peter told Anya, who assumed Finn emailed me about her fraudulent set of books. Finn had been asking questions about DreamStone's finances and she put two and two together and got five." It's strange how the guilty always assume the worst when someone asks an innocent question.

There were so many things I could have done differently. Met with Finn for ten minutes during the coal company trial, gone with him to see the Steller's Jay, not told Patrice about the email.

There was a quiet moment where all we could hear was Rupert flapping around in the kitchen muttering that he wanted more broccoli.

Then Hadiza said, "Okay, Juve wanted your laptop. How did he expect to get into your room in Banff without a card key?"

"Are you kidding?" I said. "How many card keys did you go through when we were there? Two? Three? The front desk hands them out like candy. Besides, Juve didn't need to get Louisa's cardkey, or mine for that matter, all he needed was the master key. He probably lifted one off the maid's cart. When he couldn't find my laptop in Banff, he came searching for it here, after we moved in with Madeline."

"Well, he scared the crap out of me," Louisa said with a slight shudder.

"Better than ghosts, though, right?"

Louisa picked up the white cat, it meowed in protest, and she tickled it under the chin. "I don't know. Which is preferable? A man in a black hoodie ransacking your room with you stark naked in the bathroom, or a ghost leaving bloody handprints all over your mirror?" She set the cat back down on the floor, it arched its back then headed straight for Hadiza and curled up on top of her shoes.

In the kitchen, Rupert let out a loud screech causing

Hadiza to jump. "This place is an effing zoo," she muttered under her breath.

"I'll take care of him," Louisa said, hustling back to the kitchen. Just as she reached the doorway she turned and said, "It is a shame that Russo and Laura will get away with their bribery scheme."

Madeline caught my eye and a tiny smile passed between us.

"I wouldn't be too sure about that," I said.

It helps to know a guy. Or if you don't know a guy, to know Madeline. Some of Madeline's guys are the CEOs of construction companies; others are deputy ministers in the Department of Justice. Tomorrow a government lawyer will find a new file on her desk. How it got there will be a matter for speculation, but this lawyer is a tenacious woman in a no-nonsense suit. There was no doubt in my mind. Justice would be done.

ACKNOWLEDGEMENTS

One of the greatest things about being a writer is the way people tell you things about their lives and allow you to fictionalize them and put them into your books. I'd like to thank some of those people here, starting with two of my favourite law professors, Nigel Bankes and Martin Olszynski, who generously pulled back the curtain on life in academia.

Inspiration comes from everywhere. I'd like to thank my neighbours Karren Storwick, a respected military historian who collects the oral histories of Canadian war vets and memorializes them for posterity, and Liz Gibbs, an ER nurse, who ensured I didn't stray too far from reality when a character finally met her end.

Thanks also to Shania Rose who won the right to name a character in this book. I hope Cedar James McQuinn lives up to her expectations.

A special thank you to my brilliant editor, Pip Wallace, who makes editing a joy (no, really, she does) and the writing community, particularly Crime Writers of Canada and Sisters in Crime—Canada West, for their endless support.

I'm grateful to all the lawyers, paralegals and assistants I've worked with throughout my legal career. I love the law, but you made it even more enjoyable.

Lastly, let me thank my family, first my sisters who are the inspiration for Evie's relationship with Louisa, and of course my husband Roy, the best first reader ever, and my daughters, Kelly, a nurse, and Eden, a paralegal, who were always there to answer my cockamamie questions. You guys are amazing.

ABOUT THE AUTHOR

SUSAN JANE WRIGHT studied anthropology before she became a lawyer. She worked as a litigator at a national law firm before going in-house with a multi-national corporation. Her career has taken her from the boardrooms of Houston to the streets of Hong Kong.

Fortune Favors The Dead is the third in the Evie Valentine legal thriller series. It follows the bestselling novels *The Glass Lake* and *Box of Secrets*. *Box of Secrets* was selected as a finalist by the Crime Writers of Canada and the Canadian Book Club Awards.

She lives in Calgary, Alberta. When she's not writing she's travelling with her husband and two daughters. Her favorite vacation was a trip from Prague to London on the Orient Express. One day she'd like to take the train from Venice to Istanbul.